PACIFIC HEIGHTS

PACIFIC HEIGHTS

A NOVEL

PAUL HARPER

HENRY HOLT AND COMPANY NEW YORK

Henry Holt and Company, LLC
Publishers since 1866
175 Fifth Avenue
New York, New York 10010
www.henryholt.com

Henry Holt® and 🅷® are registered trademarks of
Henry Holt and Company, LLC.

Copyright © 2011 by Paul Harper
All rights reserved.
Distributed in Canada by H. B. Fenn and Company Ltd.

Library of Congress Cataloging-in-Publication Data
ISBN-13: 978-0-8050-9393-3
ISBN-10: 0-8050-9393-1

Henry Holt books are available for special promotions and
premiums. For details contact: Director, Special Markets.

First Edition 2011

Designed by Kelly S. Too

Printed in the United States of America
1 3 5 7 9 10 8 6 4 2

To J.,

*whose patience with me
can scarcely be described,
nor gratitude expressed,
with mere consonants and vowels.*

"Secrecy is as indispensable to human beings as fire, and as greatly feared."

—Sissela Bok, *Secrets*

PACIFIC HEIGHTS

1

They ate a late dinner at Crete.

The androgynous Chinese wore a tuxedo without a tie, a clipped mustache, and bobbed jet hair. The other man was good-looking, with thick caramel hair neatly barbered, blue-gray eyes, and a strong jaw. He wore a chocolate sport coat, silk mocha trousers from Milan, and an attitude of placid self-assurance.

Sitting at a corner table not far from the white marble bar, they shared miso-glazed sea bass and coconut mojitos. The place was crowded with hip Castro scenesters swimming in the deep pink light that bounced off the rose-tinted mirrors and plate-glass windows. The crowd was cosmopolitan, too cool, *très* chic.

The Chinese did most of the talking, chatty, animated. The Caucasian sat back casually but watched his companion closely, as if he were amused by the candlepower of the performance.

They left Crete at closing time.

Their hotel in the Castro was a seedy movie set on a side street. The window looked across to Le Mesonge, a club that throbbed with a baseline you could feel all the way across the street.

They locked the door, and while the Caucasian went to the window and looked out, the Chinese pulled the cover off the bed, then the top sheet, and threw them in the corner. When he turned around, the Caucasian was right in front of him, taller by a foot. While the Chinese stood still, the other man began undressing him.

What followed was choreographed, though they hadn't rehearsed the details. The broad contours had been dictated earlier by the Caucasian, and the Chinese, surprised and intrigued by what he heard, had gamely agreed to go along. The proposed scenario was just another example of the Caucasian's extraordinary insight into the hidden nature of the Chinese. How far could he go intuiting the fantasies that the Chinese found so seductive?

Too far.

He threw the tuxedo aside, and they stood at the foot of the bed. The Caucasian carefully peeled off one side of the mustache of the naked Chinese, just the one side. She stood there, willfully unprotected, her stomach fluttering.

The sex was outré, right up to the edge of bizarre. It was intense and sublime, everything she had imagined it would be.

He went to sleep immediately after, as if she had drugged

his last drink. And it was then, while she lay awake on the sheet without cover, bare and straight as a corpse, that she began to be afraid.

In her mind she played back the saraband they had danced, movement by movement. It was everything she had imagined, and that was what scared the hell out of her.

What he had just done to her was way beyond intuitive. It was unnerving, and it made her feel as if her physical brain was no longer the sole vessel of her imagination. Her sexual fantasies were just that: *her* sexual fantasies, and yet this man had just re-created one of those scenarios with such precise accuracy that it could only be described as sinister.

It was not a frightening script in her own head; it was only now, coming to her from someone else's imagination, that it horrified her. The chill she felt had nothing to do with the Castro nights; it was because of the mind next to her.

Even when the affair began, she knew it was a cliché. Still, she welcomed it. The sexual adventure, skirting the ragged margins of propriety, the emerging special connection, the tangy odor of peril, all had been a much-needed rush in the extended story of her unraveling emotional life. But lately their uncommon collusion was increasingly troubling, moving toward weird. It was seriously freaking her out.

Tonight was too much. She couldn't do it anymore. She didn't care how handsome he was, and she didn't care how insanely good the sex was. Lying there, with pieces of her thoughts inside someone else's head, she decided she had had enough. She was going to end the affair.

But how would that work, exactly? When he called the next time, she just wouldn't answer. Could it really be that simple? Could it just end because she wanted it to end? Affairs did, she supposed. They both used assumed names. That had been the first thing they agreed on. Robert and Mei.

Did she really believe, then, that he knew nothing about her? She had played by the rules, but had he? They always met at a prearranged place and time. His idea. She never saw his car, didn't know where he lived (he had once mentioned Marin County), only vaguely knew what he did for a living (he had mentioned real estate). This protocol grew out of the tentative beginnings of their relationship and eventually developed into the rules of the affair. That's the way it was.

But she couldn't leave for the last time without knowing who he was. If he knew the inside of her head so damned well, why couldn't she at least know his real identity?

She sat up. Their clothes were in a pile at the foot of the bed, the physical debris of her psychic upheaval only a few hours before. She stood, walked around and crouched by the clothes, and began separating them by the pale wash from the window.

She picked up his sport coat and found his wallet inside the breast pocket. When her fingers touched it, she stopped, listened. His breathing hadn't changed. She took out the wallet and opened it, and looked at his driver's license in its clear plastic pocket. Too dark. She tilted it toward the window.

Philip R. Krey. 2387 Leech, Mill Valley. She examined his picture, repeating the name and address to herself several times as she went through the wallet. She slipped out the money, fanned through it, put it back. She checked the credit cards, all in the name of P. R. Krey. There was a piece of paper with phone numbers. She would never be able to remember them.

She closed the wallet and stuffed it back into his coat pocket.

"Are you leaving?"

She flinched, stood quickly to cover her surprise, holding her clothes.

"Have to," she said, dumping her clothes on the foot of the bed. Grateful for the bad light, she nervously untangled her panties, which had rolled up into a small twist.

"Want me to call you this week?"

"I'll call you," she said from the darkness. "My husband's got a couple of business dinners this week. I'll have obligations, but I don't know the details yet. Don't even know the dates."

She pulled on her underwear. Backward? Inside out? She didn't give a damn. No bra. She picked up the white shirt and slipped it on.

He was quiet. Was he dozing off?

"What's the matter?" he asked.

"What's the matter?"

"You sound . . . tense."

"How about wiped out?"

"Maybe," he looked at the windows. "It's quiet. No music."

"It's three-forty, for Christ's sake," she said, finishing the last button on the shirt. She grabbed the tuxedo trousers, pulled them on, buttoned the waist.

"You in a hurry?" he asked.

"Just need to get going," she said, stooping and feeling around for her shoes.

"You okay with the way it went?"

Why the hell was he fishing? "Sure. Why wouldn't I be?"

"Surprised?"

"Yeah, sure."

"What surprised you?"

"Everything. I don't think you missed anything, Robert. Like I said, I'm exhausted."

She found the shoes and slipped them on. She didn't want to talk to him about this. She just wanted away from him, that's all. Raking her bobbed hair with her fingers, she started looking for her black silk clutch.

"What're you looking for?"

"My purse."

At the foot of the bed again, she grimaced and ran her hands over the filthy carpet and under his clothes. There it was.

"Got it," she said. She had to walk by him to get to the door, and she was petrified that he'd reach out and touch her, want her to react somehow.

He was leaning on one elbow on the bed now, watching her.

"Okay," he said.

"I'll call you," she said, and she stepped out into the musty hallway, closing the door behind her.

He got out of bed and went to the window. A minute later she came out of the front of the hotel and disappeared down the street, walking quickly.

Turning to the bed, he bent down, picked up his sport coat, and pulled out his wallet. He dropped the coat on the bed and stepped to the window again.

He opened the wallet. Everything looked okay. Was his driver's license crooked? No. Wait. He slowly pulled the money out of its slot: the bills were upside down.

Well, damn, sooner or later it had to happen. At the very least she might Web-search the address. He would wait and see.

But now there was a new development. He'd expected her to be rattled by what had just happened, but he didn't think her heightened anxiety would take a turn in this direction. He thought it might increase the edginess of the sex, but if he was right about what she was doing with his wallet, instead of edginess, he had created suspicion. Why, suddenly, did she want to know who he was?

As far as he was concerned this woman existed only within the parameters of a very small orbit he had created for her. He couldn't let her outside those secret limits. He couldn't afford that much instability. Especially not now. There was too much at stake.

MONDAY NIGHT

2

Marten Fane watched the entrance of the Stafford from his car across the street. It was a small boutique hotel on the cusp of Russian Hill and Pacific Heights. Built in the 1930s, the art deco affair had been bought by a couple of hip entre-preneurs who restored it and spared no expense to revive its retro decor. Now it was a popular insider scene.

The hotel's entrance sat well back from the street behind a courtyard of boxwood hedges and old lime trees. A long forest-green awning led to the plate-glass front door.

Vera List had been in the room a quarter of an hour now, and Fane had seen no sign of surveillance. He often used the Stafford for meetings like this because its location made it easy to spot watchers. That, and he liked the rooms.

As he got out of the car, he looked up through the drizzle to the fourth floor, half the height of the hotel. The light was on in the room. He crossed the street.

In the foyer he took off his raincoat and glanced into the

registration lobby. A few people, but nothing caught his attention. To his left, the dusky Metro Bar looked inviting as always. He headed for the elevators.

He stepped out on the fourth floor and went to room 412. He knocked and waited for her to observe him through the security lens in the door. The latch snicked, and she opened the door, stepping back tentatively.

"I'm Marten Fane," he said.

"Hello. I'm Vera."

She was forty-four years old, with a fair complexion and thick chestnut hair that she wore in a casual shoulder-length style that framed an oval face. Her eyes were intelligent and intensely curious.

"Thank you for agreeing to meet me," she said as Fane entered the room. She pronounced her words precisely but without pretense. She was anxious but resolute, an act of will that made him feel good about her. She was determined to get this thing done, whatever it was.

"Sure. Shen's an old friend," he said, hanging his raincoat on the hook on the back of the door. "It was good to hear from him."

He followed her to a sitting area next to a pair of windows that looked out the front of the hotel onto the street. He let her sit down and then took the chair opposite her on the other side of an elliptical coffee table with a glass top, its base three art deco nudes.

Vera sat forward in her armchair, her back straight, her legs angled properly, ankles crossed. She wore a slim pearl-gray knit dress with three-quarter sleeves that accented her long, delicate fingers.

"Mr. Moretti said that you'd worked together in the police department," she said.

"Right, in the intelligence section," Fane said. "I was a detective in homicide, and then I met Shen and he convinced me to move into intelligence. I served with him nearly a dozen years before he retired."

"He spoke highly of you," she said. Though she was uncomfortable, she was doing an admirable job of dampening the body language.

"I met him through his sister," she said. "We were neighbors. When I decided I needed to . . . do something, he was the only one I could think of to go to. But when I explained that I had a problem involving two of my clients—that there were confidentiality issues, and I didn't want the police involved, no private investigators—he stopped me. He said he didn't want to hear any more, and gave me your name."

"Okay," Fane said, crossing one long leg over the other at the knee.

There was an awkward moment.

"He said that you . . . were known—among those who needed to know—as the man to go to if you've got a problem and you've run out of options. He also said," she added, "that I could trust you. Absolutely trust you."

Her last remark was a surprising act of magical thinking. She needed it to be true, so she looked right at him and said it, like making the sign of the cross.

Fane waited.

"You understand," she went on, "that even discussing this with you takes me dangerously close to violating my confidentiality agreement with my clients. They have to know that they can say anything to me, and it will go no further. Absolute trust is essential in psychoanalysis."

"I understand," Fane said.

"And I need to have that same kind of trust in you. I trust Mr. Moretti's recommendation, but I didn't tell him the things I'm going to tell you. He's not the one I'm going to jump off the cliff with."

Her choice of metaphors was interesting. "Desperate" was not a hyperbole for Vera List.

"Look," she said, "I don't even know what it is you do. Mr. Moretti said that I should talk to you, but he didn't say why. I mean, the implication was that you could help me. But, frankly, he was cryptic about it."

She stopped. Then she said, "Understand, I'm not seeking anything illegal here. You . . . you're clear about that." She tilted her head, eyebrows raised, expecting an answer.

He nodded. She relaxed a little.

"But, well, Mr. Moretti didn't tell me much, either, as I said. I've got to have more to go on than that before I can do this."

"Fair enough," Fane said. She had a good point. The people who had come to him during the past few years were already familiar with his world. They had lived on the edges of it themselves, in that unstable region where a penumbra of uncertainty enveloped everything.

But Vera List, despite her own profession, was from the everyday world, where ambiguity was generally unwelcome and mostly a matter of theoretical argument. At least, that had been the case until now.

· · ·

"Four years ago," Fane said, "I was embroiled in a controversy in the intelligence section. I'd been there about a dozen years. At that time intelligence was in the Special Investigations Division. A police department's intelligence division is where all the secrets are kept. It's a Byzantine place. The years disappear, but the secrets never do. They don't even have half-lives.

"I was eventually forced out of the police department. A few months later I got a call from a prominent trial lawyer who asked if I'd visit with one of his clients. The man had a problem, had to make a choice between two options with equally grim consequences. I helped him find another way.

"It was a favor. I didn't think much about it. Then, four months later, I got another call. The first man I helped had recommended me to someone else. It was the beginning of an accidental profession. There's no job description for what I do. I have no curriculum vitae. I don't give references."

Vera List was staring hard at him, wringing meaning from every syllable. Even the spaces between his words were speaking to her.

"Finding a solution to your problem isn't a matter of if, but of how," he said. "As for trusting me: in the intelligence business, the gold standard is the assurance of someone you already know you can trust. And sometimes it's all you've got when you have to make that decision to jump.

"If you want to talk with Moretti again before you go any further, that's perfectly fine with me. And if I don't see you again, that's fine with me, too."

Vera List lifted her chin, nodded, and took a slow, deep breath.

He guessed her heart was on the verge of fibrillating.

"I'm sorry," she said. "I'm not as composed as I'd like to be."

Fane understood. Usually she was the one waiting to hear the unsettling story. It was disconcerting to have the roles reversed.

"The situation," she began, "is . . . disturbing. Both clients are women. Very different personalities. They come from different backgrounds, have different concerns, different issues. They don't know each other. Never even seen each other. My clients arrive and leave by different doors so they never encounter each other.

"I've been seeing Elise nearly two years. Lore has been coming to me for about six months. They're both married." She paused. "And they're both having affairs.

"Elise has been involved in her affair for about five months. I don't know the man's name, but once the affair began it became the central theme of our conversations for several months.

"From the beginning it was an intense relationship. This man seduced her in every sense of the word. She tells me that he can practically read her mind, that he knows her innermost thoughts, intuits her urges, desires, fears. All of this insight is naturally very bewitching. She's mesmerized by him."

Vera's hands lay in her lap, the ends of her fingers gently laced. No wedding ring, which surprised Fane. Her posture was proper, but natural, unself-conscious.

"On occasion," she went on, "I've sensed that Elise finds something . . . eerie about it. But not so eerie that she wants to break it off. That's typical of her. She's beautiful and needy. Compassionate. Has a tendency to be self-destructive, but at the same time she's a survivor.

"The other woman, Lore, began her affair shortly after she started seeing me. Again, I don't know the man's name. When she first mentioned the affair, it seemed incidental. Unlike Elise, it wasn't something Lore wanted to talk about.

"But after several months a strange pattern began to emerge. Lore began talking about her lover, and when she did, she sounded very much like Elise. He was incredibly insightful. He could practically read her mind. He knew her like the back of his hand, knew what she wanted, what she feared, even knew what she fantasized about."

Vera stopped and swallowed once, then again.

Fane stood and went into the bathroom. He got a glass of water and brought it back to her.

"Thank you," she said, and immediately took a sip. She cleared her throat as he returned to his chair.

"At first I was fascinated by the similarities in the two affairs," she resumed, "but I expected Lore's situation eventually to diverge into its own story. But that didn't happen. In fact, the similarities became more pronounced. There were details about his sexual behavior that were identical to those Elise described. I was astonished."

Another drink.

"I really couldn't avoid the conclusion that Elise and Lore were seeing the same man," she said. "I mean, it was conceivable that two women, strangers to each other, could be having an affair with the same man. But it strained my tolerance for coincidence to believe that they could also be consulting the same psychoanalyst. I became terrified."

"You're absolutely sure they don't know each other?" Fane asked.

"Absolutely? No."

"Do you suspect they might?"

"No, I really don't. I've racked my brain about how this could be happening. Is this man getting into my case files? I really can't think of any other explanation.

"I decided to do something that, in retrospect, was foolish. I seeded my notes from the next two sessions with Elise and Lore with false information, the kind of thing I was sure he'd eventually mention to them if he was indeed reading their files. Of course, if he did mention it, there was no guarantee they'd pass it on to me."

She paused for emphasis.

"Within a few weeks each woman told me about a strange conversation she'd had with her lover. He'd wanted to talk about something that sounded completely off the wall to them. They thought it was weird."

"The information you'd planted."

"Yes."

"There's no mistaking this?"

"No. This man's getting into my case files, using my notes to crawl inside their minds."

3

Fane watched her as she held the glass in her lap. He realized that the body language that he earlier had interpreted
as her own peculiar preference for precision was more than
that. It was barely restrained panic.

"You said that neither woman has told you the man's
name. Have you asked?"

"No. At the beginning it wasn't important. Both of them
were deliberately avoiding using a name, so I respected that.
It became the norm for our conversations when they touched
on the affairs."

"Do you have any sense of how he might be using this
information?" he asked. "Or is planning to use it?"

"Well, he's obviously using it to manipulate them," she
said. "There's the sex, naturally, and maybe it's only that,
and nothing else. But . . . I don't know, something tells me
that it doesn't stop with the sex."

"Did you change your security?"

"I was afraid to. I felt like I'd already pushed my luck by feeding him the false information. When Elise and Lore were confused by his references to that false information, he might've been puzzled, but that's all. But if he suddenly encountered a new security situation on top of that . . . I was afraid he'd realize I was on to him."

"Good, that was the right decision. How long have you been sure about this?"

"Just a few days. Three days."

Fane looked at the windows. The rain, illuminated from below by the street lamps, fell like dying sparks. When he brought his eyes back to her, she was staring at him.

"You don't want to go to the police," he said, "because of the potential of public disclosure."

"Exactly. There are things in my files that can destroy these people's lives. It's just unthinkable for me to deliberately create a situation in which those files could become a matter of public record in a trial."

She checked her posture.

"Listen, Mr. Fane," she said. "I'm not sure exactly what I'm asking for here, but it seems to me there ought to be a way to stop this man without letting my clients know their files have been compromised, a way to resolve this so that no one ever knows it happened."

The tension emanating from her was almost kinetic.

"I live with secrets, too," she continued. "The way you do. I hear them every day. A dozen lives unfold every day, year after year in a certain way because I keep those secrets. If I revealed the things that are told to me in confidence, those dozen lives would unfold differently. Maybe tragically."

She fixed her dark eyes on him.

"What this man is doing is another secret that I intend to keep," she said, "but I need help with this one."

Vera List wasn't asking for advice about whether or not she was doing the right thing. It seemed to Fane that in spite of her obvious fear, she had already decided she didn't have any other choice.

"I know you realize that what you want to do here is serious," Fane said, "but there are some things you need to consider before you go any farther."

She waited.

"First of all, something like this never works the way you imagine it," he said. "No matter how cleverly you approach it, no matter how well you plan it, there's always a nasty surprise. And if that surprise unravels in the wrong way, it'll destroy you.

"You should also know that going this route exposes you to some very complicated legal challenges."

Vera raised her chin a little.

"I'm not a lawyer," Fane said, "but it seems to me that by continuing to allow this man access to your case files, you're knowingly allowing a breach of client records. If he commits a crime as a result of these illegal entries, you're at risk to charges of aiding and abetting.

"If you believe this man is planning to use the information in your case files for criminal purposes, and you don't report it to legal authorities, you're vulnerable to charges of withholding knowledge of criminal intent."

"But if it's only a suspicion—"

"And if you believe that these women are in danger and

don't warn them, don't report what's happening to the proper authorities, you're vulnerable to charges of criminal negligence, or worse, collusion."

She said nothing. This was not at all what she thought she would hear from him. She closed her eyes.

Fane noted the slight change in the rise and fall of her chest, the subtle alteration of her brow. How many other women, during the old hotel's long history, had sat by these same windows on other rainy nights, wrestling with the bewildering circumstances of their stories?

She opened her eyes. "You've used the word 'vulnerable' several times. None of these consequences are necessarily foregone conclusions, are they?"

"No."

She regarded him with a sudden calm interest.

"Something tells me that you're a very private person."

He didn't say anything.

"You'd understand, then," she said, as if his silence confirmed her assumption, "what it would mean to have your mind spilled into the public arena, your secret self suddenly the object of the world's amusement."

She stood and walked to the windows. Leaning a shoulder against the window frame, she crossed her arms and looked into the wet night. The pearl-knit dress created an elegant line from her canted hip to midcalf.

"If I go to the police," she said, turning to him, "this man will be caught; there will be a public trial. They'll subpoena my files. My clients are too rich, too pretty, too high on their pedestals not to be pulled down. So, there will be leaks, their identities revealed. Bits and pieces of their lives will dribble out, the worst bits and pieces. The dribble will become a flood, another media freak show like the many with which we're already too familiar. Two more lives will be eviscerated for the public's entertainment du jour."

"You seem awfully sure of this," Fane said.

"It's our cultural zeitgeist," she said. "Watching people self-destruct, watching lives go down the drain, is our national pastime. We're dirty-secret junkies."

It was an unsentimental observation, and Fane suspected the remark reflected harsh experience. But he couldn't disagree with her. Anonymity—privacy—was the last refuge of sanity in an increasingly hyperconnected, tell-all, digitally exposed, gossip-hungry world. It was as rare as modesty and, once lost, as irretrievable as innocence.

"And Elise and Lore may not be the only victims. The only reason I discovered that this man is reading their files is because of the way he's using the information. It came back to me like a boomerang. But what if he's getting into the files of my other clients as well? If he's using their information differently, how would I know?"

"Do you think he's doing that?"

"This kind of man," she said, "wouldn't be able to keep his hands off the others."

Vera List saw nothing but disaster here.

"You said that you thought his motive for getting into your clients' files was to be able to manipulate them, probably for sex. But you had a feeling that it didn't stop at that. What did you mean?"

"It's the way Elise and Lore talk about him," she said. "He sounds more complicated than a voyeur or sexual predator.

I . . . I just have a sense that what's happening to these women isn't . . . it's just not that simple. There's more to it than that."

"How is he more complicated?"

The question made her uneasy. "I'm . . . I'm sorry, but if I go into that I'll be going into their relationships. I'll be taking it . . . to another level."

"I need to know who we're talking about," Fane said.

Vera nodded, knowing it would eventually get to this.

"Elise," she said, "is Elise Currin."

"Mrs. Jeffrey Safra Currin?"

"Yes."

Fane suddenly understood Vera's anxiety. He could immediately think of a dozen reasons why it was justified.

"And the other woman?"

"Lore Cha. Her husband is Richard Cha, a Silicon Valley entrepreneur. Something to do with innovative software. Lots of patents, lots of money. Ambition."

"Neither of them knows what you've discovered?"

"Absolutely not, and I want to keep it that way. You're the only one who knows, besides me."

Currin was a bona fide member of the elite group of a few thousand individuals worldwide who had accrued such influence through wealth or talent or ruthlessness that their lives touched millions, even billions, of other lives by their decisions and their actions. He sat on the boards of half a dozen global corporations and owned half a dozen others. His friends were the kind of people who made broad assumptions about their privilege. They bought Washington connections, and their private planes were familiar with the tarmacs in London, Dubai, Hong Kong, Paris, and Mumbai.

Blackmail immediately jumped to mind. But like Vera, Fane had a nagging feeling that that possibility was too obvious.

"You have three things working in your favor," he said, "and without them I'm not sure your problem could be approached in the way you want. First, you were smart not to alert this guy that you're on to him. He's been getting by with this for a while now, probably feeling pretty comfortable about it. That's good.

"Second, you haven't told Elise and Lore what's happening. That gives us a little flexibility, more options.

"Third, you can keep a secret.

"I'm interested in helping you," he went on, "But you need to understand that what you're wanting to do here will set in motion a process that operates outside the system. Whenever you go outside the system, there's always a price to pay. It's easy to underestimate the cost."

"I'm not afraid of having to make hard choices," she said, "or of living with the consequences."

"It's more than that," he said. "You're going into this without knowing what currency you'll be using to pay the price. A clear conscience? Self-respect? Loss of faith . . . in yourself, in others?"

"That's grim currency," she said defensively. "There's a rule that says it always has to be that way?"

"I don't want you to have any illusions about it."

She studied him a moment, then came back to her armchair and sat down again.

"I don't give a damn about Jeffrey Currin or Richard Cha. But I have an obligation to their wives. If I allow the things they told me in confidence to become public, I'll be abdicating my responsibility. It'll be devastating for them.

"And," she added, "I'm sure it's obvious to you, but I'll make a point of it just to be fair: it would ruin me as well. I'm not going to let that happen. I'll find another way. And I'll pay the price."

4

Fane sat in his car and watched Vera List leave the Stafford, the collar of her raincoat turned up against the drizzle as she walked to her BMW parked at the end of the block. No one followed her as she drove away.

He made three calls from his encrypted BlackBerry to three other encrypted numbers.

The first call went to Roma Solís, a long-legged Colombian woman Fane had met in Bogotá a decade earlier, shortly after he joined the SID. He had gone to Colombia to follow an investigation, and Detective Felipe Solís was his contact in Bogotá. Solís's daughter Roma, educated at the University of Chicago and determined to follow in her father's footsteps, was a young detective in the Policía Nacional.

Fane became friends with the Solís family and traveled to Bogotá nearly every year to visit. In 2009, Felipe's secret investigation of a conspiracy to assassinate a hard-driving federal prosecutor resulted in two car bombings and a plane crash. The first bomb killed Felipe and his wife, and the second killed Roma's sister and her family.

Roma was on a last-minute assignment in Santa Marta and had missed her night flight to Cartagena. It went down in the jungle. A few days later she returned to Bogotá under heavy guard. She buried her family and sold their property, and within ten days she was living in Mexico City.

When Fane was forced out of the SID, it was a year before he decided to start his own business. The first call he made was to Roma. Her years in Colombia's Department of Administrative Security, the country's reckless and much-abused equivalent of the FBI, was like earning a graduate degree in conspiracy and deception. Three weeks later she landed at the San Francisco International Airport.

That had been nearly two years ago.

The second call Fane made was to Jon Bücher, a counter-surveillance specialist who ran a shop out of a cluttered converted storefront in Potrero Hill. Fane had met Bücher in the frantic year after 9/11 when some SID officers were enlisted to help the FBI update watch lists that suddenly needed immediate attention. Bücher was one of the contractors they hired to cover the tech-specialist shortage.

He had been calm and creative, two characteristics that Fane valued highly. Whenever Fane needed a countermeasure specialist, Bücher was the man he called.

"Jon, this is Marten. I've got a last-minute job for you. Tomorrow, midmorning. If you can handle it, I'd appreciate it."

"What have you got?"

"I'm guessing that Roma's going to recommend a sweep and a remote camera installation. Is that possible on this short notice?"

"You bet. You need a tech van?"

"Probably. Roma will be in touch about the details. I just wanted to see if you were available."

"No problem," Bücher said.

The third call went to Bobby Noble, whose company, Virtual Marketing Research, had nothing to do with market research.

"Bobby, this's Marten. In about fifteen minutes I'm going to be at the Shell station at California and Steiner. Have you got time to meet me there?"

"Sure can. See you there."

Fane started his car and turned back toward Larkin Street.

Noble had an interesting history. Stocky and well built, he wore his thick, straight hair well barbered and combed straight back in a vaguely retro style. He grew up in Panama City during the years when Manuel Noriega was in his sweet spot with the CIA. His father was a U.S. political consultant for Panamanian politicians cozy with the Agency. Bobby got a firsthand look at how the CIA operated in those years, and he didn't like what he saw.

He moved to the United States, got a master's degree from Stanford, and developed a highly specialized software program designed for opposition research specialists working for political candidates.

Like Bücher, Noble lived his life in several shades of gray: he ran a business in plain sight, but most of his work was in

the shadows as a secret contractor for the intelligence community. He kept a wary and jaundiced eye on the people he
worked for.

Noble was already pumping gas into his wife's car when he
saw Fane's Mercedes pull off the street. He watched it glide
into the fluorescent glow of the station and roll to a stop on
the opposite side of the pump he was using.

The driver's door swung open, and Fane got out of the
car still wearing his double-breasted suit coat, his tie snug
around the collar of his custom-made shirt. Habitually well
dressed, his lean, six-foot, four-inch frame always cut a nice
figure. He walked around and opened the gas tank door.

"Bobby," Fane said.

"How you doing, Marten?"

"Good." Fane swiped his credit card and jammed the noz-
zle of the hose into his gas tank, and the pump started clicking
away. He turned up the collar on his suit coat as Noble put his
pump on auto, and the two of them stepped to the front of
Fane's car.

"I've got a couple of names for you," Fane said.

That was the way he did business. He wasn't averse to
chatting, but the business came first, staccato, right out there
in front, laying down the game.

"Shoot," Noble said.

"Richard Cha."

"C-h-a?" Noble never wrote these things down. He got
them into his head by checking the spelling.

"Right. And Jeffrey Safra Currin."

Noble hissed. "I can spell that one. What's Cha's business?"

"Silicon Valley," Fane said. "Software patents, I think."

"Well, that really narrows it down," Noble grinned, propping one foot on the bumper of Fane's car. "I'll see what I can do."

"Here's a quick outline of the situation," Fane said, and he related a scenario held together with oblique allusions and third-party references designed to tell as much and as little as possible. The depth and detail would come later, but Fane always treated the beginning of a new assignment with a good deal of circumspection in case the story didn't develop as he anticipated.

The rain had slowed to a heavy mist, and fog was drifting in across the Presidio from the Pacific. Noble smiled to himself as he flicked up the collar of the windbreaker and listened to Fane's account, his shoulders hunched against the damp air.

Fane liked convoluted stories. Everything was a labyrinth to him, every motive ulterior. His mind worked like a ferret's, quick, curious, and wary, which wasn't all that unusual for someone in the intelligence business. He had a genuine instinct for discerning the mind behind the scheme. He was naturally inclined to unriddle.

Fane had once remarked wryly, and only half jokingly, that Occam's razor was all very well as a rule of thumb for examining scientific hypotheses. But when it came to human nature, paradox was the only model that consistently made sense.

"Holy shit, man." Noble frowned when Fane had finally finished. "What the hell have you stepped into?"

"Yeah. This is interesting."

Noble jangled the change in his pocket and watched Fane. He was leaning against the wet car fender, his weight on one leg, his feet crossed at the ankle, and his arms folded across his chest. His stern attention was turned toward the fuzzy margins of the light.

"But I don't think it's blackmail," Fane said, picking up on an earlier thread.

The serious look on Fane's face wasn't a frown, but the result of two vertical creases between his eyebrows that made him appear perpetually skeptical. His face, long and rugged with high cheekbones and a Roman nose, was in marked contrast to his immaculate grooming. His dark eyes had the beginnings of crow's-feet at the corners and were the first things to give him away when he was troubled; they grew darker.

"I think he's running something else," Fane added.

Noble's gas pump clicked.

"Like what?"

Fane shook his head. "Don't know."

Noble nodded. That was all he was going to get.

"What's the focus, then?" he asked. "There's going to be a damned library of information on Currin. Who knows about Cha."

"I'm looking for a connection between these two guys. Something besides this man sleeping with their wives."

Just then Fane's pump snapped, too, and both men moved to the hoses to hang them up.

Noble finished and stepped on the island between the two

pumps, resting his elbows on the shoulders of the pumps just as Fane opened his car door.

"Considering who we're dealing with here," Noble said, "considering what's happening, this has got 'mess' written all over it."

"Yeah," Fane said, pausing behind the opened door. He hesitated on a thought, decided to keep it to himself. He nodded. "It does."

Then he got into his Mercedes and closed the door. A moment later the taillights of his car were diminishing into the rainy night.

5

Fane was only a few minutes from his home in Pacific Heights, an old, elegant neighborhood that sat atop the ridge of one of the city's many hills. High above San Francisco Bay, it had stunning, panoramic views that reached from the Pacific on the west, eastward to Oakland. Favored by the city's wealthiest and most prominent residents, the district's quiet, tree-lined streets were crowded with grand homes in a mélange of architectural styles from Victorian and Mission Revival to Beaux-Arts and Modern. Some of the old homes had been converted into sedate foreign consulates and private schools, and only the occasional tolling of church bells disturbed the district's coveted tranquillity.

But it was the bay's unique geography that created one of Pacific Heights' greatest assets: its spectacular views. The Golden Gate at the mouth of the bay was the only sea-level break in the coastal mountain ranges, and as a result, the Pacific's varied marine weather streamed into the bay on the capricious westerly breezes that could alter the environment quickly and dramatically.

On any given day sailboats could be seen in the bay tacking back and forth on a sheen of dazzling, liquid sunlight, but within hours the fog could roll in through the Golden Gate in an impressive display of eerie beauty, shrouding the area in a veil of chilly gray. Often in the mornings fog domes formed over Alcatraz and Angel Islands, sometimes obscuring them, sometimes creating the illusion that they were levitating on serene sheets of clouds.

It was an impressive and constantly changing panorama, and Fane had made viewing the performance part of his daily ritual in the past few years, waking to new surprises every morning and taking one last glance every night before going to sleep.

His home was not among the grandest in the famous district, but it was large and handsome, and though he had lived there only three short years, it was saturated with intense memories, quickly gathered in the too-brief life he had shared there with Dana.

It wasn't his money; it had been Dana's. Fane had quit worrying about what people in certain circles said on that subject around the same time that he quit worrying about the rumors that he had had something to do with Jack Blanda's murder. Actually, Jack had managed to get killed all by himself, but if people insisted on believing otherwise, Marten couldn't stop them. And the truth was, it was Jack who had married Dana for her money. Marten had had the good fortune to actually fall in love with her.

He turned off the street into a bricked parking space

hidden behind a vine-covered wall. He parked and walked through a wrought iron gate into a small courtyard with a limestone walkway flanked by palms that led to the front door. The house was a hybrid of styles, redbrick with limestone lintels and facings, and a slate roof. Over its life it had undergone several massive changes resulting in a one-of-a-kind structure that refused to be typed. Fane liked it.

After hanging his raincoat in the entrance foyer, he went down the broad central hallway and into the living room. After turning on a few lamps, he made his way to the kitchen.

He dumped a couple of ice cubes into a glass, poured a gurgle of Glenfiddich over them, and returned to the living room. For a moment he stood in the middle of the room, sipped the Scotch, and gathered his thoughts. He had returned to the living room out of habit more than purpose. He looked around.

Photography books were scattered everywhere—some still open—on the floor and on the sofa. Always an autodidact with a restless curiosity, he habitually immersed himself in a variety of diverse subjects in which he tended to see relationships where others saw none at all.

Though Fane had been interested in photography since his Berkeley days, photographic portraits in particular had been of special interest in the past five years. It had started while he was still in the SID, working an investigation that involved several informants who were in hiding in different safe houses. One was sequestered in a small bungalow in the Russian River valley. When the informant failed to show for a prearranged meeting, Fane went to his secluded safe house and found the man dead. He lay on the floor in the

main room of his cottage as if asleep, surrounded by forty-
seven photographs, all portraits, of very young boys, adoles-
cents, and young men.

The man had killed himself with pills and vodka, and
Fane at first thought he must have been a pedophile. But
when he began to examine the pictures, which were arranged
clockwise around his body in the chronological age of the
subjects, Fane was surprised to discover that all of the pictures were of the dead man himself.

Disturbed by this discovery, Fane spent nearly an hour
alone with the dead informant looking at the pictures. For
some inexplicable reason he felt an obligation to look at each
image individually, to go through them in the order in which
the man had arranged them, taking the time to look carefully
at the changing face of the growing boy until he saw something that he identified with, the slight puckering of concern
in the brow, the beginning of a shy smile, a haunting emptiness, fleeting happiness, the eventual absence of innocence.

Why had the man kept the photographs? Why had he
surrounded himself with them in the moment of his death?
What had he been thinking as he spent his last hour arrang-
ing the pictures, looking one last time at the faces of the boy
he once had been? All of these questions haunted Fane for
weeks afterward.

He began collecting books of photographic portraits. It
didn't matter what the subjects' age was, or their nationality
or sex or ethnicity: all faces were information to him, all were
stories of their own histories and windows into the mysteries
of the individual. Fane didn't know if he understood what he

was seeing in these faces; he only knew that he wanted to, and that somehow the looking brought him closer to the possibility. He had scores of these books now, and from time to time he would pull some of them from the shelves and spend hours going through the pages.

He put his suit coat over the back of a chair and carried his drink to the French doors that opened onto the terrace. The rain had started again in just the past few moments, slowly. He looked out at the lights of the Golden Gate Bridge off to his left, and the Marina below. Maybe you could take the view for granted after a while, after a lifetime, maybe, but you could never get tired of it.

His thoughts turned to Vera List. Intelligent. Scared. She had a hell of an interesting story, and a gutsy objective. But the confidentiality issue was going to be a problem. She didn't come right out and say it, but Fane definitely got the impression that he wasn't going to have access to Elise and Lore. She didn't want them to know what was happening to them. This would have to change.

But Fane didn't go into that with her. Vera was already so stressed about her situation, almost on the verge of panic, that discussing it was best left for another time.

All in all, she struck him as a woman who could see an idea through to the end. She appeared to understand what she was in for, and his cautionary warnings didn't shake her determination. Maybe a psychoanalyst could read between the lines better than most people.

Besides, it seemed that by the time Vera went to see Shen Moretti seeking help, she had already decided that she was going to do something. He doubted if there was anything he could have said that would have changed her mind.

He took his BlackBerry out of his pocket and called her.

"What does your morning look like?"

There was a pause. "I have a ten— . . . no, she canceled. So, I'm open. But then I'm booked from one o'clock through the afternoon."

"Okay, good. There are a few things we need to do."

It was nearly eleven p.m. when he finished typing his notes from his conversation with Vera List. He closed the file, and as he turned away from the computer, his eye caught a glint from the cockpit of the model airplane on his desk. It was an old Beechcraft C-12F Huron, the aircraft he had piloted when he was eighteen, hauling what he thought was contraband down to Isla Margarita off Venezuela. A chunk of coral reef taken from the Bonaire Basin that same year sat underneath the Huron model.

Though the room was full of mementos, there were no pictures of Fane with anyone. He wasn't that kind of a guy. But there were three pictures of women on the left side of his desk: his mother, taken when she must have been about twenty-two, the Caddo mountains of Texas in the background; a young woman straddling a bicycle under the arch of Sather Gate at Berkeley; and Dana, standing in front of the bougainvilleas on their terrace, six months into their short fourteen-month marriage.

They were all smiling.

They were all gone.

Fane let his eyes rest a moment on each of the pictures, but only for a moment. Dana had been dead a little over a year now, the others longer, and it hurt too much to let his mind dwell. Dwelling was dangerous, especially this late at night. There was a time when dwelling had almost killed him. Now he had a healthy respect for night thoughts.

Instead, he turned off the lights, checked the surveillance monitors with a glance, and took his empty glass back through the main hallway to the kitchen. He put it in the sink and looked out the window at the street below.

Without giving much thought to what he was doing, he walked slowly through the silent dining room with its view to the bay and its echoes of dinner parties past. Near the far end of the room he went out the door to the central hallway, and to the French doors to the terrace. He stepped outside and stood under the dripping awnings.

On clear nights he and Dana used to put on sweaters and take a bottle of wine and a bowl of olives out to the terrace. They wouldn't come in again until nothing remained but olive pits and empty glasses. They talked about everything; with so much history behind them and so much future to explore together, they could have talked forever. Jesus. How was it that even after all the things they both had lived through, they still had been so naive?

He quickly turned away and went back inside. He went into the living room again, thinking he might spend a little time with the photography books, but the lamps were out, and the thought of turning them on again was less appealing than the darkness. A soft splash of light stretched across the floor toward him from the barrel-vaulted passageway on the other side of the room. He followed it out.

He went through the passageway, past his study to his bedroom, all of which opened onto the terrace.

After undressing, he lay awake in the dark, watching the webby patterns on the ceiling. He wished he hadn't called Roma earlier. They could have talked now, and he could have drawn out the conversation to absorb some of the night. Even if she realized he was deliberately prolonging the conversation, that would have been okay with her. She would have understood.

He thought about Vera List again. The strange situation in which she found herself must have shaken her world to its core. But despite the fact that she had obviously decided to confront her baffling difficulties with a brave resolve, Fane sensed a tone of disbelief that seeped into an occasional inflection in her voice. She knew that even to the modest degree that any of us can manage what happens to us in this world, she had lost control of her life. It had changed forever. How much it had changed now depended a great deal upon Fane.

He listened to the rain splashing on the terrace until time smeared into timeless, and he drifted off.

"You must've been a woman," she said.

"No, never was."

"How do you know?"

"Believe me, Elise, I'd know."

The glass room cantilevered into the night space in the hills above Sausalito. Across the bay, the lights of San Francisco luminesced inside the fog.

She was still unnerved, a little rattled, by what had just happened. She tried to hide it, though she didn't know why. Maybe it was time she stopped concealing her agitation at the way things were going. It was getting worse, and maybe she should acknowledge that. But something told her he already knew.

"My analyst gave me an article about this man in Greek mythology," she said. She was facing the glass wall, close to it, and her voice was coming back at her. He was on the sofa behind her.

"Tiresias. A chance event caused him to be changed into

a woman. Seven years later, she was changed back into a man. When Hera and Zeus were having an argument about who received the most pleasure from sex, Zeus said women did; Hera said men did. They asked Tiresias. He said that women did . . . nine times more pleasure than men, he said."

He was silent. In the reflection in the glass wall she saw him lift his wine glass and drink.

"Because Tiresias sided with Zeus," she concluded, "Hera struck him blind."

"Nice story," he said. "The point being, I suppose, that I must've been a woman in a past life because I understand the way your mind works."

"No, the point being, it's dangerous to know too much about what a woman thinks."

He didn't say anything, though she knew he wanted to. But first he needed to figure out what was behind the anecdote—not the meaning of it, but the mind-set. For him, their relationship was a balancing act, and it was only recently, after all these months, that she had begun to understand that.

They had dressed and were having the last of the wine before driving back into the city.

"It's dangerous?" he asked. "Dangerous?"

She waited to see where he would go with this.

"You're half-serious, aren't you?" he said. "What's the matter? Too intense?"

The question was intended to carry a tone of knowing swagger, but she heard, or thought she heard, a trace of doubt beneath the surface.

Though she was still disturbed, she managed to summon the nerve to speak what she was feeling.

"Don't get too far ahead of me," she said, cringing at the slight quaver in her voice. "Don't get too deep inside."

She knew he understood her choice of words. She wasn't mixing her metaphors, and she wasn't talking about sex.

In the reflection she saw him get up from the sofa and come across the room behind her. Even in his smoky mirror image he was handsome, the summer highlights visible in his hair as he passed through a soft beam of light. He stood beside her at the glass wall, the two of them suspended in the darkness. They were looking across the bay, and she could feel him settling in to her, trying to reestablish the psychological thing that connected them, the thing that had begun to frighten her.

"Listen," he said. "How do you want me to be? How do I temper . . . me?"

He was finding his equilibrium now, and the very fact that he was doing it so readily unnerved her even more.

"I don't understand, really," he said, "why our . . . shared . . . psychology makes you so . . . uncomfortable."

She turned to him, and he turned, too. They were still holding their wine glasses, mirror images of each other. And there beside him in the plate glass was his reflection, another mirror image. It was macabre. She could feel her own mirror image in the glass beside her as well, even though she wasn't looking at it. The four of them stood there, sharing the same mind.

She needed to think how to say it. To buy a moment's time, she lifted her glass to sip her wine. He did, too, reflexively maybe, as when one person's yawn elicits another, and they sipped wine together. She wanted to scream.

"It's not what we share," she said, feeling a wild flutter in her chest. "It's what you're stealing."

She saw his surprise. That was oddly comforting, that he seemed to be confused by what she said.

"Stealing?"

"Read my mind, if you want to," she said.

He started to speak but stopped.

"Anticipate my thoughts, if you want to."

He listened.

"Take the words out of my mouth, if you want to."

He waited.

"But for God's sake," she said, "stay out of my head. Let me have a place to hide . . . when *I* have to."

He sat in the living room of the Sea Cliff house, his computer on his lap, the text of one of the psychoanalyst's files on the wide screen in front of him. But his eyes wandered away to the glass wall and the lights of the Golden Gate Bridge, which were slowly being extinguished by the ghostly, gray breath of the bay.

He looked at his watch. It was 3:15 a.m. His eyes returned to the screen and to one of his favorite passages in Vera List's process notes from one of her early sessions with Elise Currin. The passage was a little over a year old, but it was a key event in Elise's analysis.

> Harrowing. That's the only word I can think of for this story, which is inescapably disturbing.
>
> Elise sat on the sofa emotionally lacerated by the mem-

ory and the words from her own mind and mouth. Her eyes were painful to look at, raw and swollen from crying. She had wadded a tissue into a tight ball, kneading and squeezing it until it became no larger than a grape.

She was nine when she first laid eyes on the green glass dove. It sat on a junky shelf in a booth in a traveling carnival on the dusty outskirts of Barstow. It was a prize in a game of chance, but there was no chance that it would ever be hers.

She asked the man in the booth if she could hold it. Sensing a lure for marks, he sat her on the counter and gave it to her. Try your luck, he called out to the marks passing by, win the dove for the little lady.

The glass dove was resplendent, filled with bubbles and eddies of emerald light that mesmerized her and transported her to places she had never been before, places she had never even imagined. She saw something there that gave her a sense of well-being for the first time in her life. She didn't know that it was called hope, but she knew that she couldn't live without it.

But the marks who came and went failed to win the dove, and at the end of the night the man at the booth took it away from her and sent her on her way. The next night, when the man in the booth had forgotten about her, she sneaked under the curtains and stole it.

She hid it from her mother and father. It traveled with her as the family searched for work in the dusty San Joaquin Valley, and when she could steal the privacy the way she had stolen the dove itself, she would take it out of its hiding place and hold it up to the light . . . and she would take flight, and escape.

The dove became a holy thing for her, though Elise knew nothing about holiness. The grace of the concept was unknowable to her, but when she peered into the dove's green rivers, her child's imagination was inspired.

When that night came, her mother had disappeared with paying customers. Her father caught Elise under the sheets looking into the glass dove with a flashlight. Inexplicably, he exploded. He was insanely, frighteningly furious. Already she was used to him coming to her at night, but she wasn't prepared for this.

With shocking perversity, he taunted her with the dove, threatening to use it as a phallus, toying with her before he raped her. And then he took it away from her. For weeks he returned at night with it, the same cruel taunts, the same shameful ending, until he had turned the dove into something too ugly to bear.

He killed her with it.

And then one night he came to her drunk, and when he passed out, she snatched the dove and smashed it.

It was the second death of innocence for her, and this time it was gone for good.

Opening a woman's mind was like prying a sharp blade into the crevice of an oyster. If you wanted at the pearl, you had to use the right kind of instrument. If it was too blunt, it had no effect. If it was too thin, it would snap from the pressure. You needed just the right kind of blade, and he knew that this was it.

7

(SIX MONTHS EARLIER)

The vapor-gray Escalade floated out of the night mist and glided to the curb on the side street of a Spanish-style home near the top of Forest Hill. A man stepped out of a wall gate beneath the trees and climbed in next to the woman sitting in the backseat of the Escalade, which eased away and began twisting downhill into the low-lying districts, where the streets ran straight into the windswept Ocean Beach.

"Thanks for this," the woman said.

The man said nothing and waited for the familiar routine to play out.

A glass partition separated the two from the driver and another man in the front passenger seat leaning over a laptop. The Escalade was a rolling body scanner, and within a few moments the man with the laptop would know if the new passenger presented any kind of electronic security risk.

He wouldn't, of course, but it was the same procedure for princes or paupers: everybody got scanned.

The man and the woman were not small talkers. Whatever else this meeting was about it was about trouble, and neither of them was in the mood for incidental exchanges. The man just wanted to know what the hell he was going to be facing so he could start dealing with it.

The woman gazed through the glass partition and watched the headlights of the Escalade flicker over the parked cars and street signs as they appeared and disappeared out of the fog. The dim, greenish illumination from the dashboard lights and computer screens washed the color from her face and erased the details of her features.

But the man knew those features well: she was tall and thin and fifty-two. Her hair was unnaturally and uniformly black, a physical improbability at her age that didn't seem to bother her as much as the idea of letting the gray take its course. She favored dark suits, their skirts stopping a few inches below her knees—not sexy, but not matronly either. She rarely wore jewelry.

A small green light winked below the glass partition.

"This is SCI," the woman said, turning to the man and using the letters for Sensitive Compartmented Information. It was a term borrowed from U.S. intelligence services for a way of handling information in their highest security categories. "One of our black bands has gone missing."

The man was one-fifth of the executive committee of her board. When something went wrong at this level, he was the first and only one to hear about it. If the problem could be contained or resolved, he had the authority to bury it. It didn't have to go any further.

"When did this happen?" he asked.

"Five days ago. He failed to report in, and we couldn't reach him. We sent a team to his house in Diamond Heights. It was cleaned out."

"What's our exposure with this guy?"

"He's been with us only four months . . . but the whole time he's been on the Currin ticket."

She wasn't looking at the man, but she knew his expression had changed, his mouth tightened, his shoulders stiffened. His lack of comment was a silent expletive.

"We've red-teamed him," she went on, "actually multi-teamed him, and counterintelligence is close-sifting his Currin activity. We've got forensics going on the computers. We have as many people on it as possible without taking it outside the program's core."

"You don't know anything at all yet?"

"No, but there's no sign so far that this is a result of hostile encroachment, that he was a mole. Of course, it's still early. We might dig up something in the coming days. But the guy has a long rep for being a loner, and as of right now he seems to have just disappeared on his own."

The Escalade was cruising slowly, shouldering through the murk, a mobile security cocoon for a conversation that never happened.

The woman waited for the man to gather his thoughts. She had discharged her responsibilities, and she really didn't need to say any more unless she was asked. Her experience from twenty-two years in the intelligence profession told her that it was easy to say more than you should.

The man had even more years in intelligence than she did, but he had been a corporate chieftain longer as well. Now his instincts ran closer to concerns for the bottom line than to tradecraft.

"Currin," he said. "Christ."

It didn't matter how sophisticated you were or how powerful; no one was immune to getting the air knocked out of them by a piece of bad news.

"I won't be able to sit on this one very long," he said. "If it was just a problem in one country, or even just the U.S., maybe I could carry it a while. But Currin, shit. So this guy had access to everything?"

"He came to us with incredible credentials, so we—"

"*Did* he have access to everything?"

"Yes."

He fell silent. The Escalade moved through the gray, riding on the border of light and darkness.

"Look, you're going to have to keep me informed," he said. "Hell, I want to hear something from you every few hours."

"Okay, I understand," she said.

"Even if there's nothing new to tell me. I want to hear what's being done . . . what's going to be done . . . what you think needs to be done."

"Okay."

The man was upset but under control. He looked out his window into the night. There was nothing to see but his own reflection, and even that was difficult to make out in the murk of the tinted glass.

"You ever handled something like this before?" he asked, still looking out, his voice bouncing back at him.

"Exactly like this? No." And then, not to let him get by with feeling superior, she said, "You?"

"Well, it was different for the government, wasn't it? There were . . . parameters."

She had the impression that he would have liked to continue, but he didn't. Not down that road.

"Okay," he said, settling back in the corner of his seat. "Give me his dossier."

The woman began talking. She was prepared; she was good at this. She didn't make any mistakes; she didn't leave anything out . . . technically.

But every narrative was an exercise in interpretation, especially in this new world of shadows. Though the woman's manner was dispassionate and straightforward, and for the most part she simply presented the unadorned facts, there were places where she gently nudged a word for emphasis, or attempted to guide the man's assumptions by subtle implication. And then there were places where she didn't spend too much time, where she shaded a phrase, glanced past a point . . . and very delicately finessed a critical piece of the story.

The woman spun her narrative; the Escalade whispered into the fog.

TUESDAY

"This," Roma said with a fascinated smile, "is an interesting story."

They were in Fane's car. He had begun telling her Vera List's story over a cup of coffee in his kitchen and was just now finishing it as they made their way along Pacific Avenue. The overcast was finally lightening to white and would soon be lifting.

Roma sat in the passenger seat, a small laptop in the process of powering up resting on her thighs.

"The scheme's complex," Fane said, braking at a traffic light. "That's the first thing that raises a red flag for me. Next thing is that it's played out way too long without throwing up clues that point to any of the easy answers—sexual perversions, blackmail, homicide. This is something else."

"Does Vera List realize this?"

"Yeah, this thing feels strange to her in a lot of different ways. I talked to Noble last night. He's running a first-pass dossier on Currin and Cha. Bücher's standing by. I told him you'd be calling him."

At Van Ness Avenue Fane turned toward the bay as Roma tapped Vera's office address into the computer. The sun penetrated the broken clouds in bright smears as he turned back toward Russian Hill. A few blocks later he slowed.

"Here it is," he said.

Vera List's office was in a neighborhood of gentrified addresses with lush courtyards and brick pathways, an area honeycombed with small lanes and pedestrian passageways.

The satellite image of the block popped up on Roma's computer, and she zoomed in as Fane pulled to the curb next to a tree-lined sidewalk.

"Not good," Roma said. "Too many ways to approach the place. Look at the courtyards in this block. It's a maze."

Fane leaned on the console to look at the screen.

"One, two, three, four . . . five courtyards. Can't tell if they're interconnected. Here's Vera's building. Look at the vegetation, trees, shrubs, hedges. Add the Russian Hill fog to this, and you've got a surveillance nightmare."

"Lucky guy," Fane said.

"Greenwich is a cul-de-sac," Roma said. "Leavenworth drops sharply toward the bay. No use to us. Parking on Filbert, that's a break."

She studied the screen, seeing places that concealed, trapped, allowed escape, and gave away a route two turns in advance.

"Okay," she said, "here's what I'd do: Sweep the offices. If we find bugs, leave them in place. If we find cameras, we're screwed. If we don't, then we have Jon install several micro infrared remotes. Considering the frequency of the women's appointments, the guy's probably coming every week to stay up to date. And, as you said, by now he's comfortable with his routine, maybe letting down his guard a little.

"Start with static surveillance," she went on. "Cover the approaches to the courtyards. It'll be expensive, but when you consider his targets, it makes sense. Once the guy's inside, we'll shift positions if we need to."

"Fine."

"You want to get this rolling tonight, then?"

"Definitely."

"I'll call Jon in a minute and have him start pulling things together. But first, let's drive into Greenwich, and then let's make the block. I want to see how the stairs go down through that dense shrubbery to Leavenworth."

After Roma was satisfied with her inspection, they returned to Fane's home, where Roma picked up her Pathfinder and drove off to join Bücher.

At exactly 10:00, Vera List turned on her iPod, selected a couple of hours of Mahler, and let it go.

She nervously gathered her things, grabbed two extra key cards, and walked out of her office. She took the elevator down to the small lobby, where a woman and two men waited for her.

"Vera?"

"Yes. You're Roma?"

They shook hands, but the attractive Colombian didn't introduce the two men carrying bulky metal suitcases.

Vera handed Roma the two key cards.

"The one with the blue band opens the door to the building," Vera said. "The one with the green band opens my office. I left music playing. I often do that in the afternoon when I have paperwork. Keep the cards."

"I'll call your cell after we leave," Roma said.

Vera smiled nervously, nodded at the two men, and walked out the front door into the courtyard.

When Vera had back-to-back appointments that ran through the noon hour, she often ate a late lunch at a little bistro just a couple of blocks away.

She liked the timing, usually sharing the bistro with only a few scattered patrons. That suited her. Sometimes she read or wrote up notes from the last session. Sometimes she stared out the window, letting her thoughts wander.

Today, in the middle of the morning, the crowd was also sparse, too late for breakfast, too early for lunch. She had just settled into her chair when Fane walked through the front door. He found her with a glance and walked toward her table.

"Sorry I'm a little late," he said, taking a chair across from her.

"No problem. I just got here myself."

They both ordered coffee, and she tried to quell the growing anxiety that had been with her for days now. She looked at Fane with a more deliberate attention than she had at the Stafford Hotel the night before.

He appeared to be in his midforties, but it was hard to tell. He had a face that contradicted itself: a severe brow expression with kind eyes, craggy bone structure with a patrician mouth. Expensive suit again. Cuff links again. A lot more class than she had expected, but then that was her fault for making assumptions.

"It'll take about an hour," he said. "They're fast."

"And the cameras will be on only at night."

"That's right."

The waiter came over with their coffee, and Fane's eyes followed him back to the bar before they turned to her, catching her finger uneasily circling the rim of her cup.

She stopped.

"You have to decide how you're going to deal with this privacy issue," he said. "I'll need to know more than I think you want to tell me."

"Like what?"

"I'm assuming this guy is using aliases, a different one with each woman. I need to know those names."

"I told you, neither of them has ever used a name."

He sipped his coffee. "I'll need to talk to them."

"I just don't . . . see how that . . . how that can happen."

"If you want to do this the way you described last night, if you want to contain this, then you'll have to be willing to blur the lines."

"What lines?"

"The ones you've drawn around those two women."

His eyes were fixed on her, and he was waiting for an answer. He was unnervingly observant, and despite her effort to appear resolute, she was sure he was reading her equivocation.

"When are your next sessions with them?"

"Lore will be in this afternoon. Two o'clock. Elise tomorrow morning."

"Think about it," he said. "Figure it out. You're going to have to make some choices."

She was still absorbing that, trying to get her mind around the implications, when he said, "In the meantime, I'm concentrating on Elise Currin first. The more I know about her the better. Maybe you can just give me a sense of who she is, as if you were telling me about a friend, someone I don't know."

Vera hesitated. "Well, that's my problem, isn't it? She's not a friend. She's a client. And that puts the relationship on an entirely different plane."

Fane regarded her in silence. He told her the way it had to be. He wasn't going to negotiate with her.

She felt exposed. This was going to be even harder than she had imagined.

"She's a trophy wife," Vera said. "And she knows it. She's beautiful, a strawberry blonde who is acutely aware of what her beauty means in life's great equation: not much.

"On the other hand, she knows very well that her beauty is a blunt-instrument asset and that her financial security largely depends on it. She knows that it keeps one sister in drug rehab. It's the glue that keeps another sister's family from disintegrating. It keeps her mother out of a crummy nursing home in a dusty little town in the San Joaquin Valley and keeps oxygen in the cylinder her stepfather drags around with him."

Vera List finished her coffee and shook her head at the waiter who was drifting toward her with a refill.

"Elise is a pragmatist . . . with an incompatible heart," Vera went on. "The first twelve years of her life were spent in a small, rusty trailer that her father, a welder, pulled up and down the San Joaquin Valley in search of 'work and shade and finding very little of either one,' to quote Elise. Her mother slept with locals for extra money, and her father slept with Elise for nothing.

"When she was thirteen they set up camp in a grove of trees outside some little town in the valley. One hot afternoon she hitchhiked into town and found her way to the sheriff's office. She turned in her father for molesting her and her sisters, who were nine and seven at the time.

"Father went to prison. Girls were in and out of child protective services and foster 'places.' She won't call them 'homes.' She finally finished high school in Modesto and worked her way through UC-Berkeley as a waitress. Had a blind date with another student, who turned out to be in law school. She married him just as he was graduating, and they moved to San Francisco after he signed with a firm here."

Vera stopped. "I don't know if this is the kind of thing you want."

"You're doing fine," he said.

She nodded.

"Elise suddenly found herself in a new world, and it was a long way from the one she'd come from. There was the delicate pecking order of the lawyers and their wives, firm parties, nice clothes, networking. It was a game she understood instinctively, and she was good at playing it. Her beauty was now an asset that could be leveraged for something more valuable than a big tip: it was a boon to her husband's career. And then her husband began having severe headaches. His vision deteriorated. Brain tumor. The worst kind. He was gone in four months.

"Elise was in despair. It wasn't just about losing him. She

was terrified she'd slide back into her old life. She couldn't bear it. So when a senior member of the firm, thrice divorced, gallantly gave her comfort and counseling, she played along. Seven months later they were married. It was a bald act of venality on her part: her body for financial security. It's an old and common bargain, but she didn't find any comfort in that. It immediately began to haunt her. She was twenty-seven.

"Eight months later they were divorced. And it was vicious. He threatened to expose her past, the molesting father, the prostitute mother. She folded and walked away with nothing."

Vera paused, thoughtfully nudged her saucer with the tips of her fingers, and went on.

"By now, though, she was well-known in those legal circles that had been so new to her just a few years before. There was sympathy for her, and she had learned a lot about how to handle herself.

"Then came Jeffrey Safra Currin. They dated about a year. They've been married four years."

"She's been seeing you for nearly two years?"

"That's right."

"Had she been in analysis before?"

"No. But she knew what to expect. Being Mrs. Jeffrey Currin put her in a whole different solar system than where she'd been before. The women she encountered in these circles were no strangers to psychoanalysis, and once she decided she needed help, she got a lot of advice."

"Someone referred her to you, then?"

"Yes."

"And the third marriage to Currin?" Fane asked. "Were her motivations the same as the second marriage?"

"Slightly different. This time her rationalization was more complex. She let herself be romanced. If love wasn't there, then she could buy in to the romance of it. Imitation love. The desire to hang on to the good life was more deeply buried this time, but it was there. And she knew it."

A burst of hissing and gurgling came from the espresso machine behind the bar, and in the next room someone laughed a barking laugh that died away quickly.

"Since beginning the affair," Fane asked, "does she talk about different issues, have different concerns?"

Vera tilted her head slightly to one side and furrowed her brow.

"I wouldn't say the issues and concerns have changed so much," she said, "but maybe she deals with them a little differently now. The affair . . . it's given her some relief from the isolation of her marriage."

"Isolation?"

"Trophies sit on glass shelves in glass cases. They gather dust. No one touches them for long periods of time."

"But you've seen a change in her since the affair began?"

"Yes."

"How would you describe it?"

"An accretion of sorrow."

Fane was surprised by her choice of words.

"But you said her affair had, sort of, given her a new life. You said she was bewitched by this man. Mesmerized."

"Bewitched and mesmerized aren't inherently positive

words. I believe I also mentioned that she found the whole thing slightly eerie."

"Okay, let's back up a little," Fane said. "Did she tell you how she met this man?"

"Accidentally. A casual, random meeting, one thing led to another."

"Do they ever talk about Currin?"

"If they do, she's not telling me about it."

"She's never mentioned it at all?"

"Only in the beginning. Once this guy found out who her husband was, he became obsessive about keeping their meetings secret. He was afraid Currin might have a private investigator watching her."

"Has Elise ever expressed any concern about that?"

"No, not at all."

"Before she began this affair, had she ever given Currin a reason to have her watched?"

"I don't think so. This affair was a big step for her. Something new."

Fane had forgotten his coffee, and now the cream was separating in ropey swirls on the surface. Learning about Elise Currin from Vera was a little more slippery than Fane had hoped. But he wasn't surprised.

"You said you thought the affair was a relief from isolation. Could there be more to it than that?"

She touched her saucer, traced the rim of it, stopped.

"I think," she said, looking up at him, "that being Mrs. Jeffrey Safra Currin is more than Elise had bargained for. Taken for granted, treated like property, yes. Used for loveless sex, yes. Trotted out to show people what a fine piece of meat he has whenever he wants it, yes. Elise had decided to live with all that going into it, for the reasons I've already mentioned."

Vera considered her next words carefully.

"Most women in her situation," she said, "just live with it. Their defense mechanisms are bitterness and cynicism, and those seem to serve them well enough.

"But there's something about Elise that won't allow her to grow calloused like that. It compels her to confront her life and the choices she's made, without flinching. She stoically probes her own shame. She weighs her desperation. She genuinely wants to understand the whole human mix of it. Not many people can endure that kind of confrontation with themselves. It's brutal. And it's profoundly courageous."

CHAPTER·

10

Lore Cha's legs were crossed at the knees as she sat in the corner of the sofa. She was waggling her foot, her stylish Ferragamo heel loose and dangling.

"Nobody, I swear, NObody, knows about *that* little fantasy," Lore said. "Well, you, I guess I mentioned it to you, but Christ, suddenly here we are and we're playing this thing out! Down to the least, you know, the least damned detail. It was like a . . . a weird, crazy, whacked-out hallucination!"

She was furious, and she was scared. The fright and the fury had been knotted inside her for several days, and she was still worked up. Vera waited. She wanted more; she wanted everything Lore Cha could remember.

Lore's mind caught on something, and suddenly she stopped waggling her foot. Her eyes were fixed on nothing in particular out the windows in the courtyards. She was as still as a deer, listening.

Then her foot started waggling again, and she resumed seething.

"And then he just passed out. I mean, really passed out, you know, like it had taken a lot out of him." She shook her head, and her black eyes cut at Vera. "Oh, shit, it just infuriates me."

Lore Cha was a stunningly beautiful woman, a fifth-generation Chinese American from a middle-class family. She had a master's degree in international politics from Stanford, a runway model's body, a wealthy husband, and a screwed-up psychology. If she stayed in analysis for the rest of her life it wouldn't be long enough.

She picked up a glass of water on the side table, took a quick sip, and put it back.

She told Vera about looking into Krey's wallet, about him waking up and catching her, or almost catching her, about her dressing, then leaving.

"The next day I net-searched his name," Lore said. "Nothing. Couldn't find a phone number. But I found his address. There it was, up in the woods in one of those canyons in Mill Valley. I couldn't tell much from that, and I wanted to *know*. I stewed about it all day, and then yesterday I drove out to Marin to see for myself."

She stopped and shook her head slowly, looking at Vera.

"I got up in those canyons," she said. "Made a couple of wrong turns. It was spooky up there under all those redwoods. Found it." She stopped again, furious, and now she was nodding, confirming. "Found it. I sat out there on the road and asked myself, Now how the hell do I know this is really his house? It didn't look like him. Suburban kind of thing in the woods. All wrong for him."

Lore didn't need any prompting today. She had it all bottled up inside her, and she was going to spit it out.

"I drove back into town and found a real estate office. Pretended I was looking for land, for a particular house, maybe to buy. They used their maps, and we checked out everything. Public records. The house belongs to Philip R. Krey.

"I drove back to the house and knocked on the door. A woman about, maybe fifty-five, answers. I said I was looking for Philip Krey. She gives me this startled, funny look. She says he's traveling. He's been out of the country six months and is supposed to be gone another year.

"I asked her who she was. She said, 'Jenny Cox.' I asked her how long she had known Krey. She said she didn't really know him. She just answered an ad in the paper for a house sitter. Then she got really touchy and shut up."

Now Lore calmed down and stopped waggling her foot.

"Since then," she said, her voice softer, more controlled, "I've done everything I can to verify this guy's identity, but Philip R. Krey just doesn't exist."

Just as her anger had faded to calm, her calm now evolved to a sober, grim-faced fear.

"So I'm wondering," Lore said, "just who in the hell have I been having an affair with? And why is he doing this? How come he knows so much about me? And *why* does he know so much? What's the point of all this? The sex? Is that it? But he doesn't have to be so . . . ghostly just to get the sex. I mean, I can understand wanting to be discreet, but, hell, he's nonexistent!"

Lore peaked and valleyed several times before she reached this point in her story, and by now Vera was building an entirely new universe of problems with every new revelation from Lore. She had listened to Lore's outpouring with increasing anxiety. What was Lore going to do with her discoveries? What was she going to do about the man who wasn't Krey?

"The intuition stuff," Lore said, "it's reached a point . . . where, you know, it's horrifying. He shouldn't be able to 'intuit' this stuff. He shouldn't be able to get that damned *close* to my thoughts."

Lore's voice quavered, and it seemed to take her by surprise. She blinked wildly, fighting like hell not to cry, then grabbed the water glass and drank.

"What are you going to do?" Vera asked, but Lore couldn't pull herself together enough to respond.

Vera waited. She wasn't sure where to take it next, but she knew that stopping Krey was the only way she could protect Lore's privacy and the confidentiality of her records. Think about it, Fane had said. Figure it out.

"What I'm going to do," Lore said finally, swallowing, "is never see the crazy bastard again. And hope like hell that he disappears from the face of the earth."

"Well, he's not going to do that," Vera said.

"As far as I'm concerned he already has."

"Do you think this is the best way to deal with him?"

"Why the hell wouldn't it be?"

"Pretending he suddenly doesn't exist isn't realistic. There's no real resolution."

"Resolution? Are you kidding me? If I never see him again, that's resolution enough for me."

"But you can never be sure that it's really over."

Lore studied her, waiting.

"I'm only saying that sticking your head in the sand isn't an answer," Vera said. "It's avoidance."

"It's choosing to swear off the guy."

"It doesn't provide any opportunity for a resolution."

"Some things in life just don't have answers."

"Really? That's a bit of wisdom?"

Lore didn't answer because she wasn't listening. She knew she didn't have a solution. She knew she was in really serious trouble, and she was scared to death.

Vera was struggling with her own kind of panic. She was approaching a critical decision, and she hadn't had time to think through the ramifications of the vague solution taking shape in the suddenly crowded moment.

"What are the odds that this man will let you call this off?" Vera asked. "Do you really think he'll just drop out of your life because you won't answer his phone calls?"

Lore didn't answer. Her long fingers toyed nervously with a coral bracelet.

"You'll spend the rest of your life afraid that you're going to run into him around the next corner, afraid he'll be on the other end of the ringing phone."

Lore was looking away, and her foot was waggling her Ferragamo again. She had a permanent furrow between her beautiful eyebrows.

"He's going to come after me," Lore said softly, abruptly caving in. "I don't know what to do about it. I can't think of anything else, and I can't think of any answers. It's driving me crazy. Shit shit shit shit."

Suddenly she was crying, though her face didn't crumple

with anguish. It was stonelike, and the tears poured from her eyes in startling volume, careening down her face, dribbling off her chin. She didn't bother to wipe them.

Vera stood, pulled several tissues from the box on the coffee table, and gave them to her.

"Maybe it's time to tell Richard," Vera said, testing.

Lore's head snapped up out of the tissues.

"Are you crazy? That's insane! No! No! Never!"

Relieved, Vera took another step.

"Have you told anybody about this affair, besides me?"

"Absolutely not."

"No hint of it even, to anyone? A close friend maybe?"

"You've got to be kidding," Lore spat from behind the tissues, trying to get a grip on the tears. "It's not that kind of an affair. I don't have those kinds of friends."

Vera let a moment pass, giving Lore's mind a chance to catch up with itself.

"You're going to need some help," Vera said calmly, surprising herself at the step she was taking.

"Don't tell me . . . a private investigator. Not a chance. I know someone who hired a PI for something like this, and the creep ended up blackmailing her."

Vera looked away to give Lore space, not wanting to make her feel as if she was being pushed into something. The palms outside the windows were motionless in the soft light of early afternoon, and Vera listened to the silence as if she were a musician holding a prolonged chord until she heard the precise effect she wanted to achieve.

Lore sniffled, and Vera let her eyes return to her.

"I wasn't going to suggest a private investigator."

"Well, it's fine for you to tell me I need some help. What else is new?"

"You don't want to wait until Krey tries to get in touch with you again. You need to do something—"

"Damn it!" Lore snapped, "I know that, Vera. I just don't know what."

She swore again and quickly stood, angry with herself, angry at Krey, angry at her fear. She went to the windows overlooking the courtyard and paced along them, looking out.

Vera stood and joined her at the windows.

"I know about someone who might be able to help you." There, she said it. She had begun to blur the lines.

Lore stopped pacing and turned to her.

"You know 'about' someone who 'might'—what are you talking about?"

"I know people who know people," Vera said stiffly, trying to feel the right tenor. "But I have to have your permission to initiate."

"Not a PI."

"Absolutely not."

"What is he then?"

"He'll have to explain that. I just need to know if you want to talk to someone who . . . can help you with this."

Lore searched Vera's face. "Discreetly."

"Yes."

Lore's mind was racing with the possibilities, and Vera could tell that she understood that the less said the better.

With bloodshot eyes and a puffy face, Lore looked

exhausted. She put the tissues to her nose and held them there, looking at Vera. She dropped her hands.

"How does this work?"

"I need a phone number that you feel safe with. I'll give the number to someone, and they'll pass it on to the right person."

Lore studied Vera. She sniffled.

"This guy had better be good," she said. Then she recited the phone number.

11

Fane waited on a bench in Huntington Park. On the other side of the fountain, near the trellises, half a dozen elderly Chinese women leaned into the ripples of afternoon light in a slow, somber Tai Chi sequence.

He saw Moretti before Moretti saw him. He just happened to be looking at the steps of Grace Cathedral when a clutch of tourists came out. Moretti was crossing the terrace in front of the church and fell in with the crowd.

When the group started across Taylor Street, they abruptly sheared off, and Moretti crossed to the Huntington Park steps alone.

He smiled as he approached Fane, walking with his familiar loose gait. Fane was always fascinated by Moretti's vacillant features, which sometimes favored his Chinese mother, sometimes his Sicilian father. At the moment he was more Shen than Moretti.

"You're looking elegant," Moretti said as he approached the bench and sat down.

"It's been a few months," Fane said.

Moretti smiled and settled back in his corner of the bench. He studied Fane. "You want to know about Vera List."

"She knew your sister?"

"Right," Moretti nodded, his eyes finding the Tai Chi group. "I don't know her well. I mostly know about her from my sister. But I've visited with her a few times. Very nice, I thought. You've met with her, I guess."

"Yes."

"Interesting?"

"Very."

"Did you know her husband was murdered?"

For a split second Fane was angry with himself for not knowing this. "No."

"About nine months ago. Mugged, robbed, shot. They never got anybody for it."

"What happened?"

"He was a psychoanalyst, too. They lived in Saint Francis Wood at the time. He got a call one night, a client in crisis or something. He stopped at a little grocery in the Mission and was walking back to his car. They shot him. Took everything, watch, rings, wallet. Shoes, too."

"Children?"

"No. They were all about each other and their work. After the killing, Vera sold the house, moved to a condo in Laurel Heights. That's where she met Gina. Gina is a sympathetic person, a good listener. Vera talked a lot at first, you know, the right time, right person, right circumstances. For a while they were pretty close. Then Vera moved to her new place on Russian Hill."

"Close to her office."

"Yeah. As time went on and Vera got back into her work, she and Gina saw each other less often. I have the impression that Vera's work is her whole life. Especially now. Not much time for friendships." He thought a second. "I guess when you listen to people talk all day . . ."

Moretti shrugged. They both watched the Tai Chi group drift slowly into another position.

"So," Moretti said, "how did the meeting go with her?"

Fane told Moretti practically everything, withholding enough to allow himself to feel that he was respecting Vera's confidence. Like Roma, Moretti was fascinated, and he didn't miss the potential gravity of Vera's predicament.

"That's pretty much the big picture," Fane said, shifting on the bench, crossing his legs the other way.

Moretti sat in silence, watching the thin rivulets spilling from the fountain's pink marble bowls.

"She's gutsy," he mused. "I wonder if she's handling it this way because of her husband."

"What do you mean?"

"Maybe she sees a parallel between someone stealing her files and the mugger stealing her husband's life. She's not going to let it happen this time."

"I don't know," Fane said.

Shen turned to him. "You've got to be realistic about her not wanting her clients to know what's going on. Not wanting them to talk to each other. You take that as far as you can, but when it gets in the way, screw it. You know that, don't you?"

"Yeah, I know."

"Maybe she never finds out."

Fane could see there was something working with Moretti. Something he wanted to say.

"Look, Marten," Moretti began, "I know you like this one. It's juicy. A real conundrum. And I know I sent her to you, but how the hell did I know it was going to involve Jeffrey Safra Currin? That's crazy. There's a million ways this could go wrong for you."

"It's his wife who's got the problem here."

"Don't kid yourself."

A cable car clanged and rattled up California, and the flight of Tai Chi swallows wheeled into another turn.

"I don't like the idea that I shouldn't touch it just because Jeffry Currin's wife is involved."

"Come on, Marten."

"I don't."

Shen nodded, yeah, yeah, okay. No need to throw out any more warnings. Fane was in.

Fane didn't have to explain to Moretti why he was telling him all this. It's what they did. The fact was that Shen Moretti liked a conundrum as much as Fane did, and his gut was too experienced for Fane not to pull him into it.

"Okay, what's bothering you the most?" Moretti asked.

"What she's not telling me," Fane said.

"What she's deliberately holding back? Or what she just doesn't realize is important?"

"Both. In that order."

"What about the first one?"

"I get the impression that Vera and Elise are more like sisters than analyst and client. When Vera was telling me Elise's story, she was doing her best to sound professional, but something less clinical kept seeping into her voice."

"So Vera's reluctance to let you talk to Elise may have as much to do with protecting her on a personal level as it does with her professional concerns."

"Maybe." Fane watched Moretti's mind work with that thought. A group of pigeons milling around near the steps from California Street suddenly exploded into flight, bringing Moretti back to the present.

"Whatever he's doing, this guy," Moretti said, "it's interesting that he's doing it this way."

"What do you mean?"

"He could've discovered Lore after he started prowling through Vera's files looking for information on Elise. But how did he even know that Elise was seeing an analyst? Did she tell him? Or did he discover Elise in the files, too? And if he did, what the hell was he doing in Vera's files in the first place? I'm wondering which came first for this guy. The files or the women?"

Fane left Moretti at Huntington Park, and when he was halfway to his car on Sacramento, his BlackBerry hummed. It was Vera.

"Marten, I've just finished my session with Lore Cha."

She sounded tense, trying not to sound tense.

"She's had an evening with this guy that's left her petrified.

I've got a name for you. And I think I've worked out something so you can talk to her."

By the time Vera finished describing her session with Lore,
Fane had reached his Mercedes.

"So that's it," Vera said. "She's in no mood to have anything else to do with this guy again. Ever. I don't know how
you're going to want to deal with that."

"First of all," he said, "maneuvering Lore into agreeing
to see me was smart thinking. I'll get in touch with her this
morning, make it clear to her that I got her name through
intermediaries. That'll keep you out of it."

"Good, thanks."

"So how do you read what's happening with this guy . . .
Philip Krey?"

"Oh, God, I don't know, but he's definitely not bothering
to be subtle anymore. He's focusing on specifics now, picking up explicit details from my notes and incorporating them
right into their role-playing."

"Isn't that risky for him?"

"Depends on where he's going with all of this."

"He's got to know he's scaring her."

"Of course he does. Whatever his reasons are, he's intensifying the relationship."

"Okay, I understand," Fane said, trying to sound as if he
had everything under control. He heard the rising tension in
her voice, and he needed to help her come down.

"Let's just focus on the next step: you need to fabricate
new session notes for Lore. Don't let him know about her
panic, that she wants to break it off with him."

"Okay, I'll work on it."

"What about Elise?" Fane asked.

"I have a session with her tomorrow afternoon."

"Okay, again, just try to get a name from her."

"I will."

"You did a great job, Vera. Meanwhile, I'll get in touch with Lore."

As soon as they hung up, Fane entered Lore Cha's cell number into his BlackBerry, then dialed it. He wanted to call her as soon as possible. Surprising her would help sustain the sense of urgency that was already pushing her.

"This is Townsend," he said.

"Who?"

"Am I speaking to Lore Cha?"

Suspicious hesitation. "Yes."

"I understand you're needing some help with a problem."

"Vera called you?"

"A man called me."

Hesitation. "Townsend's not your real name, is it?"

"No."

"When can we meet?"

"Right now."

Hesitation. "Uh . . . okay, I can do that. Where?"

"Are you being followed?"

The question caught her by surprise. "I . . . I . . . No."

"How do you know?"

Silence.

"Okay," Fane said, "I'll have a taxi pick you up and bring you to a place where we can meet privately."

"Is that necessary?"

"If you don't know that it isn't, then it is."

She told him where she could leave her car, and they disconnected. Fane called a taxi driver who knew what needed to be done and how to do it.

Then he dialed Bobby Noble and asked him to check out a name for him: Philip Krey.

CHAPTER

12

Lambeth Court wasn't easy to find, which was the point of doing it there. It was a little pocket inside one of Chinatown's mazes, down a crooked walking lane, through a courtyard, into an alley, a musty corridor, a stairway with sticky banisters. He finally ended up in a noisome hallway that smelled of old wood and disinfectant.

After several trips into Chinatown to find the right place, he called Traci Lee and told her to get a room there for a couple of weeks. You could do that here, week by week, and the best part of it was that when they gave you the key nobody went in there again except you, until they came looking for you to collect more money or to kick you out.

Their clientele were people who wanted to be left alone. Traci would be the only person associated with the room as far as the downstairs desk knew, or cared to know.

He had lived under so many names and addresses for so long that he didn't even know who the hell he was anymore, and sometimes he really didn't even care. This kind of life played out in increments. That was the only way you could control the reality of your situation. Compartmentalize. That was how you survived, how you kept your sanity.

In fact, even if you lost your sanity from time to time, you could always "recover" yourself if you paid close attention to what was in the compartments you created. Keep weird here. Keep sane there. Keep Joe under this. Keep Mary behind that. Keep *them* above. Keep *those* below. Keep *it* inside. Drag *them* out when you need them. Keep the lid on them when you don't. It was like counting cards in blackjack. Just keep your shit straight. You'll be okay.

But even so, he felt like he was pushing the envelope with these women. The only problem was, he wasn't sure anymore what was the envelope and what wasn't.

He rapped softly on the door with the back of his hand. It opened a crack, and her eyes frowned through the fissure, then rolled with relief when she recognized him.

"Jesus," she said, backing the door open to let him in. "Why'd you pick a place like this?"

He handed her the paper sack with the Tanqueray and tonic and two plastic glasses.

"It's gotten riskier," he said, looking around at the grim little room, at the niche with the hot plate and a porcelain sink, at the bathroom fifteen feet away, its door open and the toilet showing. "We have to talk about that. I wanted more privacy for our next few meetings."

"Oh, Christ, you know, you're way over the top with this security shit."

And that was part of the problem with Traci. Aside from knowing just too damned much now, she was getting lazy. She was going to screw up. Celia Negri was ready. He had coached her, and she had already been in once, and she had handled it like a pro. It was time.

They spent the next half hour talking and drinking. He said whatever he had to say to make the time pass and to make it sound real to her, giving the gin time to do its thing. When she got up and went into the bathroom, he slipped the first dose of Rohypnol into her drink.

She returned, and he said he was going to start paying her more because of whatever, and then she thought it was necessary to tell him about a guy she met who had a place up in Sonoma. By the time she finished that story, the Rohypnol was working on her.

He made another drink, and she wasn't even caring at all what he was doing over there at the sink. More Rohypnol. Strong.

He watched her closely, not even having to bother pretending that he was drinking anymore. He started cleaning up, covering his presence in the room, putting his plastic cup in the paper bag, wiping his prints off the bent spoon he had stirred with.

The Rohypnol was making her melancholy, fearful, anxious. As her agitation grew he decided to go ahead and finish it. He didn't even bother to get up now and just mixed the next drink, the last one, right there in front of her, with Valium, Xanax, more Rohypnol.

She drank it like a weary child taking medicine from a parent, without questioning what he gave her.

Another fifteen minutes.

Now she was too hammered to even make an effort to get up off the filthy sofa when she needed to go to the bathroom again. She sat there pissing herself, looking at him with a puzzled frown.

When she was finished, her eyebrows shrugged, and she settled into herself. Her shoulders sagged; her head settled on her neck. She eased forward and held herself in suspension at a forty-five-degree angle for an oddly long time. Then she sank further, collapsing across her own lap, her head awkwardly twisted on her knees.

Perfect. With her head torqued at that acute angle, already restricting the airway in her throat, it would happen even faster than he had anticipated. He crossed one leg over the other, checked his watch, and waited.

Soon she was snoring heavily. Within only a few minutes, her breathing changed into a grossly sonorous groan. It grew labored as the stew of drugs dragged at her brain stem, and her central nervous system lost its will to command her muscles. Her heaving for breath morphed into a weird lurching grunt.

And then silence.

He waited. Stillness. Her body coughed once. He waited. A few minutes passed. He checked her pulse in her wrist and her neck.

It took him about five minutes to finish covering the fact that she had had company and scatter the drugs around, dropping some on the filthy floor.

Unless she began to smell, the soonest they would find her would be two weeks from now when the rent was due.

13

Rumeur was a little shop near Palm Alley in North Beach. Wanda Pace ran a quirky enterprise specializing in foreign antique ink bottles and collections of old photographs of human oddities. Her three largest compilations came from the back streets and flea markets of Cairo, Hong Kong, and Mexico City.

Several years ago Wanda had bought an assortment of photographs out of Beijing from a prominent San Francisco lawyer. Before he could deliver them, he was murdered. Fane was still with the SID and had been investigating the lawyer on an unrelated issue. He helped Wanda clear her name of any involvement in the crime, then helped her get her photographs from the lawyer's estate.

After that, if he needed a little privacy for a couple of hours, Wanda always had a back room available. She also kept an eye on the street for him.

"Long time," Wanda said with a soft smile when she let

Fane into her rooms from the alley. He bent into the haze of gardenia fragrance that followed her and kissed her cheek.

"I appreciate this," he said. "A cab's going to drop her off in the front any minute."

Wanda was in that vague season beyond midlife, but not yet of a certain age. She was slim and pale and always wore stylish shirtwaist dresses. Her henna hair was pulled back in a casual 1940s style, and she moved through her rooms with the graceful confidence of a woman who didn't expect to encounter anything she couldn't handle.

They went into the front room, where Wanda had been sitting at an old desk piled with the clutter of an import business. Near the plate-glass window by her desk, two lemon canaries burbled softly in an art deco cage. The dull gray light from outside put soft edges on the ink bottles that lined the rows and rows of narrow glass shelves on the walls.

Across the street a cab pulled to the curb, headed downhill. The woman inside paid the driver, opened the door, and stepped out.

"Oh. Bless. Me," Wanda said. "That's her?"

"Right on time."

Lore wore a sapphire knit dress cut close and to perfection. Her bobbed hair was onyx; her mouth, carmine. The street was too steep for her to negotiate in her heels, so she held on to the opened taxi door with one hand and matter-of-factly took off her heels, closed the door, and came across the street carrying her shoes in her hand. Wanda watched in fascination.

Lore paused on the sidewalk outside, slipped on her heels, and came through the door.

Fane stepped forward. "I'm Townsend," he said.

Lore nodded and looked around. She saw Wanda, but Wanda was busy pretending to be busy, her head down.

They went to the largest of the two back rooms and closed the door. Lore was meticulously put together, though she seemed not to care too much about it. Fane guessed it was second nature for her to be careful with her grooming, but she was focused on something else now. Second nature was taking a backseat to fear.

"It didn't take you long to get in touch with me," she said with a trace of suspicion, as they sat in a couple of old wooden bank chairs amid packing crates and storage boxes. She was anxious but not intimidated.

"I was told it was urgent."

She nodded, and her eyes flicked all over him, taking in the details.

"What else do you know?" she asked.

"You're involved with a man, and you want to end it."

She stared at him a long time. He waited, guessing she was going to cut to the chase.

"Let's get this straight," she said. "I'm not taking out a contract on this guy. I'm not hiring you to beat him up, either. I just need somebody to get real with him, get him out of my life."

"I understand. Let me explain my fee, then if you're still interested, you tell me your story."

He outlined a cash-only agreement with a fee structure that would make her take him and the arrangement seriously. She agreed to it immediately. Then she told her story.

She was an interesting combination of methodical and

rattled. She gave him a good enough picture of her relationship with Krey to make it clear to Fane why she wanted out
of the situation as fast as possible.

When she finished, she took a small aspirin bottle from
her purse and popped two pills into her mouth.

"How are your meetings arranged?" Fane asked.

"All kinds of ways," she said, swallowing the aspirins. "It's
part of the game. He calls me. We set a time, a place. I leave
my car somewhere, a parking garage maybe, and a cab shows
up with instructions to take me somewhere. Just like you
did," she said pointedly.

"Where do you meet?"

"Houses, apartments. Hotels sometimes, motels."

"Do you carry a cell phone when you're with him?"

"No. He's hammered it into me about the GPS thing."

"But you always leave your car."

"Always." She looked at him suspiciously. "Why are we
talking about all this?"

"I can't help you with this guy until I know who he is," he
said. "Philip Krey's not his name. We need a photo, finger-
prints, things he can't fabricate the way he does IDs or a
driver's license. You're going to have to meet with him again,
somehow, to give me the chance to get those things."

"Listen," she said, "I'm afraid of this guy. I don't know if
I've got the nerve to see him again."

"Has he threatened you?"

"No."

"He's beginning to get rough?"

"That's not the point."

"You mean sometimes that is the point."

"I'm not going to get into that with you," she said, averting her eyes. Her right foot began jiggling slightly. "It hasn't got anything to do with that."

"Then what does it have to do with?"

She was irritated by the question, but she seemed to know it was within a reasonable range of curiosity for someone she was hiring to make Krey go away.

"I told you about this mind thing," she said, uncomfortable with the subject. "That's way beyond normal; it's creepy as hell. It's not the games *we* play that have gotten out of control here—it's the games *he* plays."

She sat in the dingy storeroom looking as if she had been designed, clean, with clean lines. She also looked like she was considering backing out.

"Do you call him often?" Fane asked.

"Recently, yes," Lore said.

"Why do you call him more often recently?"

"Why do you need to know that?"

"You're going to have to contact him," Fane said. "I've got to know how that's going to play with his head. Is it going to cause me some kind of problem?"

Again she thought about it, looking at him, not blinking.

"Yeah, okay, that makes sense."

She cut her eyes away, nibbled a little at the corner of her lower lip. Aside from being strikingly attractive, her face was a puzzle of unfamiliar nuance.

Finally she rolled her eyes to herself, resigned, and turned back to him.

"Because . . . lately we've been doing some role-playing."
She said it as if her response had answered something defin-
itively, and they could move on.

"Role-playing?" Townsend wasn't supposed to know
about her analysis, her penchants, the weird edges of the relationship.

She glared at him for the inconvenience of having to
explain.

"Look," she snapped, instinctively brazen, but instantly
pulling back when she remembered she needed him. "I have
these fantasies. We play them out, okay?"

"Fine. Now listen, I want you to tell me how this works—
without spilling the sordid details—because it's important
for what we're about to do."

"How it works?" She was steamed but listening.

"If we don't do this right, he's going to get suspicious.
You need to help me here so we don't screw up."

Fane guessed that her prickly behavior was mostly her
fear showing. Krey had gotten deeper into her thinking than
she wanted to talk about.

"Okay . . . I'm sorry," she said. "I see that, sure. . . .
I should've understood that."

"It's okay. We're just talking here, trying to figure it out
together."

She nodded, looking down at her hands, a little embarrassed at her defensiveness.

"Okay," she sighed. She shook her head, couldn't believe
this. "Shit."

She stood. They were surrounded by shipping crates and
there was nowhere to go, but she couldn't stay still. She

walked a few paces away, then back. The sapphire dress fit
her like a sheet of water.

She turned around and crossed her arms, looking at him.

"It's games," she said. "This has evolved. Hasn't always
been like this. Several weeks ago I gave him descriptions of
four fantasies. I was explicit, detailed. The arrangement was
that he picks one, plans it out. I know before we meet which
fantasy he's going to play out. The enactment takes up the
entire evening, sometimes all night."

"You said the arrangement 'was.' Past tense."

"The last time was the last fantasy."

"When would you normally see him again?"

"There's not any normal to it. Most of the time he gets in
touch with me."

"If you call him today will he find that suspicious?"

"I don't think so." She shifted her hips against the crate.

"If you were to contact him and suggest that he meet you
in a public place, how would he read that?"

"He'd wonder why."

"We need to figure that out, then."

Lore nodded. "When do you want to do this?"

"As soon as possible."

She fixed her eyes on him and dropped her hands in front
of her, rubbing the base of one hand with the fingers of the
other. She was an image in sharp lines, the sculpted bob, the
brightly defined lips. And her anxiety. Fane began to feel
uneasy about her.

Vera had described Lore's state of mind to him, and her
mannerisms betrayed evidence of the stress she felt. Maybe
she was a little closer to the snapping point than he had

imagined. How much more pressure could she endure? There was no way to know, and there wasn't anything he could do about it anyway. So far she was all he had.

Lore returned to her chair and smoothed the knit dress over her lap with precise, even strokes.

"You need to understand something," she said, oddly calm now. "I've had this affair with this man. And it was a little out there sometimes. But until the last couple of times we met, it was never . . . I don't know, weird."

She shifted her shoulders and long neck, a nervous settling.

"I trusted him to stay within certain boundaries. You agree on things like that, then you just let yourself go. After all, edgy, well, that's part of it, isn't it?"

Fane saw a woman so confused by her own mind that she could hardly function. For whatever reasons, reality was something Lore Cha couldn't bear. For her, fantasy was more manageable and more comforting. He suspected that she had given up wondering why a long time ago.

"But weird," she said, and she stopped. He couldn't tell whether she was trying to choose the right words or whether she had lost the thread of her thought. "Sometimes you don't come back from weird."

14

Libby's voice came over Roma's earbud.

"Okay, a guy wearing a newsboy cap and peacoat just came out of the trees on Hyde from Lombard. He's crossing to the south side of Greenwich, now he's crossing Hyde into Greenwich on the sidewalk stairs, going down."

Roma marked her place in the book she was reading and put it down. She and Jon Bücher were in Bücher's operations van three blocks from Vera List's office. Roma checked her watch. It was 2:40 in the morning.

Libby Mane was the leader of a three-member surveillance team that Roma hired whenever she needed their special kind of expertise. All former DEA intelligence officers, Libby and her partners, Reed and Mark, worked together with an intuitive efficiency that easily put them a cut above other contract surveillance teams. Roma had met Libby through Jon Bücher shortly after arriving in San Francisco, and she and Libby instinctively liked and understood each other from the start. They had been working together ever since.

"What's happening?" Roma asked the woman.

"He went into the hedge passage flanking the sidewalk steps. Okay . . . okay . . . he just went up the steps into the first courtyard."

They waited, eyes on one of the two video monitors in the van. The first monitor was divided into quadrants, one for each of the hidden surveillance cameras in Vera's offices. Bücher could enlarge any quadrant on the second screen.

Roma glanced at her laptop with its satellite image of the block where Vera's office sat. She imagined the man making his way through the three courtyards, past an apartment building, past the fountain and the park benches, and through the archway in the high hedge to the front of the building. He'd have to have an E-card to get into the building, then take a slow ride in the little elevator.

It seemed to be taking a long time.

"Maybe nothing," Bücher said. "False alarm."

"Maybe."

And then the door in the waiting room swung open.

The bill of the cap obscured his face as he closed the door behind him. Then he just stood there, waiting. It wasn't a pause; he was as still as a photograph for a minute, two minutes. Two and a half . . .

"He's listening," Bücher mused.

"For what?"

"Maybe waiting for his eyes to adjust."

Then the man reached up and took off his cap, and long dark hair tumbled out.

"Uh-oh," Roma said.

"I'll be damned."

The woman turned and put her cap in the chair near the door, unbuttoned her peacoat, took it off, and laid it over the arm of the chair.

She pulled a small flashlight out of her jeans and turned it on. She panned the waiting room with the beam, stopping on a small desk. She went to the desk, reached into a bowl and got a piece of candy, unwrapped it, put the wrapper in her pocket, put the candy in her mouth.

"Sweet tooth," Bücher said.

The woman walked to the door that led to Vera List's office and stepped inside.

Roma and Bücher switched their attention to the three quadrants that covered the office.

The woman went to the series of oversized windows that looked into the courtyard and opened the drapes.

"Bad weather's going to give her cover for the LED," Bücher said. "It's probably a blue light. By the time it's diffused nobody'll be able to see it from outside as long as she doesn't shine it directly at the windows."

She stood looking into the courtyard, and again her apparent lack of urgency was incongruous with her task.

"What's she doing?" Roma said.

"Nothing. A damned casual burglar."

After a while she turned around and walked aimlessly around the room. She went to the sitting area, with its sofa and armchairs where Vera interviewed her clients, and sat in one of the chairs. She crossed her legs, waited.

"Pull up two," Roma said.

The woman's face filled the second monitor. She was young, early twenties.

"She's . . . Hispanic?" Roma asked. "Black?"

"Hard to say."

The girl stood and leaned over the sofa to look at the photograph that hung there. Then she stepped around the other armchair and followed the pale beam of her light to Vera's desk and sat in her chair.

She picked up several objects on the desk, examined them, then returned them to their exact position. She opened the drawers, examined the contents, read a few things she found, carefully replaced them, closed the drawers.

She turned to the computer and flipped it on.

"Finally," Roma said.

The girl took a flash drive from the cord hanging around her neck, plugged it into a USB port, and started clicking away on the keys.

"Damn," Bücher said. "She's done this before. She's got to be going through security checks, passwords, all that.

"She's cool about it. I don't see any antsy glances, or hesitation."

They watched her a few minutes.

Roma spoke into her headset, her eyes on the monitor. "Anybody see anything at all out there?"

Libby's voice: "Nothing's moved on Hyde."

Reed: "Leavenworth's dead."

Mark: "Nothing on Filbert."

Roma leaned in closer to the monitor. The download must have started, because the girl pushed back her chair, watched the screen a few seconds, then stood and walked back into the waiting room. She got another piece of candy, popped it into her mouth, and again stuffed the wrapper into her pocket as she returned to Vera's office.

"Methodical," Bücher said.

She went back to the computer, clicked the keys a few times, and ejected the flash drive. She snapped it back on the cord around her neck and shut down the computer.

Roma spoke into her headset.

"Okay, everybody, we've got a girl in here, not a man. I'm guessing she's going back the same way she came in. We need a license plate number."

The girl turned around and walked out of the office.

Roma leaned into the monitor. The girl went straight to the chair by the door and picked up her coat.

"She's leaving," Roma said into her headset.

The girl piled up her hair again, pulled on the cap, and walked out.

"Okay, she's out the office door," Roma said. "Be careful. She may not be alone."

Simultaneously on three sides of the block, the three surveillants slipped off their boating shoes. When the sidewalks were wet, there wasn't a shoe made that didn't make a smacking sound. The bare foot was incomparable for silence. They stuffed their shoes into their jackets and hurried into the dark.

When the girl came down the steps of the first courtyard and into the cul-de-sac, Reed was standing under the trees at the head of the stairs that rose from Leavenworth to Greenwich. She turned toward Hyde, and he followed.

Libby rushed down the Hyde hill in advance of the girl's anticipated route. When she got to Lombard, she ran across the exposed intersection to the trees on the diagonal corner. She turned immediately and steadied her telephoto lens against a tree.

Mark ran along Filbert toward Lombard to cover a possible alternate route.

Reed followed the girl down Hyde, keeping far enough behind her to use the murky weather for cover but close enough to hear her footsteps.

At Lombard she turned left.

Reed drifted around the corner after her, temporarily losing sight and sound. Then he heard her footsteps shuffle and stop. Something raked the metal of a car. She was slipping between the cars parallel parked along the curb. He heard the snap of a car door about three cars away. No interior light. The door slammed.

Reed: "She got into a car parked on Lombard, close to the Hyde intersection headed east." He dropped back to the corner and crouched behind the last car.

The car started, the lights popped on. She pulled out of her parallel spot and headed straight for the corner, then turned left, downhill toward the bay.

Libby got a shot of the plates on the front of her car as she turned in front of her.

In the van, Roma and Bücher listened to Libby's voice recite the plate's numbers and letters as Roma typed them into the Web site already on her screen. Seconds later she had her information.

"Okay, I've got it," she said. "Thanks, guys. I'll be in touch tomorrow."

It was 3:28 a.m. when Roma left a message on Fane's BlackBerry. She was on her way to her home in the Mission, so she made it short, giving him a quick overview of what had happened and then the information he wanted: The woman's name was Celia Negri. She lived at 1360 Pomroit. She was twenty-four years old. No criminal record.

"I need to grab a few hours' sleep," she said. "Bücher's sending you a digital file of the surveillance video. I'll see you in the morning, ten-thirty."

Marten Fane was dozing, drifting in and out of wakeful-
ness, and underneath it all he could feel the comforting rush
of the car barreling through the night.

He was seven years old, alone in the backseat. "Help Me
Make It Through the Night" was on a country station on the
radio, and in the front seat his mother was snuggled up against
his father, who was driving, one arm around her. Outside the
window a waxing Texas moon raced along beside them, skimming over the mesquite and cactus flats, sailing over the Caddo
mountains that ran low and dark in the distance.

His mother was singing, her warm voice audible just under
the lyrics, and when his father whispered something to her, she
laughed softly and kissed his neck. He liked watching them
like that, their almost silhouettes so close together in front of
him. Even at seven he knew that they were a handsome couple
and that they were young and happy. The three of them were
the luckiest people in the world.

His mother turned around to check on him, and he pretended to be asleep, watching her shadow-washed face through
his eyelashes. She reached back over the car seat and touched
his leg and patted it. She was like that; he loved her so much.

When she turned back around, he sleepily rolled his head
to the side and saw the moon again, the bad moon rising.

The headlights of the oncoming rig filled the car with
lightning.

When he woke up, three months later, he was crying. There
was not enough solace in the universe to satisfy his regret,
vaster than grief itself, for having pretended to be asleep in
that last moment, for not reaching out to touch her hand.

Jesus Christ.

Fane stared straight up into the darkness, with no transition between the dream and the moment. He got out of bed,
slipped on his robe, and walked through the vaulted passageway into his study.

He was a lucid dreamer, and it was this dream that had
introduced him to his condition, or his ability, as some thought
of it. To him, it was a condition. And, really, the dream wasn't
a dream at all, but a stunningly vivid memory.

For the next nine years following the collision, he was a
stranger to himself, an untethered boy emptied of seven years
of memory by the eighteen-wheeler that had ripped into their
car that night. There was a fractured memory of his mother,
of how much he loved her, an aching nostalgia that was more
intense than the actual memory of the woman herself. They
were maddening, those misty recollections of voices and faces,
and sometimes he wondered if it was nothing more than
wishing that he felt. The impact of the crash had introduced

him to the concepts of want and need and discontent, and in place of memory had left him with an ill-defined yearning that he could neither satisfy nor escape. In a sense, he was born in that moment, already seven years into his life. The crash was his birth trauma. It was all that he knew of his past.

But he knew there was more, and he was haunted by the absence of his story. His parents' entire existence and history was trapped in those few moments of the memory-dream, and he spent a good deal of his boyhood trying to free the woman who had patted his leg in those last moments of her life.

Fane went to his desk and poured a drink of water from the glass carafe that sat on the corner. He sat in an armchair in the half light and slowly sipped the water.

At sixteen, the lucid dreams began, unbidden and astonishing. Across the span of hundreds of nights, his childhood flooded back into his consciousness, his mind thirstily drinking in the missing memories as if his life depended upon it. The scenes were filled with sensorial content so potent and poignant—and welcome—that he was often too shaken the next day to go to school.

Before tonight, he hadn't had the dream in a long time, but he knew what had prompted it: Vera List's mention of Elise Currin's childhood traumas in foster homes. Even now, all these years later, Fane, too, remembered them well, with a mixture of gratitude and grief.

The couple he was living with when the dreams began were overwhelmed by what was happening to him. They didn't, and couldn't, understand it. They were good people, but what was happening to this boy was out of their depth. It was torture for them, and he didn't blame them when they asked Child Protective Services to find another home for him.

But Marten couldn't face another uprooting. Besides, now he had found his family, returned to him in the dazzling dreams of his missing memories. The night before he was to be taken to another foster home, he slipped away into the small hours of the morning. At sixteen, he was on his own.

The city lights illuminated the drifting fog to a pale glow beyond the terrace wall, turning the bougainvillea into a tracery of silhouettes. Fane watched it and remembered the first years after he had claimed his independence.

It was the end of his isolation and the beginning of a kind of self-creation that had every opportunity to go terribly wrong but didn't. It was partly luck that he survived at all, partly his own innate ingenuity, and partly the unexpected generosity of others. He used to wonder which had been more influential in making the man he became: the isolation of his boyhood years of lost memory or his adolescence of independence, where every turn and decision he made was a roll of the dice.

It wasn't, of course, the right question in the first place. Life rarely, if ever, could be so neatly divided. It wasn't the kind of question he bothered with anymore.

He sipped the last of the water and put the glass on the edge of his desk. He needed to get some sleep, but he didn't want to go back to the dream. And he was in no mood to read or look at the books of portraits. Only then did he think to check his watch. It was 3:42 a.m. Roma and her team had probably finished at List's office, and she might have left a message.

Earlier he had silenced his BlackBerry and left it on his desk. He reached over, picked it up, and turned it on. There were several messages, but he listened only to Roma's.

As always she had been efficient, and he was glad to hear that she would be there in the morning. He liked having her there. She filled the emptiness in the house in a way that was hard to define and hard to let go of when she left.

He had to sleep, though he realized that Roma was probably only getting to bed herself about now. Jesus, he had to stop thinking.

He turned to an old diversion to settle his thoughts. He looked for something in the half light to focus on, a shape, an outline, a shadow. His eyes settled on the black filigree of bougainvillea on the terrace, and he waited for an association.

He remembered a house in the high San Angel district of Mexico City where he spent a season of summer nights in his wandering years of new independence. He chose one of those nights and began to reconstruct it. Deliberately and methodically, detail after meticulous detail, he resurrected the memory: the elegant garden behind the high walls, its paths of tropical plants, its fountain, its songbirds in cages; the colonial architecture, each room and its colors, its paintings, and furnishings; the cool stone floors on his bare feet, the wan twilight of the rooms, the soft sound of voices; the troubled woman who lived there, and the delicate, black tattoo of vines that began at the base of her spine.

16

"Here, I want you to have this," he said, putting the small package on the bed beside Elise's naked hip. He had gotten up, walked to the chair where his clothes were hanging, and returned with the package. In the lamp light she saw shiny emerald foil with a black ribbon.

"It's nothing expensive," he said, "but when I saw it in a little gift shop, I instantly thought of you."

"Why?"

"No idea. You just popped into my head."

They were sitting on a bed in a Victorian house high on Buena Vista Avenue, above Haight. Beyond the tall windows the heavy cloud cover drifted slowly in the darkness, sometimes thick, sometimes thin, revealing the city below in glimpses of shifting bands of ghostly light.

She didn't touch the package. She was sitting up, holding a glass of gin. They had been to this place before, early in their affair. When the weather was clear, you could see the city glittering all the way down to the bay.

She sipped the gin and looked down at the package. A black ribbon. Why had he given it to her while she was naked? They were about to dress. Couldn't he have waited a few more minutes?

"Go ahead," he said. He was smiling, but it didn't strike her as a happy smile, as you would expect from someone anticipating your reaction to a gift they've given you. It was a knowing smile.

"Maybe I'll open it later," she said. "Thank you."

"Later? What do you mean? Come on."

"Why did you buy me a gift?"

He frowned, puzzled by her reaction, by her reluctance.

"Look, it's just a little thing. It's nothing."

She sipped the gin to cover the impulse to swallow. They had gone straight to the sex tonight. That was the way she had wanted it. She needed to do that first because she had a yearning for it that was both a need and an escape. Their affair, as affairs must, had evolved. But it wasn't the predictable evolution toward too much familiarity. It hadn't lost its edge. In fact, the edginess had sharpened.

"I don't want to open it now," she said.

"Why?"

"Why did you put a black ribbon on it?"

He looked at the package as if he hadn't seen that the ribbon was black. He looked at her.

"The woman at the gift shop wrapped it. She chose it."

"You didn't ask her to use a black ribbon?"

He shook his head slowly, confused. "No . . ."

He was watching her closely, as if her behavior had suddenly alerted him to something. She didn't want to be anticipated, not like that.

"She said it was—I believe her word was 'elegant.' "

If it was elegant, it was too late for her to appreciate that. She already associated something else with the package. It had happened instantaneously, and it didn't allow for another interpretation. It didn't allow for elegance.

"I'll dress first," she said, and put down the glass.

"Elise?" He was smiling and frowning at the same time, gently incredulous at her behavior. He put his hand on her thigh.

She flinched. Only minutes before he had been inside her, and she had been eager and fearless. But now his hand on her thigh seemed more raw than when they were actually having sex.

"What's going on?" he asked.

She honestly didn't know, and yet his smile suddenly seemed disingenuous to her. What was it about the expression of tenderness on his face that made her think it was counterfeit? What was the actual evidence behind her sixth sense that there was something wrong here?

He gently took the glass from her hands and put it on the lamp table. He reached down and picked up the emerald box with its black ribbon and put it in her naked lap.

Their nudity was quickly becoming a significant impediment in the unfolding scene as it was being redefined in her mind. In the context of their affair, nudity had always been natural, or even inconsequential. Only minutes before it had been irrelevant.

But now his body was becoming offensive to her, taking on undercurrents of aggression, even menace. Her own nakedness had begun to make her uncomfortable. In her mind, the meaning of their nudity was quickly changing, the physical analogue of a darkening psychic mood.

"Unwrap it," he said.

Was his tone demanding? Encouraging?

She put her fingers under the box, felt its weight. It wasn't airy. Lightly, her fingers pulled at the black ribbon, and she let it drop to the floor. The emerald foil came away from the little white box and fell on the floor next to the ribbon. She opened the box, parted the crisp white tissue, and took out of its nest a little green crystal dove, perfect and beautiful and glistening.

She held it in the cup of her trembling hands, but only for a moment, before she fainted.

When she came to, she was lying on her face, one arm pinned underneath her, one leg twisted awkwardly. As her head slowly cleared, she realized that only a few moments had gone by. She had been carelessly piled onto the bed after falling to the floor. She was still naked. He hadn't bothered to wash her face with a damp cloth, hadn't bothered to cover her, hadn't even bothered to turn her over on her back and straighten her limbs.

Slowly she pulled her arm from under her, straightened

her legs, and turned over. Kern was across the room dressing, his back to her. She lay there watching him, feeling queasy, weak. She cleared her throat.

Kern turned around and looked at her, unconcerned, as he buttoned his shirt.

"You fainted," he said, tucking in his shirttail.

She summoned her strength and sat up, slowly putting her feet on the floor. Her foot kicked something. The crystal dove. The box and the wrappings were still on the floor, too. Even in the haze of recovering, she was stricken by the callous contempt implicit in these small, cruel details of disregard.

She stood, carefully steadied herself, and went into the bathroom, closing the door behind her. She washed her face, then used the toilet. She ran warm water and cleaned herself with a washcloth.

When she returned to the bedroom, Kern was tying his shoelaces. She crossed to the chair where her clothes were lying and began to dress. Kern sat back in his chair and watched her in silence. It wasn't until she was sitting, too, pulling on her panty hose, that he finally spoke.

"What was that all about?" he asked.

The question sounded oddly obligatory, having little to do with real curiosity and even less with concern. His dispassion was a new thing, and it confused her.

"It was about you," she said, looking down the length of an extended leg at him as she pulled on her hose.

He didn't say anything. He wasn't going to pursue it. How could he not? This wasn't like him. He had never been incurious about her, never. What was this new indifference?

She let the silence grow between them while she finished dressing. When she was done, she stood in front of the mirror and brushed her thick hair. He remained in his chair, watching her, and their eyes met in the mirror's reflection.

Until that moment she was still slightly muddled from fainting, her awareness dulled. But seeing his reflection gave her an unexpected jolt, as if the echo of him was his true essence. Suddenly the image struck her as deeply sinister, and she was gripped by an urge to wheel around and face him, afraid that he was doing something behind her that his reflection wasn't showing her. It took all of her willpower to focus on brushing her hair and hiding her fear.

Somehow she finished and returned to the foot of the bed without looking at him. She sat down and put on her heels.

"Not curious?" she said, crossing her legs.

"You told me last time: stay out of your head."

Now she looked at him. Such a counterfeit response was sadistic. What had just happened was all about being inside her head. The glass bird was an object from the very core of her darkest memory, one that had eaten away at her heart of hearts like psychic acid.

After months of probing and scrutinizing her, after intuiting and intruding upon her innermost self to the point that she was beginning to feel an underlying terror at the irrational idea that she might be sharing a common mind with him, he knew that she would be powerfully affected by what she would find inside the box. Her reaction wasn't a surprise to him. It was a confirmation.

They looked at each other, and the appalling truth welled up inside her as a cold rush of nausea. He was now so deep into her mind that he no longer had any need for probing. He could reach into her psyche any time he wished and pluck at the threads that made up the fabric of who she was. The casual attitude that she saw now wasn't indifference at all. It was satisfaction, a chilling arrogance.

WEDNESDAY

17

Fane drove down to Rose's Café for breakfast and was back in his study by half past eight. By this time Bücher's file was waiting on his computer.

He was able to watch the surveillance video three times before his doorbell rang. He looked over at the security monitors kept out of sight in a Chinese cabinet and saw Roma waiting outside in the palm courtyard. He buzzed her in.

She came into Fane's study carrying a takeout coffee and a pastry sack from a bakery. She walked to the ottoman in front of the sofa to put her things on the ebony wooden tray, but it was full of photography books.

"Some more new books? Portraits?"

"Yeah, a few."

She glanced at him with concerned curiosity as she moved the books to the sofa and put her things on the tray. Morning light washed into the room from the arched window that took up nearly the entire wall overlooking the terrace and the bay.

"You're obsessing," she said, sitting down on the sofa and taking the top off her coffee. "About the photographs."

"Probably," he said.

In the past eighteen months Fane and Roma had been through a lot together. Though they had known each other for years, they had never actually worked together until she came up from Mexico City.

In many ways, they were still learning, still creating the partnership. But they were comfortable with each other now. It felt "right," and seemed even more so every day. And that was good, because their new association had begun under arduous circumstances.

Roma had been working with him only a few months when Dana died, and his implosion had put Roma in an impossible situation. Still dealing with the trauma of the horrible mass murder of her own family in Colombia nine months earlier, she was in no emotional position to help him. In a feel-good movie they would have comforted each other, grief to grief, with empathy and understanding for the other's pain. But it didn't happen that way.

In truth, he couldn't remember how the hell they got past it all. They had both endured their losses alone, but they had done it simultaneously, each in the presence of the other, if not together. That, in itself, had created a relationship between them that they knew was important in a way that they didn't fully understand yet.

Eventually Fane stumbled onto a way to live with Dana and live without her, in the same moment. It was a mad kind of mind game. There was no method to it, and he wouldn't have been able to explain to anyone how he had done it. It was just a way of struggling toward a self-defined equilibrium, and eventually he was able to sleep without demons and to awaken without dismay.

However it had happened, it had happened with Roma at his side. Together they had learned to respect the other's grief, and to keep their distance when only solitude could answer loss. And they had learned, too, that when that solitude turned cruel, only the other's voice could assuage the pain they knew they shared.

But in the past few months there were signs that something had begun to change between them. They were subtle things, an occasional reference by one of them that touched upon a more intimate aspect of the other than they were used to expressing, or a remark that assumed a deeply shared understanding. However aware Fane and Roma might have been of these minutia, they were growing evidence of their evolving relationship, of their mutual acceptance of the narrowing of the distance between them.

Roma's remark about Fane obsessing over the photographs was just such an instance. He realized that she understood a dimension of his preoccupation with these images that he had never discussed with her, and her insightful observation drew her closer to him than she had been a moment before.

He looked at her a couple of beats, registering what had happened, and then he turned to the business at hand.

He told her what Vera had said about Elise Currin, then what she said later about her morning session with Lore

Cha. Then he recounted his own afternoon conversation with
Lore.

As always, he watched her with interest as she absorbed
the new information. Roma's opinion carried a lot of weight
with Fane. She was an astute reader of human nature, but it
wasn't only her words that he paid attention to. Her face
and body were rich with tells that she didn't try to hide
when she was with someone she trusted.

If she wasn't role-playing, which she did with dead-on
accuracy, Roma usually worked in a cool zone of attitudinal
reserve that might earn another woman the sobriquet "Ice
Queen." But those two words just didn't fit an olive-skinned,
dark-eyed *Rola*, as Colombians affectionately call women
from Bogotá. There was nothing cold about Roma. She smol-
dered. It was self-control with an edge, and a warning to
those who needed it not to get too close to the heat.

As he related Vera's account of her session with Lore
Cha, as well as his own conversation with her, Fane tried to
repeat Lore's words as closely as possible, because she had
done a good job of describing her growing panic.

When he finished, Roma nodded, absorbing and sorting,
but her reaction was circumspect.

"Whatever else we find out about this guy," she said, "he's
a classic creep. What he's doing is the intellectual equivalent
of groping women on a crowded subway."

"Nice image."

"He may be operating at the high end of the social scale,"
she added, "but sneaking around inside a woman's mind to
get between her legs is despicable."

"But Vera thinks this isn't just about cheap thrills."

"Does he carry this stuff into his encounters with Elise, too? Or is this just a Lore Cha thing?"

"I get the impression some of this is going on with Elise, too. But I'll bet it's in a totally different way."

Fane sat back in his chair facing Roma, and crossed his arms.

"She acts like a cutout," he said, abruptly shifting subjects. "Celia Negri, I mean."

"And what does that tell you?" Roma asked, working on her pastry, her eyes a little swollen from the lack of sleep.

"What does it tell you?"

"Uhmm," she sipped her coffee to wash down the bite. "He's careful. Willing to go to a lot of trouble to train a non-professional to take his risks for him. He's probably paying her very well, and using an alias with her, too."

"And I'm guessing she's not the only cutout he's used," Fane said.

"Because he doesn't want them to get too familiar with the contents of the files?"

"That's right. When they learn too much, they become part of his risk rather than his protection."

Roma put down the bite she was about to take and fiddled the crumbs from her long fingers.

"That raises a serious question," she said.

Fane nodded. "How many cutouts has he used? And what's happened to the others?"

"He wouldn't be letting them just walk away, knowing what they know."

"I wouldn't think so. What we're seeing here takes a lot of planning. Time. Money. I think Vera's right to be concerned that there's more to this than meets the eye."

Roma pushed crumbs with her finger into a little pile on the napkin, and Fane's phone rang. It was Bobby Noble.

"Morning, Bobby. You're on speakerphone. Roma's here."

"Hey, Babe," Noble said. "Okay, guys, short answer: I don't find Richard Cha's life crossing paths with Jeffrey Currin at all."

"You're kidding." Fane glanced at Roma.

"I don't find anything," Noble said. "I put a pretty big radius on the search, too. These guys just don't travel in the same solar systems. Nothing in common at all, not lending institutions, not business associations, no third- or fourth-party acquaintances . . ."

Fane was genuinely surprised. Despite Vera's belief that there was no connection between the two women, Fane thought an intersection between their husbands was a sure thing.

"Of course, that's just the first pass at it," Noble said. "If you've got a strong hunch on something, I can go deeper."

"Nothing?"

"I just don't see it, Marten. I'll send you a 'crypted copy of everything."

"But Cha's in the software business?"

"Yeah. Patents, a highly litigious area of patent law. Licensing issues, patent-infringement issues, cross-licensing issues. He's into building patent portfolios, arcane stuff. But he's got law and business degrees from Stanford, so this shit's right up his alley."

"Okay, so what about Currin then?" he asked.

"I looked for volatility, something with crazy profits, or something that's eating up money. They're the ones that'll get his attention.

"I found only two of immediate interest. In the crazy-profits category, there's Currin International Trading Company, with headquarters here. The global movement of goods is a high-yield enterprise. It has half a dozen subsidiaries scattered around the world. Indonesia. China. EU. Latin America. It's booming.

"In the costing-him-money category, there's only a little Web-based company in Menlo Park that's a real stinker. Another quarter like it's going now, and he'll unload it. But it's nothing in the scheme of things.

"In short," Noble concluded, "there are no red flags."

"Thanks, Bobby," Fane said. "I'll be getting back to you." He punched off the phone.

"What a surprise," Roma said drily. "You think Elise is telling Vera everything?"

"No. But then Vera isn't telling us everything, either. She can't, so she's balancing her secrets. She has to."

Roma finished the last bite of her pastry, piddling with the crumbs, thinking. Fane watched her mind churn, a subtle demonstration of her slightly furrowed brow that was as appealing to him as the graceful slant of her long legs.

"Two things jump out at me about this," she said. "First, Celia Negri. If she's just hired help, she doesn't have a personal stake in this. If she's just doing this for the money, she could be ripe for turning, and the sooner we get to her the better.

"Second, Vera's going to have to cough up some more information. I know she's worried about her confidentiality issues, but we have to focus on what we need here and really drill into her for answers.

"And three . . ."

Roma rarely considered possibilities in pairs. Her mind inevitably extrapolated in multiples beyond two, and she was quite comfortable with imagining wheels within wheels. In Fane's world, where complexity was assumed, that made her an invaluable asset.

"I keep remembering what it was like in Bogotá. Everybody spied on everybody else down there, the military, the paramilitary, FARC, the narcos, ELN, the national police, the cartels, hit squads, politicos, *contrabandistas*. . . . These guys were always running some kind of operation against somebody, somewhere. Every once in a while we'd run into one of these things and find ourselves in the middle of something very scary."

She looked straight at Fane and tapped a fingernail on the wooden tray.

"That's exactly what this feels like to me, Marten, like we've stumbled onto somebody else's operation."

Fane nodded. "I agree. If this is seepage from something happening at that level, then . . ."

He shook his head and stood. He walked around to the French doors, hands in his pockets, and looked out across the terrace toward Angel Island. The sun was breaking through the clouds and throwing splashes of light across the white sails tacking in the bay.

He opened the doors and stepped outside. The bougainvilleas that draped over the terrace wall vibrated neon magenta in the flashes of sunlight.

He heard Roma's footsteps as she followed him out and stood beside him.

"Let's do this," he said. "Go ahead and contract your people for a two-week block. Continue the static surveillance in Vera's office. Since Bücher didn't find any bugs, this guy's getting everything from Vera's notes. That's good."

"Maybe we'll get lucky with the surveillance," Roma said. "In the meantime, I'll check out Celia Negri."

She reached out and plucked a magenta bract from the bougainvillea, and in doing so, her arm brushed against Fane's. She didn't bother to readjust her touch, but stood there, turning the delicate wings of the bract in her fingers, the space between them gone.

"It looks professional," he said. "But maybe it's not professional business. Maybe he's just using tradecraft for something personal. Either way, it looks like he's been doing this awhile and nothing's happened to make him doubt his security. He's settled in. He's comfortable."

"That's one for us," Roma said.

They stood together at the terrace wall, the bay glittering in the sunlight below them. But the thoughts they shared tended toward the shadows, and in that they were more alike than not, even more than they knew.

18

He sat alone at a long glass table in the dining room of his home on the cliffs overlooking China Beach. He was eating Dungeness crab as if he hadn't had a meal in days, and while he chewed he stared out the glass wall at the international orange expanse of the Golden Gate Bridge looming in the near distance. A freighter churned underneath the bridge's girders on its way out to the open sea.

The house sat on Sea Cliff Avenue. The owner on record lived at an address in Nassau. The house was sparsely furnished. He had moved in eight months earlier and had had neither the time nor inclination to do much with it.

Still chewing, he stood and walked to the other end of the glass dining table, wiping his hands on a linen napkin. He sat down again and slipped a memory stick into the Vaio. He logged into Vera List's case files, went through the security measures, and pulled up Elise's and Lore's files in two separate windows.

He possessed the entire files of each woman, nearly two years of Vera's notes on Elise, and six months of notes on Lore. He had both the clinical case notes and Vera's process notes, sometimes called working notes, which are the analyst's private thoughts and observations about the client and the analytic process.

Not all psychoanalysts keep working notes, and among those who do, the method is idiosyncratic. Some keep a kind of shorthand, mere bullet points to be used later to fill out the case notes of record.

Vera, however, was of that rare variety who kept private working notes as a way of thinking things through. Her notes on her clients were like vignettes, short stories that recounted her general thinking during a particular session, and in the context of their overall analytic history. They were, in essence, chronicles of dark thoughts.

He had spent his entire career trying to discern people's inner worlds so he could shape their thinking in order to control them. Interrogation was a tedious cycle of observation, assessment, and designing stimulus, and every kind of deception was his delicate instrument. Every chink in the target's psychic defense system had to be exploited.

But Vera's files were so complete, so detailed, that he was able to cut through hours of trial-and-error experiments and go straight to the triggers, the most vulnerable elements in her clients' psychic worlds. Over the past nine months he had been able to glean incredible insights into psychological manipulation. And in the process he had had some crazy sex.

Now he was close to being able to actually accomplish

the very thing that he had been forced to stage with Britta Weston. She had been his first guinea pig from the List files, his initial experiment to see if he could duplicate and refine his desert successes.

But Britta almost got away from him because he wasn't subtle enough with her. He went too fast, pulling things from her session notes and using them like a goad. She never caught on that he was reading her files, but instead of bending to his persuasions, she freaked out. Fast. It happened overnight.

So he had had to stage her suicide. There was so little precursor basis for it in her files, and it was so rushed, that he was afraid the police wouldn't buy it. But the two homicide detectives who caught the case weren't the brightest boys in the division. She was in psychoanalysis? Well, shit, she must've been a whack job. Suicide made sense to them. He had been lucky.

Though he was very near his goal, it was still a delicate situation. Push them too far, too fast, and you get surprises like Weston. Don't push them fast enough, and you lose the advantage of aggregated stress. Still, he was getting there. It was working. And he even thought that, if he played it exactly right, Lore Cha might actually be ready after one or two more sessions.

His cell phone vibrated on the glass table. He watched it gibber and slowly drift on the slick surface, and then he picked it up.

"This is Jenny Cox," a woman said in a hesitant voice. "Have I got the right person?"

"Go ahead."

"I had a visitor, here at the house in Mill Valley."

She waited again for some kind of further confirmation.

"I understand," he said. "And . . . ?"

"She was looking for Philip Krey."

Despite himself, he was caught by surprise. From the very beginning he had taken elaborate precautions. After all, considering who these women were, he was risking his own possible extinction by targeting them. So this phone call was part of his protective system, and the fact that he had gotten the call proved that his system was working the way he had designed it to work, as a kind of trip wire.

On the other hand, it also meant that he had slipped up somewhere. A little piece of his security mosaic had come loose.

He knew the answer before he asked the question.

"Who was she?"

"She never said, but she was Asian. A very attractive Asian woman. In her thirties I'd guess."

Kroll disconnected and sat perfectly still, staring at the page of notes on his computer screen. If they had been written in hieroglyphics he wouldn't have noticed. His mind was instantly focused on reassessing a triad of significant details. Was it possible that in his last sessions with Lore and Elise he had overplayed his hand again? Had he, in fact, repeated the same mistakes he had made with Britta Weston? How could he have done that?

He was incredulous, but he had to stay grounded, pay attention only to the facts.

First there was that thing three nights ago in the Castro when he woke up and found Lore rifling through his wallet. He had pretended he didn't know what she was doing, and she said she had to go, mumbling something about her husband and obligations.

It was such transparent bullshit that he was surprised at her for coming out with it. But there was no mistaking what had happened. He had heard the self-consciousness in her voice. The woman was screwed up, but uncomfortable? Never. Not like that anyway. Neurotic, but not nervous.

And then there was the situation last night with Elise. He thought he had designed that with just the right emotional precision, just the right amount of surprise, insight, and menace. But her reaction wasn't what he had expected. He had seriously misread that, and then he got angry when it didn't go his way. Shit, the whole thing had gone wrong.

And now there was this, Lore's turning up in Mill Valley. Dangerously curious. Shit! In this business, ignoring the odd remark, the incongruous incident could be costly. But ignoring *three* of them within just a few days . . . that could be fatal.

Two things were certain: these issues were problems, and he was running out of time. He had this one shot to prove that he could do this. They wouldn't give him a second chance.

He quickly planned the next step. Lore had had a session with Vera List the day before, and Elise would have hers this afternoon. He knew they would spill their concerns to her about the disturbing events of their last two meetings with him, and he sure as hell didn't want to wait another week to find out what they said.

He was still staring at the screen, his mind riveted on the assembly of bad omens. Jesus, when he thought about how all that added up, it looked serious. He decided to get in touch with Celia Negri, get her to go back into Vera List's office tomorrow night, after Elise's meeting this afternoon. Even though she wasn't due to do it again for another week, she would. For the money.

19

It was nearly eleven a.m. when Fane called Vera's cell phone. It was half past eleven when she called back.

"I'm sorry," she said. "I was with a client."

"I'd like to show you the video from last night," he said. "Can I come over now?"

"I'm not at the office," she said. "I'm just above the Marina, near Green and Union. Could we meet somewhere?"

"You're five minutes from my place."

He met her at the front door. She was wearing a straight black sleeveless dress with a collarless top that turned white at midchest. Her dark hair was gathered at the nape of her neck, revealing small oval onyx earrings bordered in roped silver.

"It's not long," he said, as they started down the corridor. "About seventeen minutes."

He offered her a chair at his desk and clicked on the link from Bücher. As she viewed the pantomime that had played out in her office only hours before, he watched her face. Her concentration was laserlike, her back straight as she watched Celia Negri eat her candy, prowl through her desk drawers, and examine her personal items.

When it was done, she shook her head. "What happened there?" she asked.

He thought she might be angry; people often were infuriated by watching intruders prowl around in their private world. Instead she was more intent on understanding what she had just seen.

"Her name's Celia Negri," he said. "Does that mean anything to you?"

"Nothing."

He told her the little they knew about Celia and what they thought she was doing. She listened intently and kept her agitation well under control.

But she tensed when he told her that because of the way this man was conducting his business—the elaborate security measures with Lore and Elise, using multiple aliases, using Celia Negri as a cutout to distance himself from risk—it looked suspiciously professional.

"Someone hired him?"

"I don't know. Maybe he's on his own, but either way, it may be a more serious situation than we first thought."

He explained that if this man was a professional they would have to be much more careful and move more quickly because of the sensitive nature of the information he was holding.

Fane doubted if Vera missed any of the implications that came with the new assumptions.

He told her about his conversation with Lore the day before and said he thought he could depend on her when he needed her. But he wanted to see if he could talk to Elise before he made a decision about what to do.

"I'm going to have another session with her in a couple of hours," Vera said. "I'll see what I can do to put her in touch with you. Something like I did with Lore."

"Good," he said. He hesitated.

"Look, I know you feel you can't tell me as much as I'd like to know about these women," he said, "but keep in mind that when you withhold information you may be withholding something that's critical for me to have to be able to help you."

There was no way to make this easier for her. She was in an untenable situation. The more she withheld from him about her clients out of a legitimate concern for their privacy, the more she could be a stumbling block to the solution of her own dilemma.

Uncomfortable, Vera let her eyes drift to the pictures on his desk, her gaze moving deliberately from one to the other. She took in the model of the old Huron on its stand, then looked at him, nodding thoughtfully.

"I know," she said. "I've thought of that. I don't know what to do about it."

"I can't help you without knowing who this guy is, and they hold the keys to his identity."

She regarded him quietly. Despite her ramrod posture and firm expression, Vera List knew she was facing a wrenching concession. Fane felt sorry for her. Despite his warnings and cautionary observations that first night in the Stafford

Hotel, there was no way to prepare her for that inevitable moment when she would have to compromise her professional ethics.

He watched her somber eyes soften and one corner of her mouth pucker slightly as she wrestled with her decision.

"Christ," she said. She looked away to think, and again her eyes fell on the mementos on his desk. He watched her and imagined her mind moving obliquely, holding her decision momentarily in abeyance.

"Your father was a pilot?" she asked, tilting her head at the model on the desk.

"No," he said.

She looked at him. "You're a pilot?"

"Hard to believe?"

"Well . . . no, I don't know why I'm surprised."

"That model's in great shape compared to the old Beechcraft I actually flew."

"In what other life was this?"

"When I was sixteen, seventeen, eighteen . . . nineteen."

She smiled skeptically. "Come on."

"Okay," he said. "Short version: Parents killed in a car crash in Texas when I was seven. Foster homes. Lots of them. On my own by the time I was sixteen. Got a job helping a mechanic at an airfield near San Angelo. Old crop duster pilot taught me how to fly. Got my license. Woke up one morning in El Paso, and I was a pilot in the murky business of transborder 'transport,' flying 'stuff' across the border, both ways.

"I was cocky and young. Good at brush-top flying, dodging radar, skimming the night waves in the Gulf of Mexico or the Caribbean or the Pacific. I never saw any of the stuff I was carrying, so I told myself that I wasn't in 'the business.' I was just flying. That's how stupid I was.

"One day this sleazy guy came to me and said he had an old C-12F Huron." He nodded at the model. "He needed a pilot. Crazy good pay. So, for the better part of three years I flew back and forth from the States to all points in Latin America. Flew all the time, loved it. This guy was on nearly every flight. We hauled people, equipment, in and out. Again, I didn't ask any questions. Really cool, I was."

"How did you finally end up on the right side of the legal system?"

Fane smiled.

"The sleazy guy became my friend, too young to be a father figure. More like a disreputable older brother. Even though I didn't know what he was doing, I knew it wasn't drug running. I minded my own business, but I paid attention, too. This guy was up to something complicated, and it was fascinating.

"A couple of years went by, and one day he showed up at the airstrip outside San Diego where I was having the Huron engine overhauled. He looked like a different man. Clean-cut, suit, different manner, very smooth.

"At his instructions I flew us up to Napa. He had reservations in a fancy hotel there. A woman joined us. That first night we met at dinner, and he introduced the woman as his wife. I had no idea he was married.

"'Welcome to your new life,' he said. 'You're through flying.'

"Those three days in Napa flipped my life around," Fane

said. "It turned out that he was a CIA intelligence officer. For two years I had been flying support missions for clandestine CIA operations all over Latin America.

"My friend had been working out of the San Francisco office but was being pulled out of the field, transferred to Washington. He arranged for me to take high school equivalency exams, then entrance exams at Berkeley. He paid for my first year, and then set up a legitimate flying job for me so I could work my way through university.

"For the next couple of years he really stayed on top of me. Held me accountable, taught me self-discipline. He and his wife put everything they had into setting me on the right track. Must've spent a fortune on cross-country airplane tickets. When I began to find my feet, he eased back, but he never really let go. Neither of them did."

Vera regarded him in silence for a moment. "That's simply an incredible story. Do you still fly?"

"No, I quit after getting my master's at Berkeley. I discovered that life was bigger and richer than I was living it. There were other things I wanted to learn and do."

"Are you still in touch with this man?"

"Sure. He's still in Washington."

"How do you feel about what he did, taking you under his wing like that?"

"I was headed for prison, or worse, and he decided to save my life. I feel the way anyone would feel if someone did that for them. It's hard to talk about."

Vera continued looking at him as if she might see something different now that she hadn't seen before.

She said, "Do you mind if I ask . . . what were the circumstances that caused you to be dismissed from the Special Investigations Division?"

Fane smiled. After what he had just told her, the question was understandable.

"About five years ago, when I was running a human-smuggling investigation, I uncovered a corruption scheme. A fellow SID agent named Jack Blanda was working undercover. I began to suspect that he was working both sides of the street. I knew way too much about Jack, and I thought he was a sorry excuse for a man. But I was in no position to make that judgment, because I was having an affair with his wife. He knew it, and I knew he knew it. It was a mess, and neither of us was being very adult about it.

"Anyway, I filed a confidential report presenting all my evidence against Jack, but it looked bad because my affair with Dana had become known. Understandably some people assumed I was stacking the deck."

Fane stopped. He didn't like talking about this, but for some reason he felt that Vera had a right to hear it. Disclosing the personal information seemed justified.

"The two cases grew more complex," he said, "and finally we realized that some very prominent names were involved. And a lot of paths crossed through Jack Blanda. One night during a surveillance operation something went wrong, all hell broke loose, and there was a really sloppy, confusing shoot-out in the Tenderloin. I fired shots, Blanda fired shots, two other undercover guys fired shots, and so did some bad guys we never even saw. Jack was shot in the face and killed."

"Oh—"

"There was an investigation. I was cleared of the shooting. Everybody was cleared. But Jack was dead. An investigation found that he was on the take, paid by the smugglers to steer them around the traps and surveillance set up by us and the Feds. Some of his fellow conspirators were in high places, and they promoted the rumor that I was behind Jack's murder.

"I was asked to leave the police department. It was a matter of 'appearance of wrongdoing,' I was told. Five months later Dana and I got married. Fourteen months after that, she died from a brain aneurysm."

"When was this?"

"Just over a year ago." He paused. "Yesterday."

Vera nodded, understanding. She tilted her head at the three pictures.

"Last question," she said. "Who are they?"

"My mother, Georgia. Helen, met her at Berkeley. She introduced me to that bigger, richer life. And Dana."

Fane watched her gaze dwell on each of them, then she dropped her eyes to her hands in her lap.

"I'll do my best to get Elise to talk to you," she said. "And I'll be as . . . forthcoming about all this as I possibly can."

2 0

It wasn't only the cruelty of the memory that had caused Elise to faint when she opened the package he gave her. It was also the fact that he was, incredibly, connecting to something that was buried deep inside her.

Vera was stunned, too, when Elise told her what had happened the night before, though she was careful to hide it. Elise's lover had chosen a particularly vicious memory to let her know that he was plugged into her unconscious.

Vera's decision to keep Lore and Elise in the dark about what was happening to them was even more difficult to justify in light of this brutal turn of events. For Vera to let their torture continue, whatever her reasons, seemed nothing short of heartless. She was mortified by her silent complicity in their suffering.

Yet, as in Lore's case, Vera knew that the only way Elise could be rid of this man was for Fane to stop him before he realized someone was on to him. And Fane couldn't do that unless Elise continued the affair.

"What are you going to do now?" Vera managed to ask. "Are you going to keep seeing him?"

Elise put her damp tissues in her lap and plunged the fingers of both hands into her strawberry hair at her temples, raking it back away from her face and holding it there while she considered Vera's question.

"What's happening here?" she asked, staring hard at Vera.

Vera stiffened.

"What . . . ?"

Elise dropped her hands. "What kind of a freak is this man that he would know such things? Am I going crazy? Of all the things in the world . . . I mean, he said he thought of me when he saw it! What is that? How could that *happen*?"

"Are you sure you've never mentioned that childhood memory to him?"

"Oh, please."

Vera braced herself. "Then, how do you account for it?"

"I can't. I just can't, and that scares me. More than I can tell you, that scares me."

Vera saw what she had often seen in Elise: a woman who was a complex fusion of broken and brave. And, at times, Vera was taken aback at how broken, and how brave.

"Maybe . . . maybe I'm losing it," Elise said. "I'm not sure. I'm really not sure."

"What do you mean by that?" Vera asked.

"Something's going on," Elise said. "He's different somehow. And it doesn't feel . . . safe."

"If the relationship's changing," Vera said, "why do you think that's happening? And why do you think it's happening the way it's happening?"

Elise sat with her knees together, her hands in her lap, kneading the tissues.

"I asked him to step back," she said. "Give me some room, some distance. Then he does this, this thing last night. It's just the opposite of what I'd asked."

"Do you think he realizes that?"

"Yes, he knows." She seemed grieved and perplexed. "It used to be that his intuition was nurturing. He could be so understanding about what he saw in me. But I don't know what's happening now."

She looked up and tilted her head back and from side to side, stretching the stiff muscles in her neck. When she stopped she closed her eyes in a weary shrug.

"I don't understand," she added, "but now I'm beginning to wonder what I was missing during the early part of our relationship."

"What do you mean?"

"I haven't known him that long, just five months. I think his ability to get inside my head kind of accelerated the relationship. We got in very deep, very fast."

She stopped and, like Lore, looked past Vera to the palms outside the windows.

"And?"

"I think he was manipulating me from the very beginning, and I just didn't see it."

Elise had just given Vera the opening she needed to take

the conversation in a direction that might have seemed out of the blue only a few minutes earlier. Now there was a logic to it.

"You don't really know that much about him," Vera said. "Why weren't you ever curious to learn more?"

"We agreed to leave each other's private lives behind when we met. It was about us. Not others."

"But, Elise, when I think back over our conversations about your affair, it strikes me that it's mostly been about you, not 'us.'"

Vera cautioned herself to be careful.

"You agreed to share your 'selves' with each other," Vera continued, "but, honestly, it seems to me that you're the one who's been doing all the sharing."

Elise looked at Vera unblinking, her mind racing back through the months.

"What do you know about him, really?" Vera asked. "You both agreed that you'd honor the privacy of each other's lives outside your relationship. Yet, when you examine the progress of your affair, it turns out that you've actually taken him into your life to an amazing degree."

Elise looked away but said nothing. Vera went on.

"If I asked you to write down all the facts that you know about him, I doubt you could fill a page."

Another pause, this time for emphasis.

"For instance," Vera's heart labored as she edged up to the question, "you've never spoken his name. I've assumed that you wanted to keep his identity anonymous. But now, I'm wondering, do you even know his name?"

"Ray Kern."

"And you *know* that's actually his name?"

Elise snapped her eyes back to Vera.

"It never occurred to me to doubt it." She shook her head slowly. "No . . . I never even wondered—" She frowned. "My God, what have I done here?"

"Now wait a minute," Vera said. "Before you go there, remember the context of your situation. Until recently he's been nurturing, supportive. He's been good for you. If that was deception on his part, a scheme to gain your trust, then you can't blame yourself for believing him. It would've been counterintuitive to be suspicious of a man who appeared only to wish you well.

"But, now everything's changed," Vera went on. "You've got to deal with the fact that something's gone terribly wrong."

She watched Elise's demeanor slowly change as she confronted the arc of her relationship.

Vera faced an entirely different set of problems. When she first talked to Fane, both women were feeling uneasy about the subtle changes in their affairs. But literally overnight, this man had ratcheted up the psychic tension with them. There was an edge to it now, and it was sharp. The situation was suddenly freighted with far more risk than when she first talked to Fane. It didn't take a lot of effort to imagine one of her clients being murdered. It was horrifying.

"This thing with Ray," Elise said, her dry-eyed gaze fixed on Vera with a sober new reality, "if it isn't what I thought it was . . . then . . . what is it?"

For months Elise had lived a kind of magic affair with Ray Kern. But now it had become something twisted, and the magic had been replaced by a foreboding anxiety.

"What are you going to do now?" Vera asked again.

Elise didn't answer immediately. During the hour, Vera had watched her demeanor evolve from hurt and bewildered, to bewildered but determined.

"I've got to find out who he is," Elise said. "I want to know why he's doing this to me. And I want to know how he does it."

The first two parts of Elise's answer were exactly what Vera wanted to hear. But the last part presented a host of problems, for all the reasons that Vera had already discussed with Marten Fane.

"And how are you going to do that?"

"I have no idea, but I can't just walk away from it . . . as if it never happened."

"What if he's been playing you, Elise? What if he's got a scheme of some sort? Blackmail. Extortion."

"I'd be stunned."

"You can't afford to be stunned. You need to be very careful how you handle this man."

Elise nodded.

"This sudden change in him has caught you by surprise. His reaction to what you do now could catch you by surprise, too. It could be ugly."

Vera couldn't bring herself to actually speak her deepest fears.

"I realize that," Elise said, "but I've got to find out what's going on here. How the hell can I *not* do that?"

Vera could only imagine her consternation.

"I'm going to make a suggestion," Vera said. "I know about a woman who was in a situation roughly similar to this. She found someone who could help her. I'm going to contact her."

Vera was relieved to see Elise's aggressive attitude regarding Ray Kern. It would make it easier for Fane to work with her. But she was also surprised. Elise was tough, but it was an inner toughness that did not translate to an especially assertive personality. Vera had never seen her quite so overtly forceful.

Lore's response had been something of a surprise as well. While she presented herself as an emphatic, in-your-face, and independent woman, her increasingly eerie experiences with Philip Krey had shaken her. Instead of responding to Krey's growing menace with belligerence, she desperately wanted to get away from him.

To see these two damaged women reverse their characters in the face of this man's manipulation was sobering to Vera. It spoke to the power of Kern/Krey's personality and influence over them. And it was frightening. What kind of a man could have such an effect on these two very different women? And why would he want to?

At half past two, Fane's BlackBerry hummed. Vera had finished her session with Elise, and she was upset. Could he meet her at her place only a few blocks from her office on Russian Hill?

The building dated from the '30s and had an ornate Spanish-colonial portico entrance and a lobby with wrought iron grillwork. But Vera's apartment near the top floor was *très* modern: ebony wood floors, brushed chrome furniture with chocolate and smoke upholstery, white on off-white walls. There were glass bookshelves, sleek abstract sculpture on stone pedestals, and a view of Alcatraz.

The day had turned gloomy, and Vera's dark mood matched the weather. They were standing in her stainless steel and slate kitchen. It was immaculate, as if it had never been used.

Vera was heating water for tea when Fane arrived, but turned it off when he declined to have any. Too preoccupied and agitated to think beyond that simple act, she leaned her hips back against the cabinets and started talking about her session with Elise Currin only an hour before.

As Fane listened, he realized that this last session had changed the nature of the game for Vera. There was an urgency in her voice now, along with the anxiety, and Fane could tell that the situation had crossed a threshold. She was a few clicks away from panic.

She turned to him. "This man's doing something really terrifying," she said. "I don't know. Maybe I'm way out of line here, not telling them what's going on."

If that was a leading question, to draw him out about her dilemma, he wasn't going to help her. He thought it would add more pressure on her not to talk it out. She was imagining the possibilities, all of them grim.

"Don't forget to edit your notes from today's sessions with Elise," he reminded her.

"But . . . it'll be another week before he comes again," she said.

"He could change his mind. What if he wants to know how they reacted to what he did the last time they met? Keep your notes . . . uneventful."

"But he's got to know they're upset by what he did. What if . . . what if that's even what he wants, to see them agitated, even fearful?"

"Well, I don't want to give him that right now," Fane said. "We don't want this to accelerate. We need to put a damper on it."

"What if his inability to agitate them agitates him?"

"Look, let's don't overthink this. We just don't know enough about what's going on yet."

"This is happening . . . so fast all of a sudden."

"And we've got to control that if we can. You need to feed him information through those files that will buy us time. Try to read this guy, try to slow this down."

She nodded, her eyes sliding to the side.

Fane said, "Elise knows someone's going to call her?"

"Yes, she's beside herself. I think you'll find her easier to talk to than Lore. If you . . . you're going to stick with the same scenario, right? That I don't know you . . ."

Fane nodded. "Yeah, the same way." He pulled his Black-Berry out of his pocket. "Do you mind if I step into the next room? I need to give this name to someone."

She nodded, her thoughts already distracted, and he stepped into the living room, where a fireplace framed in black marble dominated the far end of the space.

He called Noble and told him he had another alias for him, then dialed Roma. He told her where he was.

"Elise was with this guy last night," he said, "and it was crazy stuff, like Lore's last experience with him. He's picking up speed. Make sure Bücher's in place every night along with your people. I'll call you as soon as I'm through here."

When Fane turned back to the kitchen, he caught Vera with her face in her hands. For an instant he thought she was crying, but when she looked up, unaware that he was watching her, she shook her head slowly in disbelief.

He looked away as he moved, knowing that she would see him out of the corner of her eye. When he entered the kitchen, she was adding water to the teapot.

"Maybe a cup of tea wouldn't be a bad idea," he said. She nodded and again turned on the heat under the pot.

They sat in her study with cups of tea that neither of them wanted. There were no lights on in the apartment, and as the day grew gloomier the fading light leached the color from the room leaving them in an ashy haze.

Though Fane was gentle about it, he went straight to the subject of her husband's murder. He apologized for asking about it, but it was unusual, and he wanted to know.

She didn't seem at all surprised that he knew about the death. Nor was she surprised by the question. She nodded and was silent for a moment.

"It was incomprehensible, really," she began, "hearing that Stephen was dead. The detective who came was too young. That sticks with me, that he was too young to bring me news like that. For a while after that, I was the center of the universe. Nothing mattered to me but my grief. The pall was . . . indescribable."

"When was this?"

"Nine months ago this week."

"They never arrested anyone?"

"I don't think they've even come close." She hesitated. "But, to be honest, 'getting' the person who killed Stephen isn't a priority for me."

"What do you mean?"

"In the greater scheme of things, 'closure' or 'justice' or 'revenge,' however you feel about it, whatever you choose to call it, it's not an essential requirement for me to be able to go on with my life. As far as I'm concerned, lightning struck him. It was just that random, that senseless."

"You haven't been following the police investigation closely, then?"

"I haven't been following it at all. The psychic and moral weight of Stephen's murder belongs to the man who pulled the trigger. It's not my burden. My grief isn't affected by what happens to Stephen's killer. The two aren't related. And I know that my sorrow isn't unique. It's special only to me. I try to keep it to myself."

She stopped but kept her eyes fixed squarely on Fane as if defying herself to turn away.

"But I'll tell you something," she said. "As tough as Stephen's death was for me, my real moral confrontation with a senseless death came a few months later. And it had nothing to do with Stephen."

She raised her cup to her lips but didn't sip.

"It's cold," she said.

Fane heard the double meaning in her choice of words. Vera's cool attitude about her husband's death was excruciating for him to watch. He knew what she was doing and why. Dana had died only a few months before Stephen List, and even now he would rather pretend to have bravely dealt with it, to have put it a little distance behind him, than to admit to others—or even to himself, really—how raw and close to the surface it still was for him. And how profoundly it still hurt.

So he wasn't surprised when Vera abruptly shifted the conversation to something else, and though she made a stab at a seemingly logical transition, someone else might have found her sudden change of subject off-putting.

"Britta Weston had been my client for four years," Vera continued. "One night she went to a movie alone, as she often did when it was a foreign film. Her husband didn't like dealing with subtitles. Afterward, she drove to a remote spot in the Presidio, took a massive dose of Demerol, and started drinking Skyy. She left behind a scathing note blaming me for ruining her life, for driving her to suicide."

Fane was surprised but said nothing.

"The police investigation confirmed that it was a suicide," Vera said. "But the unnerving thing about it was that there was nothing in our sessions over the years that would lead anyone to anticipate this. There was no analytical context for it. No precursor behavior. It was . . . out of the blue. Didn't fit with anything.

"As for the accusation," Vera said, "I talked with Britta's husband about it at length on many occasions. In the end he didn't put any credence in it. He didn't understand the suicide note any more than I did. We both were perplexed by it. It was . . . just terribly unfortunate . . . and disturbing."

Vera set her tea cup on the corner of a small writing desk. She looked out to the bay. Alcatraz was gone. It was raining.

"Believe me, there was plenty of guilt about that," she said. "What did I miss? How could I have read her so wrong?"

She stood and went to the window, reminding Fane of the way she had gone to the window at the Stafford Hotel only two nights earlier. She stood with the same posture, looked out with the same bewildered gaze.

Fane waited a moment before he asked his next question.

"I'd like to go back to Elise for a moment," he said. "It seems to me that when you talk about her, there's something in your voice, maybe even your choice of words, that makes me wonder if you might not have the same clinical distance from her as you do with your other clients."

Vera had no reaction. She didn't move, didn't take her eyes away from the somber afternoon light. Fane couldn't read her face at all, and her prolonged silence was totally unexpected.

Then she turned from the window and came back to her chair and sat down. She looked at him.

"I guess I'm not surprised that you sensed that. You're unusually perceptive. The fact is, I haven't done a very good job of 'distancing' myself from Elise. And that's a breach of a cardinal rule of psychoanalysis, as you know.

"You can imagine from what I've already told you that her life has been horrendous. But it's been worse, much worse. Understand, as a psychiatrist and a psychoanalyst, I see people like this all the time. All the time. She is not unique. And yet, to me, she is. To put it bluntly, she's simply the only client I've ever had that I *couldn't* be objective about. I don't know why. And believe me, I've struggled with this. I should have referred her to another analyst a long time ago. But I haven't. I don't want to let go of her.

"I'll be honest with you about this: I know that with Elise I'm being absolutely unprofessional. I've even been to her home, a number of times, when she needed me." She stopped, reflecting. "She fights so hard, she's so brave . . . and fragile. I cannot be objective about her. I cannot. And I don't want to be. God help me, she breaks my heart."

Fane didn't know how to respond to this admission. Her confessional tone surprised him, and he felt as if Vera had brought him into her confidence in a way that was rare and unusual for her. She didn't give him much time to reply.

"I can't imagine what this man's intentions are," she said. "But even if you can stop him before he hurts someone, it's not going to be easy for me to live with myself after deceiving Elise and Lore like this, after willfully putting them through so much hell."

Vera List was already paying the price, and not liking herself very much for being willing to do it. The truth was that Fane had known from the beginning that Vera would underestimate the cost of her decision. People who were desperate to deliver themselves from their dilemmas usually weighted hope against reality. It was one of the sad and wonderful things about human nature.

22

Roma sat in her car outside the parking garage on Carl Street. When Celia Negri's old Volvo pulled onto the street and headed east toward Stanyan, Roma followed. A few minutes later Celia turned a corner and stopped at a small corner grocery.

Roma waited. Too many casual passersby. But she didn't want to approach Celia inside her car or at her apartment, either; both could be bugged.

When Celia came out of the store, the light was falling, and Roma followed the Volvo into the maze of crooked streets near Kite Hill. She gambled that Celia wouldn't be able to park right in front of her apartment and would have to walk a short distance.

The houses were close here, a mixture of three-story Victorian homes and stark stucco moderns. When Celia stopped nearly a block from her apartment to parallel park, Roma drove past her and parked at a fire hydrant in front of Celia's apartment, uphill from her parking spot.

Roma got out of her car, went around to the sidewalk side, and opened the passenger door, pretending to get something from the seat. Just as Celia approached, coming under a canopy of ficus trees only a few steps from Roma's car, Roma turned around.

"Celia," she said, as if surprised to see her.

Celia looked up, smiled reflexively, then lost the smile as she realized she didn't recognize the woman.

Roma's eyes guided Celia's attention to a single-fold ID case that she held discreetly at her side. The gold shield and the large letters "FBI" were clearly visible in the fading light.

"I'm Linda," Roma said.

Celia looked up, her jaw slack with an 'Oh, shit,' expression. She looked like she was going to bolt.

"Now wait a second," Roma cautioned, "Relax, okay?"

Celia was trying to figure it out.

She was attractive, a mixture of Hispanic and African American blood, Roma guessed. She had thick, wiry hair, which she controlled by pulling it back and gathering it at the nape of her neck. She wore silver loop earrings.

"Just act as if we're friends," Roma said, "no need to make people take notice."

"What's going on?"

"I'd like to ask you a few questions. So if you'd get in the car, I'd appreciate it."

Celia glanced at the opened door and the empty rear seat. The woman was alone, not so threatening.

"Questions about what?"

"Please," Roma said. Celia hesitated.

Roma smiled again. "Celia, we have a surveillance video of you in Dr. Vera List's office last night."

Celia swallowed and shifted the bag of groceries in her arms. She looked down the sloping sidewalk. "Shit," she said. Then she got into the car.

They wound down from Pomroit to Clarendon and Laguna Honda. The traffic was lousy, and Celia was silent as they made slow progress through the edges of Forest Hill and Miraloma Park. By the time they headed down the long slope of Taraval Street, the fog was rolling in from the Pacific to meet them. It swallowed them at dusk, under the hazy blue neon sign of the Sunset Motel.

Roma parked on the street, and they left the groceries in the car and entered the motel office. The television-watching night clerk glanced up, then went back to his program as Roma led the way outside and down the stairs to the barebones units behind the office.

Room twenty-six. Roma knocked. The door opened, and they entered.

"Hello," Fane said approaching Celia. "I'm Townsend." He was holding open his ID. His suit coat was thrown over the back of a chair.

Celia's eyes clipped over the ID but locked on Fane.

He gestured to a nightstand. "There's some coffee."

Celia shook her head; then she saw the laptop on the bed.

Fane stepped over and tapped a key, starting the surveillance tape of Celia entering Vera List's office. Five minutes later Fane tapped another key, freezing Celia's image.

Celia hadn't moved a step since entering the room. Fane pulled a chair over, and she sat down. He pushed the laptop back and sat on the foot of the bed, facing her.

Celia looked at him.

"I don't care so much about that," Fane said, tilting his head toward the laptop.

"Oh, you don't?" She wasn't an idiot.

"Not really." He sipped the coffee. "Why don't you just tell me what's going on?"

Celia glanced at Roma, who was stirring her coffee, looking at Celia. She looked at the laptop again and shook her head at the shit she was in.

"Well, I'm in the middle of something, I guess," she said. "If the FBI has surveillance cameras in there."

She stared at the hem of the bedspread, dejected.

"That was just my second time in there," she nodded at the laptop. "But I guess you know that."

Fane said nothing, as if her conclusion was obvious.

"Five or six weeks ago," she said, "this guy calls me at my office. I work in computer services at UCSF Medical Center. The guy says, 'You have my computer bag.' I'd stopped at this totally crowded bakery that morning, and the bags had gotten mixed up there, I guess.

"I couldn't meet him until after work, so he said he'd buy me dinner, apologies for screwing up the bags. Fine. We met at the San Juan Grill in Noe Valley.

"His name was Robert Klein. Early forties, maybe. Nice

looking. Nice guy. Dinner turned out to be a lot of fun. Said he was in real estate, a sort of broker for high-end properties. Appointment only, exclusive."

"You tried his computer sometime during the day?" Roma asked.

"Yeah, I did. You know, curiosity. It was locked down. Anyway, we saw each other a few times. Nothing serious. He was divorced, twice. No children. He wasn't looking for anything, and I wasn't either. It worked out fine."

"You've got his phone number?" Fane asked.

"Uh, no. He said he was in the last stages of his second divorce, and that it was nasty. He wasn't giving out phone numbers. To anybody." She shrugged. "Whatever."

"So he always called you."

She nodded.

"Did you ever go to his home?"

"I don't know where he lives, either. Same story. I guessed he was hiding from her lawyers."

"So, this guy just shows up when he shows up," Roma said. "And you're okay with that?"

"Sure. Look, he was intelligent, fun, and as I said, neither of us was looking for anything. It was easy; it wasn't going anywhere. And he always paid."

"You didn't sense anything odd about the guy?"

Celia leveled her eyes at Roma. "Should I have?" Beat. "What's going on here?"

"You just seem to be pretty accepting of the sketchy outlines of this guy's life."

"Listen, this city's full of men with sketchy outlines. If I didn't accept some of that stuff I'd live like a nun."

Roma nodded.

Celia looked from Roma to Fane, "So . . . if you're FBI, then you're not working for his ex-wife, I guess." Pause. "So . . . then, he's in some kind of really serious shit."

"We're actually interested in what you were doing in those offices," Fane said.

"You don't have anything besides coffee, do you?"

"Water."

"There's gotta be some kind of soft drink machine around here."

"I want to hear about the business proposition."

She thought about this, staring at nothing, just thinking how she was going to do this. Then her shoulders sagged, and she shook her head again at her situation.

"Robert found out his wife was seeing a psychoanalyst," she said with a tone of resignation. "He wanted to know what she was telling the shrink, so he hired a private investigator to break into the shrink's office and copy his wife's files. But the guy couldn't get past the computer security, so Robert asked me if I'd go in and do it."

"Why didn't he do it himself?" Roma asked.

"He couldn't get around the security, either."

"You could?"

"That's what I do for UCSF, security for medical records. Knowing how to hack them sort of goes with the territory, like reverse engineering."

"And you agreed to do this, just like that?" Roma asked.

"No. I was sort of shocked, told him he was crazy, forget it. But he kept on. Said he could tell me exactly where everything was. I'd just go in, do it, and leave. But I still thought it was weird. Then he said he'd make it worth my while, pay me for every time I copied the files."

"And that changed things for you?"

"It sure as hell did. It was almost a week's salary."

"Really?" Roma said.

"Yeah, my reaction exactly," Celia agreed. "I said I'd think it over, but he knew he had me right then. I just couldn't turn down that kind of money."

"How often did he want you to do it?"

"Every week."

"So, you don't go again for another week," Fane said. "Do you talk to him afterward?"

"No, I leave the flash drive at a dead drop—right out of the spy movies. Different place each time."

Fane nodded thoughtfully and looked at Celia. Then he stood and said, "I've got to make a phone call."

Outside Fane walked along the balcony, the dim porch lights hazy along the way. Whoever Klein was, he was a real piece of work. They weren't going to learn much more from Celia. She had met Robert Klein but, unfortunately, he didn't exist.

He stopped at the head of the stairs near the soft drink machine and called Bobby Noble on his BlackBerry and asked him to check out the name Robert Klein.

"Damn, this guy's busy," Noble said. "Looks like he's an Rs-and-Ks man for sure."

"Apparently. The sooner the better on this, Bobby."

"Okay. Well, so far I haven't had any luck on the others.

There's a Frank Krey, Interpol, Buenos Aires, but the guy's still there. And there's a Bryan Klein, FBI, Detroit, but he's still there, too."

"You said he's an R-and-K guy," Fane said, "but the two first names you just gave me start with an F and a B. Maybe the initials have to be R and K—in that order."

"Okay. I'll run a another search, get right on it."

Fane bought a Pepsi from the vending machine and walked back to the room. Celia was pacing, and her face had gone from sober to anxious. He handed her the soft drink.

"Celia's going to help us out," Roma said.

"Listen," Celia choked down a mouthful of Pepsi. "I can't do this!"

"It's not that complicated," Fane said.

"I don't believe I'm hearing this," she said, trepidation tightening her voice. "This is insane. Regular people don't just . . . just start doing this kind of stuff."

"You don't have to do anything different from what you're doing now," Fane said. "You can even keep his money."

Celia put the Pepsi on the nightstand and buried her face in her hands, thinking. Fane knew she was reviewing her options and kept coming up against the surveillance video. She knew she was screwed.

She looked up. "How long do I have to do this?" she asked.

"I don't know." That wasn't the answer she was hoping to hear. "Look, you're in a bind here. The good news is that you're going to be able to work your way out of it."

23

Elise Currin lived in the lush lap of a Pacific Heights archi-tectural beauty, a three-story neoclassical hybrid on the crest of a hill. It was only one of the three homes Jeffrey Currin owned in the city.

As with Lore, Fane introduced himself as Townsend, who had been contacted by a friend on behalf of a third party whom he did not know.

Elise didn't want to meet in her home. She asked Fane to pick her up there, then she asked him to drive. She didn't care where.

While Fane worked his way over to Geary and headed out toward the Pacific, Elise expertly limned the context of her situation. She had a softer approach than Lore, but she got in more information about her predicament in less time, and she had a firmer idea of what Fane might be able to do for her. Because Vera had a closer emotional connection with Elise than with Lore, Fane guessed she had done a better job leading up to the suggestion that Elise consult him.

Also, Elise simply had more experience reading between the lines. Life had presented her with a cynical text, and she had survived by learning to interpret the shadowy languages of implication and innuendo.

Fane gradually acquired an impression of Elise from the composite of glances lighted by oncoming cars and city lights. She smelled faintly of perfume, more like sachet, and she spoke softly, with a graceful, precisely modulated cadence.

Vera's description of Elise's beauty was on the mark: her hair was the color of a faded '50s Kodachrome photo of a redhead, and it framed her face in lazy waves. Her mouth was a pleasure, and he liked the way it doled out her words. But her skin was the showstopper. It was a paler shade of white, almost translucent, and Fane couldn't imagine any man looking at her face without wondering what a fine sight the rest of her must be.

But that crass observation was quickly put in its place by her personality. She was, quite simply, a nice person, and talking to her would've been a genuine pleasure if the circumstances hadn't been so strained and peculiar.

Fane already had a soft spot for Elise. Her rocky childhood wasn't so different from his own, and he knew from harsh experience that those years created a psychic DNA that informed everything you came to believe about yourself. Trying to understand the ways in which a childhood experience could affect your life was like trying to chart the vaporous undulations of a mirage.

By the time they were approaching Sutro Heights Park,

Elise had made her case for needing his assistance. They headed south along Ocean Beach. In the darkness only fifty yards on the other side of Elise's window lay the galactic black hole of the Pacific.

"My biggest obstacle to helping you," Fane said, "is that you know virtually nothing about this man. His name almost certainly isn't Ray Kern, which leaves me with no place to start."

"Yes. That's . . . incredible, isn't it?" She looked straight ahead at the highway receding into the foggy night beside the sand dunes. "It's embarrassing."

"Maybe, but you need to remember you're a victim here, not a coconspirator against yourself."

"You know what's surprising?" she said. "As I was telling you about this rela—affair—just now, it sounded . . . bizarre. But, as it was happening, day by day, week by week, it didn't seem that way at all. It was just a little bit unusual sometimes."

Her remarks were consistent with Vera's observation that Elise was atypical in her willingness to confront the "whole human mix" of her life. Vera said she was profoundly courageous. Fane decided to take advantage of that.

"I'll be honest with you," he said. "It sounds to me like this man is setting you up for something."

"Yes," she said, her face turned away from him.

"What do you think he wants?"

He could feel her stiffen at the question.

"You mean," she said, "apart from the sex?"

"I didn't mean anything. You think it's only about the sex? Or not?"

She didn't answer immediately. A couple holding hands and leading a Labrador on a leash appeared out of the dark at the edge of the dunes, coming from the beach. They stopped and squinted into the headlights as Fane drove by.

"I've always been used for sex," she said. It was a sad remark because it was spoken without sadness. "I'm not surprised by what men are willing do for it, or by what they're willing to do to someone else for it. But it's not the only thing men are willing to take to extremes.

"It's funny, but in the beginning I didn't even think it was about sex. We met by chance—"

"How did that happen?"

"We were both picking up clothes at a laundry. There was some confusion about his dry cleaning, and while we were waiting for it to get straightened out we started talking. He was good-natured about the mix-up. We found that we had similar likes and dislikes about many things. We had lunch together. A few days later we met for drinks. Dinner one night. It just kept going.

"He knew I was married. I knew he knew, but both of us avoided the subject. After a while it went from not being about sex to being all about sex."

"That's when he started getting paranoid about security?"

"Yes, when I told him who my husband was. That almost ended it right then."

"Why didn't it?"

"We were pretty heavily involved at that time. He made all these security rules. It was also about this time that I began to realize that Ray had these uncanny insights about me. As if he could read my mind. It was crazy. Over a period of several months it turned from crazy to intense to just plain tense. Then cruel, which I've already told you about."

Her account of the stages of her affair wasn't easy on her. There were long pauses, and she steered clear of the psychic aspects of Kern's "insights." Fane was glad to let it go at that.

"Look," Elise said finally, clearing her throat, "I've been emotionally wrapped up with Ray Kern for five months now. Four months of serious involvement. I never thought he had ulterior motives until the last couple of times we met."

She stopped. When she spoke again her voice was tight.

"This . . . sick turn of events," she said, "is . . . wrenching. I don't have any hunches about it. I just find it disorienting. And frightening. And I want it to end."

At Sloat Boulevard, Fane made a U-turn and started back. The visibility now was no more than a few yards.

"This obsession Kern has with avoiding your husband's private investigators, do you think it's justified?"

"I'll tell you something," she said. She hesitated, as if second-guessing what she was about to say. "Ray's paranoia, if that's what it was, made me wonder if he could be right. Without telling him, I hired a private investigator. His people worked on this for a month. Nothing. No bugs. No one following me. No tapped phones. No GPS in my cars. Nothing."

Fane was jolted. "Did they pick up any signs of Kern's security measures?"

She shook her head. "I told them I was having an affair, and I wanted them to stay away from it. I just wanted to know if my husband was having me watched."

"Did it surprise you that they didn't find anything?"

"Until Ray, I'd never been unfaithful to Jeffrey," she said. "It's humiliating to admit, but the reality is that Jeffrey doesn't give a damn about my fidelity, one way or the other. Sexually, he's ADD. He's never bothered to hide his infidelity. It's just not an issue with him."

"And you didn't tell Kern what you did."

"I said I didn't tell him what I was going to do. I did tell him afterward."

"How did he react?"

"Well, that's interesting. I thought he'd be relieved, but he was . . . shaken. It rattled him for some reason."

At Balboa, Fane turned into one of the parking lots facing the esplanade. Again, out of the corner of his eye he saw Elise look at him, but she didn't say anything.

He parked, facing the Pacific. Occasionally the lights of the Cliff House were visible through the haze off the water, glimmering on the heights in the distance. In front of them the surf breakers rolled onto the beach in florescent ribbons, ghostly visible through the night and haze.

Fane turned off the motor. All of this was done for emphasis, so she would definitely remember this part of the conversation. He turned to her. A street lamp in the parking area behind his back reflected off the moisture in the night air and threw a muted moonlight into the car.

"I never want to have anything to do with a private investigation agency," he said. "I never want to be known to any private investigator or to any agency. You need to understand this."

Elise was facing him, her back against the door.

"Anonymity is everything. Without it I can't do what I

do. If I'm going to help you, you must never—ever—mention me to anyone. If I help you with this, then this piece of business has to exist in a world all its own. You don't let it bleed over into anything else."

They looked at each other in silence. Even as he was intent on getting her to understand a point of critical importance, he was aware of her incredible beauty. In that moment, he realized how thoroughly the aesthetics of her overpowered the deeper reality of who she was.

"You understand that," he said.

She nodded. "Yes, I do."

She wasn't intimidated, Fane could see that. Living with Jeffrey Currin had been nothing if not an education in power and how it operates. She had seen it up close. For her this was merely information about the rules.

"I'm going to explain how I think we should approach this and why," Fane said. "If you can't agree with it, then you need to find someone else to help you."

"Before you go on," she said, "What do you think about what I've told you, about Ray Kern?"

"I said earlier, I think he's setting you up for something. His behavior's changing. The intensity is escalating." He hesitated a beat. "It doesn't sound good."

Elise nodded. She was looking at him with eyes that betrayed drifting thoughts, and suddenly she seemed sad. He was surprised that melancholy should override anxiety at this point. This thing she had with Kern had to be anguishing.

"What do you want me to do?" she said.

2 4

After taking Elise home, Fane drove to Fillmore and parked near Wilmot Alley. He walked half a block to Florio and was lucky enough to get a table after only a ten-minute wait at the bar. He sat next to the wall, a favorite spot, and ordered the hangar steak, pomme frites, and a carafe of Zinfandel.

An hour and a half later he was pulling the Mercedes into the drive at home. Just as he cut the motor, his Black-Berry buzzed. It was Noble.

"Marten, I've got something for you. I don't know if it's good or bad, but it's sure as hell interesting. When I ran searches for your RK combo, I immediately got five hits:

Randall Kirsh
Richard Keyes
Ruben Koper
Ryan Kroll
Ralph Koch

"I took all of those names deeper. One dead, two in Europe, one in Dubai, and one right here in San Francisco. Ryan Kroll. His last contract came out of VS."

"Oh, shit," Fane said.

"Yeah, really."

Vector Strategies was one of the largest private intelligence companies in the world, a $10 billion per year spying behemoth headquartered in San Francisco.

In the years immediately following the end of the Cold War, the CIA and other U.S. intelligence agencies dramatically pared down their personnel. The clandestine services dumped hundreds of spies and spymasters.

Left to their own devices, these uniquely trained men and women melted into the public sector, where they eventually found uses for their unusual skills on both sides of the legal system in just about every country in the world.

Then came September 11, 2001. Suddenly the intelligence community found itself underfinanced, understaffed, and woefully unprepared for the new threats they were facing. They turned to the very men and women they had let go a few years earlier. Overnight, scores of private intelligence companies sprang into being, founded and run by former government intelligence operatives and administrators.

The result was a boom in intelligence contracting, and private spies were hired by the government to do what the government could no longer do for itself. Spies, now working for themselves, were making five times what they had made while doing the same thing as government employees.

The era of private spying—what some called the Intelligence-Industrial Complex—had been born, and it was huge. More than 70 percent of the U.S. intelligence budget was now spent on private contractors. The public interest was now in competition with the bottom line.

Many people in the national intelligence community thought it was a colossal mistake to shift so much secrecy and power from Congress, the people's representatives, and put it into the hands of corporate boards and CEOs. But that had been the trend for the past dozen years. And now that global corporations had gotten a taste of the billions of dollars in government contracts—and of the infinite ways in which having access to the secrets of world governments could be used to make them even billions more—they would do everything in their power to keep the trend going. It was an awesome and questionable shift of power, and the average citizen wasn't even aware that it had happened.

"I've done contract work for these guys," Noble said. "I can't go there. They've got the goods on my computers, and I can't penetrate their systems without leaving a trail."

"I know. You've done great work, as always, Bobby, and you've brought me this far. Many thanks."

Fane disconnected and dialed another number.

"Shen, this is Marten. I need to talk to you."

The photography books lay beside him on the sofa, the Scotch glass empty on the ottoman. He had selected several books with two kinds of portraits: people who were unaware that they were being photographed (the subway photographs of Walker Evans) and people who were achingly aware of being photographed (Diane Arbus, Avedon). Then he spent some time with a collection of portraits by Claude Serna, a Spanish photographer who told his subjects to think on specific ideas (happiness, horrors, death, forgiveness, violence) as he photographed them.

He spent about half an hour with the books before he stopped to watch the rain. Finally his mind was settled enough to think back on the events set in motion forty-eight hours earlier when he had walked into the Stafford Hotel and met Vera List. She had quietly unleashed a maelstrom.

Ryan Kroll had crept into Vera's world of tortured souls as if he had entered dark, but familiar, waters. Whatever business he had there, it was grim business, and he was going about it with a fearsome precision. Fane knew in his gut that he didn't have much more time to figure out what Kroll was up to before it would be too late. It made his stomach knot.

He thought of Vera List looking at the three pictures on his desk. He wished he had a photograph of her silently studying the images of the three women. Would that photograph say any more to him about her than theirs had said to her about them?

In the end a photograph provided little more than a momentary triumph over the enigma of the individual. Though it was enough sometimes to ignite the imagination or sustain the weight of memory, in the end it was never enough. More secrets were hidden in a photograph's shadows than were revealed in its captured light.

25

This, Kroll had never done before. But it didn't matter, because the consequence of his misstep, if it *was* a misstep, was nothing short of failure. So, what was a little backtracking if it saved you everything in the end?

At half past two in the morning, Lambeth Court was even more rancid than it was in the warm, muggy midday. There was no sound other than dripping, the wet night materializing into a foul, slick lubrication on the stones that made his shoes smack with every step. In this dank minute he allowed himself one last scolding. How could he doubt himself on this? He had checked her fucking pulse.

But . . . he'd seen it happen before, in Kabul, in Peshawar. Everyone thought he, or she, was already dead, and while they stood around ignoring the corpse, smoking and shooting the shit—the damned thing coughed! And they were back.

He'd seen it happen. More than once.

The alley's night was thick, suffocating. He pulled a small

LED from his pocket and hid it in his palm, letting a splinter of light leak from between his fingers to help him find the doorway. Then into the corridor and up the stairway which smelled of the dead air of disappointments that had haunted these treads for decades.

The odds of seeing anyone were low, but even if he did, this was the kind of place where people averted their eyes at hallway encounters, or even turned their faces to the walls.

He found the doorway, slipped on a pair of latex surgical gloves, and inserted the duplicate key. There was only a flutter of apprehension before he pushed his way into the room. And closed the door.

Darkness. The LED again, a splinter of light. And there she was, slumped forward on her own lap, forehead on her knees, long black hair draped over her bare legs like a shawl to ward off the chill.

Okay. Here was the question: he knew she was dead, so why the hell did he start thinking that maybe she wasn't? He thought about it, and thought about it, and finally it drove him here to see this. Shit, Lore Cha's magical thinking was creeping into his head, like nematodes crawling into his mouth, eating him from the inside.

It was supposed to be the other way around. He got into *her* head, and he put thoughts into *her* head, and he did it again and again until she imploded into herself. *Her*, not him. What was this shit, this magical thinking shit, driving him here so he could see this dead monkey?

He sat down at the dinette table and looked at Traci Lee.

His mind drifted back, and he remembered the first time in Peshawar—

Footsteps stopped in the hallway. He listened. They started again and went on, into the infinite silence.

He was interrogating a Pakistani Inter-Services Intelligence agent who had spent a lot of time in New York and spoke excellent English. Kroll learned that while the man was in New York, for some really screwed-up reason, he had gone to a psychoanalyst. Kroll got his counterparts in New York to break into the analyst's office, copy his notes, and send them to him in Peshawar.

The Pakistani was a double agent, or triple agent, or just nuts: he couldn't figure it out. The guy was so crazy up that after a while they decided to take him out and shoot him. Kroll intervened and convinced them to give the guy to him. He promised them that the man's fate would be the same in the end. It just may take a little longer. They didn't give a shit.

For the next several months, Kroll worked with the Pakistani. He knew from the guy's analyst's files what his obsessions were. He knew about his fears, his terrors. The guy was haunted by the shit he'd done, by the incest in his family. Childhood miseries. Guilts. Fantasies. Despairs. Everything, the usual human wreckage of sick secrets that people always pretend are in other people's lives but not their own.

Kroll used the whole mess of it to create a concoction of horribles that he cobbled together from his analyst's notes. After a couple of months of force-feeding this guy his own mad nightmares, Kroll had poisoned and twisted his mind so severely that he finally felt like he could trust him to act exactly as Kroll wanted him to under certain circumstances.

One hot summer afternoon, he took the Pakistani out of his cell and into a small courtyard surrounded by mud-brick walls. The two of them sat in the shade of black mulberry trees in wooden chairs, the Pakistani's bare feet on the hot dirt. The guy was so broken, so despondent, that being out in the fresh air for the first time in months didn't even faze him.

Kroll gave the man a cigarette, lit it, and lit one for himself. They smoked. When the Pakistani was finished, Kroll reached into his jacket pocket and handed the man his Beretta. The guy could have just pointed it at Kroll and killed him. Instead, he turned the barrel of the Beretta around and shot himself in the eye.

Kroll sat quietly. The LED was turned up toward the ceiling so that Traci Lee's body was only faintly illuminated by a pale, cold suffusion.

He didn't know how long he sat in that hot garden in Peshawar staring at the dead Pakistani lying in the dirt beside his empty chair. Kroll was mesmerized. He knew he had discovered something astonishing, that a man's mind, his own thoughts, could be used by others to destroy him. Suddenly he understood the incredible lethal power of every man's own inner darkness.

For a couple of years, Kroll was able to do this with another prisoner . . . and then another . . . and another. Each time he did it he became more efficient at using the man's own grim shadows to convince him to kill himself. But that had happened in a world in extremis, the black sites of Afghanistan, Pakistan, and elsewhere . . . in the lands of nightmare.

Could this be done in a "normal" world? he had wondered. We're all human, and nothing human is really alien to us, is it? If we're honest with ourselves. The darkness is there, in all of us. All we have to do is pick its scab, let it ooze.

Kroll studied Traci Lee's slumped body, collapsed upon itself in the misfortune of an indignant death.

He knew that he was on the brink of a revolutionary accomplishment. The received belief used to be that only men were suicide bombers and that only men could be stone-cold assassins. Now everyone knew that was bullshit. Psychiatry and psychoanalysis used to be thought of only as tools for healing. But someday everyone would realize that that was just bullshit, too. When he could finally prove that he was capable of turning the mind against itself, that he could use the mind's own inward darkness to cause it to devour itself, then he would really be able to wield the true, full powers of the psyche.

He looked at Traci Lee's swollen ankles, her shoulders rounded and tightened with gas.

He would prove to them that he could do this. It would blow them away, the doubters ... and the believers. Lore would be the easiest, but Elise would come along. That is, if he hadn't already screwed it up with those last two meetings. He would soon find out where he stood on that.

Traci Lee's long black hair fell over her pale legs like shadows spilling out of her head.

THURSDAY

They sat at Fane's favorite table at Rose's Café, next to the front window just to the right of the entrance partition. It was in a nook and gave him as much privacy as he could reasonably expect in a popular café.

Outside it was raining steadily, and the cozy restaurant was quiet with few customers. The morning's nasty weather was keeping the normal crowds away.

"It doesn't do us any good at this point to worry about what Kroll's up to," Fane said, pushing his last cup of coffee to the side. "There's no time for that."

"Maybe we should take it to the FBI," Roma said. "Vector Strategies? We don't have any business getting into that. We need to hand it off."

"Let's see what Shen tells us. If Kroll's on his own with this, then it's not a Vector story, it's a Kroll story. And I'm not going to let go of that."

He looked at Roma's tired eyes.

"I want to turn the tables on this guy," he said. "After we talk to Shen, I'm going to tell Vera she's got to let these two women in on what's happening. We've got to get them together, figure out a way to flush out Kroll."

"Vera's not going to allow that."

"If she wants to salvage this, she'll have to."

Roma frowned skeptically at him, and he noticed two droplets of rain beaded to a strand of jet hair at her right temple. It was typical of her that she was unaware of them, these tiny accidents of beauty to which she was prone.

"And you think she'll do this?"

"I do because this situation's eating her up inside," he said.

Roma shook her head and plucked at a bra strap through her knit blouse. "This whole thing is just crazy," she said. "I mean, to me, it seems like Kroll has actually treated Elise more cruelly than Lore. And yet Lore's the one who seems to be the most afraid of him."

"I imagine the explanation for that lies in Lore's fantasies," Fane said. "Kroll's crawled right into the middle of those. Even if she's not in danger, he can make her feel like she is. Maybe he gets juiced by that."

"You think she's not in danger?"

"I didn't say that. But she's more high-strung than Elise, more inclined to let her imagination sweep away reason. And then there are Vera's files. Kroll's holding a ton of confidential information. All he has to do is tap once on his computer keyboard, and all that stuff flies into ubiquity. That could explode a lot of lives."

Fane's BlackBerry hummed. It was Moretti.

Moretti didn't want to talk over the phone, so they agreed to meet back at Fane's home, which was midway between Moretti's place in Presidio Heights and Rose's Café.

Fane and Roma were no more eager to hear what Moretti had to tell them than he was to tell it. He had actually called his contact at Vector Strategies immediately after talking to Fane the night before, and the two men had met a few hours later at the Lucky Penny on Geary.

"My guy—call him Parker—knew Kroll," Moretti said, tossing his raincoat over a rustic four-foot-tall clay jar. "He didn't like him, and nobody else did, either. But he was good. He's no longer with VS, though. Left six months ago."

"Six months?"

"He quit. Disappeared is more like it. Just didn't come back one day, and that was it. But the important thing about Kroll is his background. What do these things have in common: a brick-making factory outside Kabul; Al Jafr prison in Jordan; Rabat, Morocco; Peshawar and Kohat, Pakistan; Romania; a Gulfstream V."

"You've got to be kidding," Roma said. "Black sites?"

"Hey, that's good," Moretti smiled, surprised. "Kroll was a CIA psych specialist, a qualified C-Level SERE instructor—"

"Hold it," Fane said. "Explain."

"Survival, Evasion, Resistance, and Escape. It's a military program that teaches secretive survival techniques to elite special operations forces. There's a powerful psychological component to the program in which they teach people how to endure torture if they're captured.

"After 9/11, the SERE techniques were reverse-engineered by former military psychologists hired as contractors by the

CIA to oversee interrogations at their black sites, where they used 'enhanced interrogation techniques' on suspected terrorists. The CIA had gotten their hands on these suspected terrorists by using extraordinary rendition. These new techniques Kroll was using were known as 'The Program.'

"Kroll traveled to all the black sites I just mentioned, plus Guantánamo, to advise the interrogation chiefs. That's the official story.

"In 2008, he left the Agency under some kind of cloud. Something about how he was handling some of the interrogations. Parker wouldn't tell me more than that.

"Then, like hundreds of other intelligence officers had done, Kroll showed up at VS. They're the biggest commercial employer of former government intelligence personnel in the world. Everybody shows up there eventually. He had recommendations out the wazoo, plus a lot of dirty baggage about some kind of weird experimental interrogation techniques he was rumored to have been working on. Vector snapped him up, put him to work immediately."

Moretti shook his head.

"Then, for whatever reason, he's put on the Currin ticket. He has one of the highest clearances you can have. When those guys leave the Agency and go into a contract intelligence firm, they take their clearances with them. He had access to all of Vector's intelligence files."

"How long was he on the Currin ticket?"

"Not long. About four months of that, and he was gone."

"Did something happen?"

"Parker swears he doesn't know. VS initiated a massive

manhunt for Kroll. . . . He knew way too much sensitive stuff to leave the way he did. Apparently they've scaled back the manhunt now, figuring he's on the other side of the world by now, but there's a permanent watch notice on him."

"Why did they put him on the Currin ticket?"

Moretti smiled. "You're going to like this. He wasn't contracted out *to* Currin. He was *on* Currin."

"He was spying on Currin for Vector?" Roma was incredulous. "They were covering their own client?"

"Kroll was very deep at Vector," Moretti said. "He was as black as it gets in that business."

"No wonder they tried to find him when he left," Fane said. "I guess we can't get a picture of him?"

Moretti shook his head again. "I understand he was movie-star handsome," he said. "And, apparently, movie-star aware of it, too."

"Do you have any biographical information?" Roma asked.

"Sketchy. Master's degree in psychology from Johns Hopkins. Served in U.S. Army intelligence, in Eastern Europe. Worked for the Defense Intelligence Agency. Worked for the CIA. Served with the U.S. Army Special Operations Command, psychological directorate. SERE instructor, Fort Bragg. Served in the Middle East."

"That's it?"

"When Vector puts someone in a black situation on one of their own clients, they're elevated to an elite corps," Moretti explained. "Vector empties their 'Blue Band' files, the top-secret personnel files, and replaces them with a 'Black Band' file.

Everything in the old file is replaced with a single flack sheet that tells you what I've just told you. From then on that's the only official file they have."

Roma and Fane exchanged glances.

"Look, Marten," Moretti said, "that pretty well sums up all I can tell you. I, uh . . . since I sent this thing your way, I feel I can say this: if this were a Vector operation, I'd say, go to the FBI with it, get rid of it as soon as you can. But it looks like Kroll's on his own agenda here."

Moretti hesitated again, then went on.

"In light of that, my advice to you would be: go to the FBI with it, get rid of it as soon as you can."

"It's complicated," Fane said.

Moretti looked at him, and from the expression on his face Fane knew that Moretti wanted to give him a lecture. He also knew that he wouldn't do it. But it mattered that he cared enough to want to. That was the thing about Moretti, why he had been so good in the SID. He rarely underestimated anyone, rarely oversimplified. He respected complexity, and he never presumed that the men and women working for him needed complexity explained to them.

Moretti put his hands in his trousers pockets.

"So, you both know how this works," he said. "Vector's going to be picking my life apart to find out how I know about Kroll and why I want to know more. Eventually they're going to be looking at every man and woman who ever worked with me in special investigations. Kroll's important to them, Marten. You're not going to have a lot of time."

Fane nodded. "Thanks, Shen. I'm sorry about putting you in the crosshairs."

Moretti shrugged and stood there a moment, then took his raincoat off the old jar and turned to Roma.

"I worked with him a long time," he said, as if Fane wasn't in the room. "He doesn't seem like a stubborn man. Or reckless. Even when he acts that way, you tend to give him a lot of slack. You think: well, I can see a certain logic in that; I can see why he did it. It's a judgment call. And it's true. But it's still stubborn and reckless."

He smiled ruefully at her, then with a glance that took in both of them he said, "Be careful, you two. This one could set your hair on fire."

He walked out of Fane's office, and they could hear his footsteps receding down the stone hallway to the entry. They were still staring at each other when they heard the heavy glass and wrought iron front door close.

"Go ahead," Fane said. "What is it?"

"Vector's a global intelligence contractor that works for some of the biggest corporations—and best intelligence agencies—in the world. They're scary good."

Fane nodded. He knew what was coming.

"But they couldn't find one of their own agents who's gone missing? We're supposed to swallow that?"

"We've both seen it happen before," Fane said. "You can't be so big or so good that betrayal never touches you. Human nature is the Achilles heel of this business."

"It's too convenient. We stumble onto this thing and when it leads to Vector, oh, surprise, they've been looking for Kroll themselves. They're shocked to learn he's been right here under their noses all the time. Really?"

Fane ran his fingers through his hair.

"Come on, Roma. Inside knowledge is a hell of a big advantage. That's why spy scandals can go on for years."

"You're willing to bet that's what's happening here, and not something else?"

"What have we got as an alternative? The possibilities are infinite, and we have nothing to point us in another direction. No matter how uncomfortable we are with this, we have to go with it. We've got to get this guy, and we're out of time."

27

It was 1:22 p.m. when Fane called Vera at her office and told her that he had identified the man with all the aliases. He said he needed to talk to her and asked if she could cancel her appointments for the rest of the day.

The blunt request caught her off guard.

"What's the matter?"

"Take care of your appointments," he said, "and I'll be there in twenty minutes."

When Fane arrived at Vera's offices, she was keeping herself together with practiced poise. But he recognized the telltale signs of suppressed anxiety in her heightened mannerisms: the correct posture was tense, her searching glance was edged with concern, and there was an air of apprehension in the careful way she moved.

She sat on the sofa facing the glass wall that looked out into the gloomy courtyard. Fane took one of the armchairs.

He brought her up to date, telling her of his and Roma's

meeting with Celia Negri, who gave them the third alias (Robert Klein; it meant nothing to her), of his long conversation with Elise, and then of the call from his researcher with Klein/Kern/Krey's real name: Ryan Kroll. Then he told her what he had learned of Kroll that morning.

Stunned, she opened her mouth and took in a slow, silent deep breath. "This is unbelievable," she said. Then, warily, "Why did you have me cancel those appointments?"

"We're not in a good place," he said. He wasn't going to waste any more time with this. "We still don't know what Kroll's doing, much less why. We don't know where your files are. He's intensifying his activity, but we don't know why. And now that we know about his background, we have to assume that Elise and Lore are in danger."

Vera waited, expressionless.

"If we're not smart about what we do next, Kroll could suspect something and just vanish. With your files."

Vera closed her eyes.

"If I picked up the phone and called the FBI right now," he said, "I'd be justified in doing that."

Her eyes remained closed. "What do you want?"

"Tell Elise and Lore what's happening. You can't keep this from them any longer. After what we've learned, it would be irresponsible."

She opened her eyes. "I know," she said.

Fane said, "I'm willing to try one more thing. Let's get Elise and Lore in here and tell them everything. Then let's put our heads together and create an entry in your files that will force Kroll out into the open when he reads it. We need to know where he lives, and hope we're lucky enough that he's keeping your files there."

For the first time Fane saw Vera's eyes glistening. He had seen fear there, and anxiety, and panic, but never this.

"You told me," she said, swallowing, her voice thick. "You told me . . ." But she didn't finish. Maybe she was afraid that to speak now about the price he had told her she would have to pay would only tempt the fates to make it higher. She said, "I'll call them, right now."

As bad luck would have it, both women arrived at the same time and actually came through the waiting room door one after the other, Lore first.

When they saw Fane, they stopped, just far enough into the room for the door to close behind them.

Lore's eyes flashed at him, and Elise's face went blank.

"Vera's inside the office," Fane said. "You're both her clients. Elise and Lore," he said with an introductory gesture between them. "You both know me as Townsend."

They flicked their eyes nervously at each other, both scrambling to make sense of what was happening.

"This is confusing, I know," Fane said. "But if you'll be patient for a few minutes in there, I'll explain what's going on. Okay?"

"Oh, shit," Lore swore under her breath.

Fane opened the door to Vera's office and followed the two women inside. Vera was at the windows and turned around as they entered.

"I'm afraid we all have a problem," she said, her voice strained. "There's a lot to talk about. . . . please, just bear with us a little while. . . ."

Fane asked them to sit down, and there was a moment while the two women surveyed their surroundings, moving as carefully as cats among the furniture before they each found a place to settle.

Elise sat at one end of the sofa, while Lore suddenly changed her mind, shook her head testily, and paced a couple of turns around one of the armchairs. Both of them were warily compliant, as if they had forfeited their free will to the great conundrum of what was about to happen.

Elise was handling the tension better than Lore, but her eyes were locked on Fane. She was braced for something.

"Okay, look," he said, preferring to stand also. "This is going to be awkward until some basic facts are laid out."

Lore again snapped a glance at Elise, who kept her attention focused on Fane.

"The names I just used to introduce you are all that you know about each other. That's important for you to remember as we go through this.

"I met Vera for the first time three days ago. She contacted me at the recommendation of a trusted friend. Three days prior to our meeting—six days ago—she came to the agonizing conclusion that both of you are having an affair with the same man."

There was no drama except the involuntary look of shock on their faces. Lore slowly edged around the armchair and sat down. Elise closed her eyes and tilted her head forward.

Fane felt terrible for them.

"It took Vera several weeks to realize what was going on. Each of you know him by a different name. He's been breaking in to this office and reading your files. He knows everything you've ever told Vera, everything you've discussed with her, and he's used what he knows to shape his relationship with each of you."

Elise's head snapped up, and Lore gasped.

There was no use elaborating. It was excruciatingly clear to each of them how Kroll might have done that. Each woman was going through her own personal humiliation. Their silence concealed the explosions in their minds, but their dismay was palpable.

He went on. "Vera was beside herself. It took her three days to decide what to do. The first thing she emphasized to me when we met was that whatever happened, her primary concern was protecting the confidentiality of your sessions with her. Protecting your privacy."

To Fane's surprise, it was Elise who spoke first. She looked at Vera, but her question, personal and poignant, was addressed to Fane, her tone of voice dead with pain.

"Why . . . didn't she come to us? How could she . . . not come to us and tell us this?"

Fane glanced at Vera, who was looking squarely at Elise, not averting her eyes or hanging her head. She was facing the nightmare with all the dignity she could muster.

"She was, and is, in an impossible situation," Fane explained. "This man had access to *all* of her client records. You aren't the only two she's had to consider. She couldn't go to everyone because she didn't know who might be involved with him. The only reason she discovered the situation in your cases was because she began to see . . . similarities. Patterns, common . . . behavior."

"Oh—this is . . . ," Lore moaned.

Elise seemed stupefied and grievously embarrassed.

"As you can imagine," Fane went on, "He might be abusing"—he used the word deliberately—"other women in ways that have no recognizable similarities. Or in ways that aren't, in fact, similar. There was no way for Vera to know. She had to give every client the same consideration."

Fane glanced at Vera, who swallowed hard but kept her attention on her two astonished clients.

"Now," Fane went on, "his name is Ryan Kroll, and this whole situation is complicated by Kroll's background."

He told them of Kroll's history, leaving out specific names, referring only to "international intelligence." He explained about black sites, the psychological techniques, and the abuses. They needed to know the context in which Kroll was manipulating them.

Both women were overwhelmed. Fane didn't stop until everything relevant was out in the open. It was a lot to absorb. When he finally stopped, there was only silence.

Vera stepped forward, her arms still crossed, standing erect. "We'll answer your questions as well as we can. I'm sorry. I know this is shocking."

During the next hour and a half Elise and Lore asked a torrent of questions. After Lore got over her shock, she was alternately furious and frightened, animated and weepy, combative and panicky.

But Fane was more concerned about Elise, whose relationship with Kroll had undergone the greatest and cruelest change. To discover now that even the kindness and generosity Kroll had shown her early in their affair was insincere and cynical must have cut her deeply.

Finally the questions slackened, and eventually the two women again fell silent.

Fane said, "Keep in mind that everything you've said in confidence to Vera is in Ryan Kroll's hands. We don't know what he intends to do with those files, but as long as he has them, he's got all of you by the throat."

Lore hissed a curse.

"What we need to do is get them back," he said. "Once we do that, then we can decide how to deal with Kroll."

"This is too much." Lore could hardly believe what was happening to her. Elise was still quiet.

"I'll tell you what I've got in mind," Fane said. "And then we can talk about it."

2 8

The man Parker needed to talk to had been en route from London on a Vector corporate jet when he got Parker's call early that morning. Parker had used the code word for "urgent," which ensured that the two men would meet as soon as it could be arranged after the Gulfstream landed at SFO.

At a quarter past five, Parker's phone rang. The man told him to be at the head of the Vulcan Stairway in an hour.

In a city of hills, stairways were unavoidable and indispensible. There were hundreds of them in San Francisco, each with a character of its own, grand and humble, pristine and grimy, public and secluded.

The Vulcan Stairway was in Corona Heights, in the hills above the Castro and Ashbury Heights. Its highest point began on Levant Street, and then fell in multitiered flights through overgrown vegetation that crowded the stairway and formed a canopy over its long descent. The houses and cottages that flanked the stairs were mostly hidden by the dense foliage on the ivied slopes, though some of the homeowners culti-vated lushly planted flower beds adjacent to the steps.

Parker waited in the margin of shadows near the top of the stairway. He heard a car stop in the street twenty feet above, a door open and shut, and the car drive away. Foot-steps. The man appeared at the top of the stairs and nodded at Parker as he fished a pack of cigarettes out of his pocket and lit one. He blew smoke into the dusk and descended a few steps.

"Long damned flight," he said in a soft baritone. "What've we got?"

He didn't move, and Parker got right to business.

"Late last night I got a call from Shen Moretti, used to be in the SFPD's Special Investigations Division."

"Yeah, I remember him."

"We got together, and it turned out that he was asking a lot of questions about Ryan Kroll."

The man's hand stopped on its way to his lips with the cigarette.

"Someone had asked Shen to make some inquiries about Kroll. These people have been hunting him—and they've found him."

"They *found* him?"

"Well . . . almost. They've got him nailed down here, in the city—"

"Oh, shit."

"And they've got people who are in personal contact with him somehow, but they don't actually have him. Apparently he doesn't know they're on him. It's been a delicate run, and they're sweating it out, pushing it. They found out that he'd worked for Vector, and they were hoping for a break from us."

"Are we dealing with another intel corp here?" The man started casually down the stairs.

"Moretti says no." The Vulcan Stairway was easily wide enough for them to walk side by side. "And he assured me they weren't law enforcement. He said he was just doing a favor for a friend, and I think that's what he's doing. I got the impression these people were a small, elite operation. Moretti seemed to have a lot of respect for them."

"What's their interest in Kroll?"

"I don't have any idea, but they've moved pretty damned fast."

"What do you mean?"

"They've been at this less than a week."

The man stopped, looked at Parker. "Bullshit."

"No. That's what Moretti said. They're flying. That's how I came into it. They reached out to Moretti to reach out to us. They want it over fast."

"Is that from duress, or are these people just cowboys?"

"Duress, I think."

The man smoked, regarding Parker. "What the hell's Kroll gotten into? He did something, got into something. He screwed up somehow and triggered this hunt. That's why they're so far along so fast. Was Moretti aware of how Kroll left Vector?"

"No, I gave him the picture on that."

The subject of Kroll's disappearance—and Vector's inability to find him—had quietly subsided into oblivion in the inner circle of Vector's intelligence division. Nobody talked about it anymore, not openly anyway. It was anathema. Kroll was now the ghost that haunted their counterintelligence, the bane of their lives. The only thing that made his disappearance bearable at all was that, try as they might, Vector could find no evidence that Kroll had sold or otherwise used any of his inside knowledge about Vector.

On the other hand, others argued, that's exactly how a good spy worked. Vector wasn't going to be blasted out of the water by what Kroll had taken away with him. Instead, whenever things went wrong in Vector's operations, they might never be quite sure why, whether it was bad luck or incompetence or a superior opposition . . . or Kroll's inside knowledge at work, secretly sold to Vector's highest-bidding adversary.

The man dragged on his cigarette and then started moving down the shadowy steps again. Here and there lights were coming on in the houses along the hillside, their glow instantly deepening the shadows by contrast, turning the ashy vegetation to black silhouettes.

"In a hurry," the man said. "They've got a time frame problem."

"Definitely."

"You know how these people got the contract on Kroll? Or is it a contract? Maybe it's something else."

"Moretti was fuzzy on that, but I didn't get the impression it was generated out of their own shop."

"How did you leave it with him?"

"I gave him the basics, stuff I figured he'd get anyway in a few more days. That saved him some time and made it easier for me to ask for a favor in return if I needed to."

"Good. Okay." The man fell silent again as they progressed down another tier of steps.

Parker was a little puzzled by the man's reaction to the stunning news that Parker had brought him. Parker had expected an explosion of anger, but instead, aside from his obvious surprise, the man was more thoughtful than outraged. And there was a lot to be outraged about. Not only did another intel operation practically have their hands around Kroll's neck, but it was all happening right here in San Francisco, not in Bangkok or Bahrain as everyone had speculated. This was even more humiliating.

But the man seemed to be absorbing Parker's shocker revelation as if it amounted to a small move in a much larger game, something to be factored in to his calculations, rather than something that required him to marshal his resources to counter a major threat. This definitely wasn't what Parker had expected.

They continued in silence, slowly. At one point the man dropped his cigarette on the stairs, stepped on it, and ground it out with the slowness of preoccupation. Then he continued on, his hands in his pockets.

After a minute or two, the man stopped and turned to Parker. When he spoke, he lowered his voice.

"If Shen Moretti didn't know about our situation with Kroll," he said, "then that means that after your conversation he would've realized that his friends were smack in the middle of a matter of major importance to Vector . . . and that by talking to you he'd let the cat out of the bag. He had to have known that you'd do exactly what you've done, report to somebody at Vector what you'd just discovered. He's going to expect us to jump all over this, do everything in our power to get our hands on Kroll."

Yeah, exactly, and that's what Parker was expecting, too. He had actually thought he was bringing news to the man that would put into play a massive operational scramble . . . but that didn't seem to be what was about to happen.

"It sounds like these people are wrapping this up," the man said. "Time's short. And if they think they know what we're going to do, they're going to be on the defensive and moving faster. I don't think we've got any realistic expectation of taking this thing away from them. At least not without attracting a hell of a lot of unwanted attention. The truth is we've fucked up the Kroll thing from the beginning. We're just going to have to make the best of that."

The man paused, his silhouette looming in the murky light. For all his calm, his hesitation betrayed a racing mind. He was right about Vector and Kroll; if it hadn't been disastrous for them yet, it still could be. They didn't have a lot of options.

"I want you to get back to Shen Moretti," the man said, his baritone even softer now. Parker leaned in, listening closely.

In three minutes it was done.

They were already near the bottom of the stairway, and Parker saw the taillights of the man's car waiting for him in Ord Street below.

Parker stayed where he was as the man turned and descended the last dozen steps to the street. He heard the car door open and close. The brake lights winked, and the car was gone.

Parker waited a moment. He shook his head. He turned and headed back up the stairs, the tiers of steps unfolding before him into the deepening shadows.

Lore had kicked off her shoes and crossed one long leg over the other, her stockinged foot waggling impatiently. She was boring in on Fane with her black eyes.

Elise sat at her end of the sofa. She was leaning forward, her elbows on her knees and her hands clasped together, the back of one hand resting against the side of her face. She had been quiet for a long time.

"Okay," Lore said briskly, "so, basically, we need to create an opportunity for your surveillance people to lock onto him so they can follow him."

"That's right. Until we can physically get to him, we can't do anything about him, can't find out where he lives, can't find out where the files are—"

"Which you think are at his home," Lore said. "Okay. So, then, why don't I just call him and ask to meet him somewhere?"

"You've both told me that you rarely initiate meetings,

that he usually does that. So how is he going to react to a call from you all of a sudden?"

"I guess it depends on what I say."

"What will you say?"

"Whatever you want me to say."

"There's a reason Kroll always initiates your meetings," Fane said. "All of his training, his entire life, is built around the knowledge that the only action he can trust is action that *he* initiates. When someone else initiates, he can't be sure of their intentions. Is he being set up? Is it a trap? Why does she want me to do this now? Why there? Why then? His obsession with security is all about controlling the situation. If he controls it, he's safe. If someone else controls it, he just can't be sure."

"The bastard," Lore said, "he choreographed everything. And, Jesus, wasn't he good at it."

She stood suddenly and tugged down the hem of her dress that had crawled up her thighs. "You know what? I never wanted to see the sorry bastard again, but now I can't wait to get to him."

She grabbed her shoulder bag. "I've got to go to the bathroom," she said, and headed for the toilet in the waiting room.

Vera was exhausted by the emotion of the past couple of hours and sat down in one of the chairs in front of her desk.

Elise was watching Fane. She was still sitting forward, her forearms on her knees. She studied her clasped hands.

"Let me ask you something," she said softly. "Last night you said that you believed that Ray—Ryan, was setting me up for something."

He nodded, remembering.

"I . . . was just wondering if you have any better idea now what his intentions were?"

"I think I may have been wrong about that," Fane said.

Elise frowned, puzzled.

Fane was aware of Vera listening. "Since last night, I've learned a lot more about him. A lot more."

He paused; he really didn't have any right to say these things. She picked up on his hesitancy.

"It doesn't matter anymore," she said, "what hurts and what doesn't . . . or why. I just wondered . . . if he got what he wanted."

Fane was touched by her sad curiosity, poignantly clinging to the last shreds of those remembered moments before Kroll's cruelty turned everything to disillusion.

"I'm afraid I don't know the answer to that," he said.

"But . . . ?"

"But . . . I think that, at the core of it, he wanted something else."

She waited, tilting her head a little to the side.

"I don't understand," she said.

Fane couldn't forget Elise's story and the echoes of his own desolate childhood that it evoked. There is a spiritual debasement in that kind of loneliness for a child, in that kind of solitude. It savages the heart when you believe, deep inside of yourself, that you really don't matter at all . . . to anyone.

"That idea," Fane said. "I was on the wrong track, trying to understand what was happening. I think I misunderstood what I was seeing."

She regarded him in silence. He was sure she saw through

his lie, and he wondered what she thought of him for doing it. Then Lore came back into the office.

"Okay, so where are we then?" Lore asked. "Is there a plan or what?" Her bob was freshened, her attitude was recharged, and her determination to nail Ryan Kroll was set firmly in the forefront of her mind.

Fane looked at Vera, who had been silent during his conversation with Elise. He had the feeling that she was anticipating what he was about to say and was trying to figure out how to deal with it.

"We need to talk a little about that," he said. Vera stood and walked over to sit on the sofa with Elise. Lore was back in her armchair, one long leg crossed over the other.

"We want to plant bogus entries in the daily session notes that Vera makes for each of you. We want those entries to contain something that will draw Kroll in close to us. Literally. We need to get a physical fix on this guy. Whatever we put in those files needs to attract him, not repel him. And keep in mind, if he reads something that doesn't ring true, or makes him suspicious, we lose everything."

All three of them were looking at him.

"Elise and Lore, your last meetings with Kroll were . . . stressful. You need to remember that he did what he did for a reason. Maybe he wanted to provoke a reaction from you. Maybe he wanted to hurt you. Who knows what he was doing. But if anyone knows, or has any insight into what he was after, it would have to be you two."

He paused, giving this time to register with them.

"As much as you've talked to Vera about this," he said, "you can't have said everything there is to say about those two meetings. And now that you know more about Kroll than you knew at the time, maybe you have a new perspective about your relationship with him."

Elise dropped her head at this point, from embarrassment or chagrin or confusion he couldn't tell and couldn't know. Lore started waggling her foot.

"You need to blend what you know with what you suspect, even what you intuit, about him. You need to create a mixture of truth and lies that will be like nectar to this guy and make him want to meet with you again—soon."

"Just a minute," Vera said, glaring at Fane and leaning forward on the sofa, challenging, but Elise interrupted her.

"No, Vera, he's right," she said, not taking her eyes off Fane as she spoke. "At the first sign of something wrong, he'll disappear. If that happens, none of us will ever be free of him again. I have to do this."

When Fane looked at Lore for her reaction, he was startled to see her crying, silently. She stared at him with a haunted expression that caught him off guard. He couldn't tell if she was furious or frightened, but there was no doubt she was deeply agitated. Her cocky, in-your-face attitude was gone, and Fane suddenly realized how brittle and fragile her act was.

She couldn't speak, but she nodded, forcefully.

3 0

When Celia Negri left the Medical Center, a gloomy, early dusk was settling over the city. Lights were coming on everywhere as she turned off Carl Street onto Parnassus and headed into Ashbury Heights.

As she approached Cole Street, she immediately starting looking for parking places. The brake lights of a Volkswagen parked at the curb next to La Boulange Bakery popped on.

"Yes!" she hissed, and shot across the intersection to claim the parking space as the Volkswagen was pulling away.

She locked the Volvo and crossed Parnassus to the Alpha Market on the corner. She picked three oranges and two onions from the baskets on the sidewalk in front and quickly paid inside.

Next door at Cole Hardware, she bought some glue to repair a metal strip coming off the front of her oven door. As she stepped outside on the sidewalk again, her thoughts wandered back to what had occupied her mind all day: to Robert

Klein, to Dr. Vera List's office, to the two FBI agents, to whatever the hell Klein was up to.

She crossed Parnassus thinking she might go into the bakery to get something for breakfast the next morning but decided against it by the time she reached her car. She unlocked the car from the curbside, stepped down, and put the sack on the front seat.

"I would've put money on you going into the bakery next," he said behind her.

Celia flinched and spun around, banging her head on the car door.

"Damn it!" she snapped, her stomach knotting instantly. "That was deliberate."

"I scared you?" Klein asked.

"You can really be a prick."

He frowned skeptically at her. "Go ahead and lock it. Let's walk a little."

There was a slight incline up Parnassus into the Upper Haight, a more gentrified area than its famous hip neighbor farther down the hill. Here the old three-story houses tended to be neat and orderly. Cars lined the street under the trees in their always hard-to-find parking places.

Klein kept his council for half a block, his silence tightening the knot in Celia's stomach. She couldn't believe she was living this. How the hell did this happen?

"Something's come up," he said, "and I need you to make another run to the psychoanalyst's office."

"Oh?" Her heart skipped. How did that sound? Natural? Nervous?

"Yeah."

"When?"

"Tonight."

"Tonight?" Oh, shit. "Why . . . what's—"

She stopped.

"What's the matter?" he asked.

"The matter?"

"You, uh, you can't do it tonight?"

"Well, yeah, I can do it," she snapped, a deliberate tinge of sarcasm in her voice. It was easier to hide her fear behind an attitude.

"You're a little touchy," he observed.

Shit, was she overdoing it? "You scared me back there," she said. "That makes me touchy."

He guided her to the right onto Belvedere, a quieter, tree-lined lane with clean clapboard houses and stoops leading to the sidewalk. Again cars were jammed in every spot along the street.

Klein said, "There seems to be something else."

"Oh, really?"

"You have . . . some concerns?"

"About what?"

"The change of routine?"

"No."

"No? You seem preoccupied."

"Well, I'm not. I could do it with my eyes closed."

"That's confident."

"If I was worried sick about it would you want me doing it?"

"No . . . but maybe a little respectful caution would be a good thing."

"I don't want to get caught," she said. "How cautious do you think that'll make me? And I really want the money. How respectful do you think that'll make me?"

A dog in a backyard got wind of them or raked them in with his sixth sense and started barking. In the misty dusk the bluish jitter of television screens flickered in rooms here and there. The street was still.

They walked past a couple of houses in silence.

"You seem . . . tense," he said.

Her heart lurched; the wind whooshed out of her diaphragm.

"I thought you were concerned that I was too confident," she said.

"Brash, but tense."

Shit. Does this guy know something? She decided to come back on him.

"What's the matter?" she said. "You sound a little equivocal yourself. Are *you* having second thoughts about something?"

He didn't respond. She could actually feel him weighing her words. The son of a bitch was picking up on something, and it was freaking her out.

She had always had a tendency to be cocky, but that's what had made her such a hell of a ride in bed. It's also why he knew she would be fine with this. That and the money. She really wanted the money.

But, still, there was something going on with her. Maybe it was jitters, and she just didn't want to admit it. He'd seen it before. There's a sinus-clearing, jazzing kind of thing that happens before a new thing goes down. Everybody feels it.

"So," he said, "I'm pretty sure this needs to be done tonight."

"I thought you said it was happening."

"I did."

A waft of something cooking came on the damp air from one of the houses. Something rich, spicy it seemed, but he couldn't peg it.

"I don't understand. Is it or isn't it?"

"Maybe, I don't know."

He was having mixed feelings. He wanted to push her a little, see if there was something behind what he was picking up on. See if he could get a better feel for it. But if it was nothing, he didn't want to rattle her just before she was about to do her job.

She stopped and turned to him. They were standing at the edge of a wash of light spilling off a front porch. He could see the look on her face.

"What's going on here?" she asked. "If you're wanting to tell me something, then just spit it out. I don't need the innuendo. I don't know what it means. Don't know what you're getting at."

Well, he didn't expect that. But he liked it. It felt right.

"You're spooked," he said. "And that spooks me."

She stared at him, and it was just a couple of beats too long. Even in the washed-out light he could tell that she didn't know what to do with her face.

"Okay, yeah," she said, suddenly giving in. "I'm . . . I'm pretty nervous about this. I . . . I don't really know why. It's

not any different from the other nights, I know, but . . . I
don't know, you scaring me like that and then popping the
last-minute run. . . . What would be different? Maybe different people around the building . . . different routines . . . it
just . . . hell, it just got to me in a way I didn't expect, then
that got to me and . . . shit, it's just caught me by surprise and
I didn't want you to see that, and I guess I didn't do a very
good job of hiding it."

Finally she stopped. It was a good recovery, or at least a
good stab at one, but it was too late. For one flicker of an
instant her artifice had slipped, a fatal mistake.

"That's okay," he said. "I understand. Come on."

He turned away from the light and headed back toward
Parnassus. He put his mind on dual operation. He pretended to talk to her as if he were trying to steady her
frayed nerves, make her believe that he had swallowed
her performance. What he said came out of the rote behavior part of his head. It didn't require any thought or any
reasoned calculation, just a recitation of tradecraft on a
superficial level.

But the other track of his mind used that rote language
like a flywheel and kicked into action at a rate of speed that
quickly shot past the white noise of his own voice to focus
like a laser on her deception.

Why was she lying? What were the most logical, the most
obvious options?

One: Maybe what she had just rattled off, that she was
getting cold feet, was the truth. He had seen something like
it before with professionals, so it certainly could happen to

her. But, if what she said was true, then her lying must be about something else.

Two: Maybe she was getting ideas of her own about what she could do with those files. Maybe she had decided to make copies for herself, too. Was she thinking of a little blackmail scheme? Did she think she could sell the information in those files? She was always hungry for money. Maybe she was hungrier than he realized.

Three: Maybe she had been caught during the last break-in, and someone had flipped her. But he couldn't really make that one work in his head. First of all, when he met her less than an hour afterward she had been a hell of a lot calmer than she was right now. Whatever was causing her nervousness had happened after their last meeting.

Beyond those immediately obvious possibilities, he couldn't come up with any other logical explanations. But something was drifting out of focus, and alarm bells were going off.

"I'll tell you what," he said, as they approached Celia's car. "Let me check one more time, make sure the stuff I need is going to be there. No reason to do it if it's not. I'll let you know."

She gave him a look, double-checking his face in the light of the bakery. Then she turned, stepped off the curb, and walked around her car. She unlocked the door and looked at him once more over the top of the vehicle.

"I'll let you know," he said again.

She opened the door and got in. He watched her lock the doors. Then she started the car and pulled into the street and drove away.

31

While Vera was working with Elise and Lore to create the bogus session entries, Fane walked down the hill on Hyde into the coming dusk. When he reached Hastings Terrace, he turned into the stubby dead end of the alley where Jon Bücher had parked his van next to an art and antiques store.

He tapped on the door, and Roma opened it. He stepped in and sat down.

"I think we're in pretty good shape," she said, putting the plastic top back onto her coffee. "Libby's team is already in the area, drifting around the edges—staying out of the way."

"You've given them the general picture?"

"Yeah."

"Nothing from Celia?"

"She hasn't called, and I'm not calling her. That's the plan. We agreed that the less we communicate, the better it'll be for security. Besides, I think if she could talk to me every time she got butterflies, it would just keep her keyed up."

Fane turned to Bücher.

"Erik's standing by?"

Bücher nodded. "When we're sure the run is on, I'll call him. He's ten minutes away."

Erik Kao was an assistant professor of data management in computer sciences at Berkeley. He was Bücher's regular hire for these kinds of jobs. Once they found Kroll's computers, Kao would have to determine on the spot the best way to secure Kroll's cache of files, copy them, or physically take everything away. If taking the hardware wasn't feasible, Kao would have to copy everything in Kroll's possession, then wipe everything clean. No trace of Vera or her clients was to be left behind.

"And you've tagged their cars?"

"We're in the process," Bücher said, nodding at the monitors. Each of the six cars in the operation (Fane's, Roma's, Libby's, Mark's, Reed's, and Bücher's) were tagged with tracking devices so that each one showed up on the monitors as a different colored dot. Each of the cars also had monitors, so everyone knew where everyone else was at all times.

Fane had decided to tag Elise's and Lore's cars as well, though without telling them. Reed was now in the process of locating their cars and placing the tags on them. Libby and her crew were experts at this kind of surveillance, which enabled them to "shroud" the target while staying out of site a block or more away.

As soon as Kroll showed up to meet whichever woman he chose, they would tag his vehicle as well—if they could locate it.

Fane and Roma stepped out of the van and stood under the awning of the art and antiques store. A light rain was dripping off the awning.

"How is it going at Vera's?"

"It's tense. They're cooperating, but they really haven't had time to get their minds around what's happening to them."

"Do you know what they're going to say?"

"No, and they can't know either until they're face-to-face with Kroll. I understand that. But I spelled out what we needed, how they should handle it to avoid spooking him. We went over it and over it. They don't have any illusions about the situation they're in."

Roma looked at him. "Are they going to be able to do this?"

Fane shrugged against the damp. Roma always got right to the heart of the matter. "We've got a shot at it," he said.

They both knew that Elise's and Lore's emotional involvement with Kroll was the biggest wild card of all. Maybe they could control that. Maybe they couldn't.

"How's Vera holding up?"

Fane shook his head. "Stunned. They're all stunned. Not knowing why Kroll's been doing all this has really rattled them. I imagine Elise and Lore are rethinking every word they've ever said to him. It's got to be disorienting."

"And neither of them have heard from Kroll since their last meetings?"

"No. But apparently it's not unusual for a week or so to go by without hearing from him." He looked at his watch. "I'd better get back up there."

. . .

It was 8:45 p.m. when Vera finally finished entering her bogus notes into Elise's and Lore's files. It was an awkward process with the two women taking turns huddled with Vera at her computer at one end of her office to talk about her entries so that neither Fane nor the other woman could hear what was being said. If the consequences reliant on those hushed conversations hadn't been so frightening, the process might have seemed ridiculous. But considering what was at stake, nobody was feeling absurd.

Whoever wasn't talking to Vera passed the time in silence. They paced the floor or sat in stupefied thought or stood at Vera's windows gazing out into the growing darkness.

When Lore was returning to the sofa after conferring with Vera for the last time, and Elise was taking her place, Lore motioned to Fane to join her by the glass wall. They stood there a moment, staring into the moist night, then she turned to look at him.

"What happens when . . . you've got everything you want from him?"

This wasn't something he wanted to discuss with her.

"I don't think I can know that until that time comes."

"I'm not an idiot," she said. "You've thought about it. In your business—whatever the hell your business is—you would've thought about it. What are you going to do with him?"

"Look," Fane said, "there are so many variables about what might happen that it's impossible to play that out with any accuracy."

"Then don't be accurate," she said acidly. "Scenarios, give me some scenarios." Lore had found her voice again, and she didn't want to be humored.

She said, "You can't turn him over to the police, can you? He knows . . . shit! who knows what he knows . . . and he could just spill all kinds of stuff to whoever would listen. And that would defeat your purpose, to keep all of this quiet. Make it disappear."

"I can't talk to you about that," he said.

"Oh, really?" She caught her rising voice and glanced back at Vera and Elise. "I'm in no position to be demanding anything, is that what you're thinking? Right?"

She glared at him. The question was rhetorical but it didn't stop her from delivering a withering look.

"You can't *possibly* know what this feels like," she said, "being in this . . . 'situation.' You know what it does, more than anything? Next to wanting to be out from under this hallucination, I mean. It makes me want to know . . . to know for *certain*, what's going to happen to him."

She moved closer to Fane and lowered her voice for emphasis. "In the past couple of hours going through this humiliation," a tilt of her head toward Vera, "knowing for certain what's going to happen to him has become a burning concern for me, an obsession."

She was close enough to Fane when she said this that he could feel the breath of her last two words on his face.

"That's it," Vera said from her computer behind Lore.

Lore didn't even blink. She held Fane with her eyes, telegraphing something he didn't recognize.

"It's done," Vera said, standing up while Elise walked

away from the computer, her eyes averted from the others. Vera was exhausted, her face drawn, as if she had been through something brutal. She looked at Fane, seemed to want to add something, but didn't.

Again he checked his watch.

"Okay, the sooner we leave here the better."

"What's the next step?" Elise asked. "I mean, right now?"

"Everyone goes home," he said, looking at both women. "If he tries to contact you before you hear from me again, don't talk to him. Call me immediately. Otherwise, as soon as we know he's got the files, one of us will contact you and we'll set up another meeting to decide the next step."

"Can't we talk about that now?" Lore asked.

"No, because we don't know which of you he'll contact first. He might contact one of you just to talk and then call the other one to arrange a meeting. There's just no way to know how he's going to handle what he reads."

He looked at Vera. "But you think you've got something here that will make him want to contact them?"

"Yes," she said, "I think we do." Her tone was troubled.

"Okay, then," he said. "Now we wait."

3 2

At 9:45 p.m., Kroll pulled into a side street across from Celia's apartment and cut the motor. All through the evening he had shuffled through his concerns about Celia's skittish behavior earlier. He finally decided that she was working her own scam.

That didn't surprise him. Celia was a lot more savvy than Traci Lee, and more resourceful. She had recognized the potential in List's files the very first time she entered List's office. That was a flaw in his system: if someone is smart enough to jigger computer security, they're also going to be smart enough to recognize the value of what they're stealing.

So Celia probably went to someone with as much gall as she had, someone she could trust, and enlisted their help. It was nothing to copy more flash drives. An hour on the Internet would give them the identities of all those women. Celia was smart, but unsophisticated. She was thinking of blackmail.

He was pissed off. He couldn't trust her anymore, and he didn't have anyone else trained. And he didn't quite yet have Elise and Lore where he wanted them. Even after reading List's session notes from the last meeting he would have more work to do. But Celia was a threat now. Shit.

When he considered Celia's situation along with the uneasy last sessions with Elise and Lore, he saw a sobering trend toward instability. He had to eliminate the weakest link first, settle things down. Then he'd figure out a way to continue accessing List's files.

He got out of his car and walked to the end of the side street and crossed Pomroit. Celia lived in the top floor of an old two-story house on the sloping street. He climbed up the narrow outside stairs leading to her apartment and knocked on the door.

The clock started ticking.

"Who is it?" Celia sounded concerned, cautious.

"It's me, Robert," he said.

"Klein?"

"Yeah. I've got instructions for you."

Silence. Was she calling someone? The door snicked open, and Celia peered out.

"Hey," he said. "Got some info for you." He tried to sound casual, at ease.

"Christ, why'd you come here?"

"I've got a proposition for you. A lucrative one."

She hesitated. "Why didn't you just call?"

"What's wrong? You want me to go back down the stairs and call you from the sidewalk?"

She rolled her eyes and opened the door.

They were in her tiny living room; a door led to the kitchen, another to her bedroom. The furnishings were thrift-shop retro. The general feel was there, but the budget was missing. Celia wore an old pair of jeans and a snug black turtleneck. She retreated a short distance from him, across the small room, arms folded. Wary.

"A proposition," she said.

"My wife has hired a private detective to look into my finances," he said. "He's in Vegas where I've moved some of my assets. I've hired my own PI out there to find out what's going on. He's got a flash drive for me, and I don't want him to send it commercial. Too damn risky. I can't go tonight, so I want you to fly out there and bring it back in the morning."

Celia frowned. "Tonight? What about the List thing?"

"We'll do it first, then I'll take you to the airport."

Her eyes bore into him.

"Lucrative, you said."

He could always depend on her to zoom in on the money.

"I'll cover everything, the flight, hotel room, meals. And pay you three grand. Clear."

She didn't say anything, just looked at him. But he knew her mind was churning, wondering what the catch was, calculating the ins and outs of his proposition in light of her other scheme. There wasn't any downside for her.

"I get the three thousand up front. Plus the regular amount for downloading the files."

He reached into his coat pocket and took out an envelope and handed it to her.

She opened it. Looked at him. Counted the bills.

"It's got to be tonight?"

"My guy's waiting in Vegas."

"But I've got to work tomorrow."

"Look, for this kind of money you can call in sick. Tomorrow's Friday. Call your supervisor, leave a message that you're throwing up, have a fever. You'll be in Monday."

She was holding the money, and he was betting she wasn't going to let go of it.

He didn't seem particularly worked up or tense or calculating. He just wanted it done. She held the envelope for what seemed like a ridiculously long time as she calculated the results of doing exactly what he wanted.

She knew that Linda was already set up to monitor her "break-in" at List's office. She could tell her what was happening while she was in there.

And how would Linda and Townsend feel about her flying off to Las Vegas? Whatever they were running on Klein, Celia would wager half of what she was holding in her hand that they didn't know about this little business in Sin City. Go ahead, they would say, and keep them informed.

She couldn't see a downside to this. After all, hadn't they pressured her to be an informant? Hadn't they said she could keep whatever Klein paid her for working for him? Damn right they had.

"Okay," she said. "I'll do it."

. . .

Celia immediately called her supervisor's voice mail at UCSF Medical Center and reported in sick, then started throwing a few things into a small carry-on for the overnight to Vegas. While she packed, Kroll told her how to get in touch with his lawyer in Vegas and gave her his cell number. He told her which hotel had her reservation and that he had her e-ticket down in the car.

For a moment, watching her pack her underwear, he thought about getting her into bed—she would do it, wouldn't want to piss him off and risk losing the three thousand—but he let it pass. The clock was ticking.

Roma was reading a year-old copy of *Wired* she had found under a computer monitor in Bücher's van when he said, "Hey. Look at this."

She looked up at the bank of monitors and saw Celia Negri walking into Vera's office. Roma looked at her watch.

"What's this? Why the hell didn't she call?"

Bücher reached out to touch the audio dial, a nervous tick.

Roma's gaze was locked on Celia as she hurried through the waiting room to Vera's office. She didn't waste any time turning on the computer and inserting the flash drive, which was hanging from a lanyard around her neck. Her fingers flew over the keys, and when the download started, she looked up from the computer and looked around the room.

"I don't know where the cameras are," she said needlessly.

"Listen, I couldn't call you because he's been with me every minute since he told me he wanted to do this tonight. After I finish here he's taking me to the airport, and I'm going to Vegas for him."

She told them quickly about Kroll's surprise visit with her that afternoon and that he had come to her place an hour or so ago and what he wanted her to do, what he was paying her, and when she would be back from Vegas.

"If you don't want me to do this you'd better call me, but I've already got the money right here with me . . . and, I guess, he'll think something's funny if I back out now."

Roma was incredulous. "He drove her here? Is that what she's saying?"

Bücher touched the audio dial. "Sounds like it."

Roma's mind suddenly flooded with possibilities.

Celia was just sitting there as if she were listening to the night noises of an empty building. She didn't know where to look to be facing the cameras.

"You gonna call her?" Bücher asked.

"I don't . . ."

Celia tapped a couple of clicks on the keyboard.

"You calling Libby?" Bücher asked.

Roma's attention was riveted, her mind racing to play out all the possibilities.

Celia said, "Okay this is almost finished. Doesn't take that long to dial a phone number, so I guess you don't want me to change anything I've told you."

The computer beeped, and Celia pulled the flash drive out of the USB port.

Roma couldn't take her eyes off Celia.

"No, I'm not going to do it," she said to Bücher. "She'll be out of there in five minutes, and that's not enough time for us to reset our plans in this fog. Besides, tailing him to SFO will expose us too much. If we had a different target, maybe. If we had his car tagged, sure. But we can't tail him, not this guy. We've already got a better plan. We'll stick with it."

Celia began shutting down the computer.

"She's got what we wanted her to get," Roma said. "So far so good."

They watched as Celia turned out the lights, walked through the waiting room, and closed the door.

"Christ," Roma said. "He could be a block away. Damn!"

She picked up her BlackBerry and called Fane.

33

Kroll was parked just two blocks away on Larkin at Lombard, the car pointed downhill. He stood across the street in an alley, and when Celia got into the car—he heard her as much as saw her, the fog was so dense—he looked at his watch.

He waited five minutes. Celia knew the drill. Then he crossed the street and opened the car door and got in. The interior light didn't come on, an old habit that he had taught her as well, so she was used to it.

"Piece of cake," she said, taking the lanyard with the flash drive from around her neck. While her arms were in the air, his arms went up, too, and in an instant he slammed them down, each fist gripping one end of a braided rope garrote.

He jerked it tight and leaned back for maximum torque, lifting her off the car seat. But her thick hair caught under the rope preventing him from having a clean, efficient wrap. It wasn't a fast death. She flailed like a blue marlin, hammering his dashboard so hard with her feet that he heard knobs and handles smashing and snapping. He gave the garrote a couple of brutal jerks for punishment.

After she went limp, he released the garrote and rammed his hand down her blouse to fondle a lush, warm breast before he moved up to her carotid to check her pulse. Nothing.

He put the flash drive into a coat pocket, took her phone and keys out of her shoulder bag, and retrieved the nearly four thousand dollars he had just given her. Then he shoved her down onto the floor of the car.

The next fifteen minutes were critical, with Celia's body clearly visible to anyone who approached the car windows. But it wouldn't do to put her in the trunk. He needed quick access to her, and besides, they were going only a few blocks.

He started the car, and moments later he was crossing Chestnut where Larkin Street dropped sharply in front of him. Only four blocks away, but far below in elevation, was Ghirardelli Square and the cable car turnaround. Immediately in front of him Larkin turned sharply to the left along the edge of the hillside. To the right was his objective: the crumbling roof of the old, abandoned Russian Hill reservoir built into the hillside.

He pulled to the curb and took night-vision goggles out of a black carry-on bag. He slipped them on and quickly checked the turnaround below that separated a group of townhouses from the reservoir. A thick hedge fronted the derelict reservoir, and a chain-link fence surrounded it. A pedestrian walkway with a railing led around the perimeter.

He let the car roll down and around the corner. In the

middle of the steep block, he turned back onto Francisco Street. As he approached the turnaround, he reached over and unlatched the passenger door without opening it. He continued slowly into the dead end, pulled up close against the bank of dense hedges, and cut the lights.

Moving fast, he walked around to the other side of the car and wrestled Celia's body onto the ground. He shoved her up into the hedges near the entrance to the walkway, then got back into the car, drove out of the lane, and parked half a block away on Polk.

Carrying his night-vision goggles, he returned to the turnaround. Pulling on the goggles for a second time, he slipped off the walkway into the undergrowth. The only living body his goggles picked up was a cat creeping along the path against the fence halfway down the length of the reservoir, coming his way.

Celia's body, still black with heat as seen through his goggles, was only an arm's length away. He hauled her down into the bushes, undressed her, and laboriously dragged her naked body under the chain-link fence and through the tangle of shrubs to the edge of the reservoir. Through his goggles he could clearly see the caved-in hole in the shabby roof.

The view to the north side of the reservoir dropped down to the waterfront. On the south side, uphill from him, two high-rise residential towers dominated the hillside. The view of San Francisco Bay made it expensive real estate. The reservoir was also in full view from the towers. For a couple of minutes—forever if the conditions hadn't been perfect—he would be totally exposed as he dragged Celia's body across the reservoir roof.

But the night and weather were on his side as he pulled her out into the open and started toward the hole in the roof. It went smoother than he anticipated, though he could feel her buttocks snagging on the nails and rough edges of the composite roofing.

The roof structure around the ragged hole was flimsy. Being careful not to slip into the opening himself, he grabbed one of Celia's hands and held on to it as he circled the hole. From the other side, he tugged and inched her toward the opening until the gravity of her own weight sucked her over the edge into the reservoir.

A millisecond . . . and then the thud of her body hitting the dry reservoir floor.

In five minutes he was off the roof, lying up under the shrubs at the edge of the turnaround, breathing heavily. In a pinch for time, the reservoir was better than the bay or the Pacific, both of which had a bad habit of coughing up the bodies dumped into their waters before the bodies had a chance to disintegrate. No telling how long it would take her body to be found in the dusty silence of the dilapidated reservoir, but with luck and time the rats and the damp would take care of her.

He gathered up her clothes and walked back to his car. A few minutes later he tossed the clothes into a Dumpster.

In twenty minutes he was back on Pomroit, climbing the stairs to Celia's apartment as he pulled on a pair of latex gloves. When he got to the landing he unscrewed the porch light. Inside, he went straight to her bedroom and dragged out two suitcases from under the bed. He took all of the clothes out of her closet and put them in the bags, along with the clothes from her chest of drawers. Her shoes and boots went into the second bag.

In the bathroom, he emptied the contents of her medicine cabinet into a pillowcase, along with her shampoo from the shower and her sanitary napkins from under the sink. He wanted it to look like she had gone on a trip and intended to stay awhile.

Carrying the bags to the sidewalk, he turned downhill and walked half a block to her car. He put the two suitcases into the trunk with the pillowcase, then put the keys in the ignition. He left the car unlocked.

While walking back to his car, he flipped open his cell phone and made a call.

"Pablito, this's Bob May. Got a clean one for you."

He gave the address and license plate number.

"It's unlocked," he said, "Keys in the ignition. Make it disappear."

In twenty-four hours her car would vanish into Mexico. It would be five or six days before somebody would get serious about checking up on her. They would discover that her clothes and toiletries were gone. In a city heavily salted with young women runaways and lost causes, it would take an energized family to convince the police that she was truly missing and hadn't deliberately made herself scarce.

If she didn't have that kind of family, and if there was no one else who really gave a damn that she wasn't around anymore, then Celia Negri would simply cease to exist.

34

When Roma called Fane and told him that Celia had picked up the bogus files, he and Vera were sitting at her kitchen table finishing the last of the Thai take out they had picked up near Fisherman's Wharf. They were surprised by Roma's news and realized they had left Vera's office only a couple of hours before Celia showed up.

Fane assumed that Vera had asked him to come by her place so she could either tell him something or ask him something about the past few hours at her office. But Vera had been subdued throughout the meal, and now she seemed to have lost what little appetite she had. She put down her fork and sipped her green tea, studying her plate.

"This feels like a mistake," she said, raising her eyes to him.

"This?"

"The whole thing."

"Why?"

"Every time I think about all the possibilities of what might happen next—about the potential ramifications that could result from each of those possibilities . . ."

She shifted her eyes away from him, past him, into the dimly lit living room.

"I don't see how the rosy expectations that I imagined when I came to you nearly four days ago could reasonably survive all those dark possibilities."

"You don't see any good possibilities?"

"Not enough."

"Not enough for what?"

"To justify the risks that seem to be multiplying by the minute."

"I'm not sure Elise and Lore would agree with you."

It wasn't Fane's place, nor his inclination, to cheer her up. They were all in a nasty situation.

"What did you put in those fabricated notes?" he asked.

She nodded, then stood and absently picked up their plates, needing something to do with her hands while she thought. He gathered up the paper takeout boxes, and she pointed to the trash while she rinsed the dishes and put them into the washer.

"I wanted to talk to you about that," she said, drying her hands with a towel as she sat down at the table again.

"Remember I told you about my client, Britta Weston, who, inexplicably, committed suicide when there was no reason for me to believe that she would even try?"

Fane nodded.

"Well, if that had been either Elise or Lore I wouldn't have been surprised," she went on. "Both of them have made attempts. Both of them were legitimate efforts, nothing half-hearted. Both of them were saved by flukes, but even so Lore almost died.

"All of that happened immediately before they came to me," she said, "and it's been a long slog, working through the emotional traumas that contributed to the despair that lay behind those attempts."

She paused for tea, to think.

"I shouldn't be telling you this, and wouldn't be," she said, looking up at him again, "except for the fact that when I was talking to them this afternoon about what they thought we should put into those fictitious files, they both homed in on scenarios directly relating to their suicide attempts. I wasn't so surprised with Elise. The incident with Kroll the other night was directly linked to her suicide attempt. It was still fresh with her, still raw.

"But when Lore also came up with a suicide scenario, I was shocked. That was too much coincidence. And then there's Kroll's training, his work in interrogations. Psychoan-alysts have studied those techniques, the theory behind them. I've read articles on it." She fixed her eyes on him. "Quite a few of those prisoners committed suicide."

"You think he was trying to get Lore and Elise to kill themselves?"

"I do. And I think they now have an inkling of what he was up to. Why else would they bait him like that? Neither woman knows what the other woman talked to me about, yet they both came up with variations on the same scenario."

"That's what they wanted you to put in their files?" Fane was as shocked as Vera. "That they were thinking of suicide?"

"Lore even imagined a scenario in which Kroll mentioned that he might want to be present when she did it. They framed their scenarios in different contexts, of course, but their own suicides were their bait."

"That . . . it's hard to make sense out of that. Why the hell would he be manipulating them to do that?"

"It's sick," Vera said. "It probably wouldn't make any sense to anyone but Kroll."

Fane left Vera's place at 11:50 p.m. and walked to his car in the wet, drippy silence. He began to rethink what to do about Kroll once they had retrieved Vera's files.

One of the basic tenets of his and Roma's business was that regardless of the problems they were hired to resolve, they would manage them in a way that left no traces of a problem having been there in the first place. Invisibility. Anonymity. Silence. No loose ends. Lacunae, perhaps, but that would be the closest thing to evidence that they would ever leave behind.

That was where Kroll presented a special difficulty for them. Fane sensed—and he was sure that Vera was sensing this as well—that the man didn't understand stalemate. Or checkmate. Or threats. Even to know that he existed meant that sooner or later you would have to deal with him in a manner that had to be final.

As he got into his car, Fane punched Roma's number on his BlackBerry.

"Five more minutes," Roma answered, "and you would've heard from me."

"Where are you?"

"Home. I'm just now undressing."

"So what's happened?"

"After I talked to you, I called a source at SFO and got her to tap into the flights to Vegas. No Celia Negri."

"Using another name?"

"I don't think so. After I left Bücher I drove to Celia's place on Pomroit."

"Not smart," he snapped, then quickly checked the flash of temper. "Damn, Roma."

"Celia had given me a key. The place is empty, Marten. Everything's gone, clothes, empty medicine cabinet. She's gone."

"Maybe she was more afraid than we thought."

"The porch light was out. Unscrewed. It wasn't out two nights ago. The inside of the place felt creepy."

"What do you mean?"

"I don't think she ran. I think it's Kroll." Roma's voice was flat. She was sick about it.

"If you're right," Fane said, "then he's deliberately cut himself off from Vera's files. Either he thinks he doesn't need them anymore, or something's spooked him and he's shutting down his operation."

Roma didn't say anything. Fane told her about creating the fictitious files in Vera's office and the disturbing conversation that he had just had with Vera about suicide.

Roma was floored.

"Can you believe that! My God, this man is sick."

Fane agreed. "But I've been thinking about this. There may be something more important here than Kroll's personal psychopathology."

He could almost hear Roma's mind churning as she tried to anticipate him.

"Moretti told us that Kroll left the CIA under a cloud," Fane continued, "because of the way he was experimenting with 'The Program's' interrogation techniques. You put that information together with what we've seen him doing with these women, with what Vera just told me, and we've got some pretty frightening possibilities."

"Like what?"

"What if Kroll's experiments involved psychologically manipulating his prisoners until they killed themselves? If he could exploit their psychological weaknesses and steer them to despair . . . and suicide, if he could reliably do that, he would have acquired a lethal, highly marketable skill.

"Think about it. He leaves the CIA and goes to work for Vector. He's put on the Currin ticket and learns that Currin's wife was seeing a psychoanalyst. This was a perfect opportunity for him to test the results of his experiments. Up to that point he had only been able to do that in the torture cells of the black sites. He needed to prove that he could do it in the 'normal' world, too."

"Suicide as assassination?" Roma was thinking her way into the possibility. "But how many potential targets could there possibly be whose psychology would make them vulnerable to this kind of approach and whose psychological histories would be available to him? That doesn't seem too practical to me."

"Proxy spying has come far and fast in the last decade," Fane said. "Maybe we need to rethink the old spy game's idea of a 'target.' If you're a spy-for-hire corporation, your personnel roster is brimming over with former intelligence operatives, and you're representing the interests of global corporations as well as sovereign states. It's easy to see how the lines between the two kinds of clients might begin to smear. When hundreds of billions of dollars are at stake, the difference between 'competitor' and 'enemy' can begin to get fuzzy."

Roma was silent for a moment.

"This is hard to get a grip on," she said. "You're saying that if Kroll is offering the invisible, perfect kill, it could be a tempting option to high-stakes players in the global corporations?"

"I'm saying that if Kroll can prove he can really do this—I promise you there are plenty of people who will put him to work."

Roma again was silent. Fane knew she was pushing his theory through her own filters.

"No wonder Elise and Lore were so rattled by this guy," Roma said. "They were getting bad vibes about him long before he turned mean on them."

"I think we're in real trouble here," Fane said.

3 5

Lore Cha was swimming naked and alone. There were palms around the pool, and beyond a sprawling green lawn, an old Victorian mansion, derelict and deserted. She dived to the bottom of the pool, then ascended through the water toward the fading light of dusk.

When she reached the surface, she hit something clear and soft. An impenetrable film covered the water. Confused, she swam to the edge of the pool, but the transparent covering had sealed her in. She panicked.

Then the smeared image of a man appeared at the edge of the pool. She screamed for help. He crouched on all fours and slowly moved onto the transparent film. He was naked, too, and crawled on his stomach like a lizard, slithering over the surface toward her. It was Kroll. He offered no help. Instead he lay there, sprawled directly above her face, grimacing viciously at her.

Suddenly Lore was choking . . . drowning. . . .

She opened her eyes, gasping for air. The world was inverted. The lights of the Bay Bridge glittered beneath her, and the lights of Oakland spread out above her.

Her neck hurt. She wiped her mouth and rolled to the side as she grabbed the sheets and pulled herself back onto the bed. How long had she been like that?

She lay still, letting her equilibrium return. Raking her hair out of her face, she looked over the sheets at the bridge, its strings of lights slowly coming into focus. One of these nights she would take too much of that damned sleep medication, wash it down with too much liquor, and kill herself out of extreme stupidity . . . a dumb-Asian-chick death.

Rolling her head to the side, she looked at the clock. Just after midnight. She remembered that Richard was in Chicago. Not that it ever mattered. She was always alone. Stunning rooms, stunning views. Stunning solitude.

Then she remembered Elise. When they left Vera's office earlier that night, they paused in the foyer and Lore impulsively gave Elise her cell number. Elise was taken aback but seemed grateful. Then she gave Lore hers, as if they shared a rare blood type, and it only made sense to be able to contact each other. It was a bond, and that mattered when little else seemed to.

She sat up, crossed her legs yoga-style, and gathered the sheets into her lap, twenty-eight stories above the Bay Bridge. She thought about the strange afternoon, she and Elise taking turns huddling with Vera, spilling their guts in whispers about that freaking ghoul Kroll.

And Townsend, as handsome and elusive in his way as

Kroll, but without the stink of hell on his breath. The guy was a puzzle, but Vera trusted him, and she trusted Vera. Even so, she didn't trust him without reservation.

How did Elise feel about Townsend? Did she tell him as much about her relationship with Kroll as Lore had? Was Elise's relationship with Kroll different from Lore's? Townsend explained that Kroll used Vera's notes about them to customize his affairs with them. What the hell was Kroll *doing*?

Shit, this whole thing was so whacked.

She reached over to the nightstand and picked up her cell phone. She punched the telephone number.

"Hello?" the voice was husky. Awakened? Drunk?

"This is Lore . . ."

Hesitation on the other end, and then, "Oh, yes, of course."

"I think we should talk."

The place was near Sutter and Larkin, one of the few late-night grills in the area and roughly midway between Lore's place on Rincon Hill and Elise's in Pacific Heights.

They sat at a table near the front plate-glass window, apart from anyone else in the place, grateful that the crowds had seeped away leaving only a few couples and a handful of loners at the bar. Closing time was only an hour away.

They ordered coffee and started talking. Even in the small window of time they had, it was a process: generalizations first, then circling in with more specifics as they began to trust each other more. Soon they weren't holding back, and they couldn't share enough to slake their relief at discovering that they weren't alone in Kroll's nightmare. They were the only members of a select survivors group, a secret sisterhood of two.

But it wasn't exactly the same for both of them, and Elise was far more aware of this than Lore. For her, there was a pain in Kroll's deception that went deeper than Lore understood. It cut to the heart, and no amount of objectifying could heal it.

Finally there was a lull in their conversation, and Lore said, "One of us is going to have to get close to that bastard again."

Elise nodded. She hadn't let herself think about that.

"Townsend," Lore went on. "Not easy to get to know that guy. He's complicated, but I guess he seems to know what he's doing. Do you trust him?"

"I do, yes."

"So do I." Lore glanced around. "But . . . you know, he really hasn't told us how he's going to get rid of Kroll, has he? I mean, that's the whole point of me talking to Townsend—do you know his real name?"

Elise shook her head.

"Anyway, that was the whole point in talking to Townsend in the first place, to get that bastard off my back. But how's he going to do that? All of this has been so rushed, I know. But what's next?"

"I think it's first things first," Elise said reasonably. "We need to get the files back. It'll be a load off of my mind knowing Kroll can't hold that over my head any longer."

Lore nodded in agreement and looked away. She sat with her body turned slightly to the side so she could cross her legs, and she had begun waggling her foot. Elise had watched her do that at Vera's when she got impatient or irritated.

"Okay, what's on your mind?" Elise asked.

"I guess, once he gets the files, Townsend has a plan up his sleeve," Lore said, her tone contradicting her words.

"You sound like you don't think he does."

Lore looked at Elise. "I keep thinking about what Townsend told us about Kroll's background. Shit, I didn't know any of that when I asked him to get Kroll out of my life. I thought . . . I don't know, that he was some kind of a sick creep, somebody Townsend could scare off. But the Kroll Townsend described doesn't sound like the kind of guy who scares off. And that really freaks me out."

Lore turned her eyes to the rainy night street.

"I suspect Townsend's thought about this," Elise said.

Lore's eyes snapped back to Elise. "Then why hasn't he told us? We're the ones at the center of this insanity. This is happening to *us*, right? But they're not telling us what they're going to do with this maniac?"

"Townsend plays his cards pretty close to his vest," Elise said. "He'll let us know when the timing's right."

"Well, that's not good enough. We thought we were hiring somebody to look after our interests. Turns out he's working for Vera."

"Her interests are our interests."

"As far as it goes."

"What do you mean?"

"Well," Lore shot back, "for one thing, Vera hasn't been screwing Ryan Kroll, has she?"

Elise's face burned. It wasn't Lore's way to think that Elise's relationship with Kroll might not have been like hers. Elise didn't hold it against her, but it only added to her bitterness at the way Kroll had treated her to hear Lore assume a similarity and to express it so crudely.

"And she didn't put up with his stupid security shit for months and months," Lore went on. "And she didn't endure his sudden humiliations or his flashes of cruelty that went way beyond what"—her voice broke—"whatever."

Elise looked at her, and her stomach knotted as she remembered the same indignities. And the memories were all the more shameful because they didn't even have the value of being exclusive. Knowing that Lore, and maybe others, had been through it, too, only demeaned her relationship with Kroll even more.

Christ, it was repellant to remember that she had thought that what she had with him was unique. It was loathsome to realize that every casual revelation by Lore gave the lie to that delusion. And it reduced Elise's role in her affair with Kroll to nothing more than the gullible partner of a serial rapist.

She felt stupid and savagely enraged. Suddenly she was so agitated that she felt as if she were about to explode.

"I've got to get out of here," she said, standing suddenly. "I've got to go."

Lore sprang to her feet also.

"Wait! Go where?"

"Home."

Lore reached out and gripped her hand. "But . . . what about me—?"

The shocked look of anxiety on the face of the normally intrepid Lore stopped Elise short. Instantly she saw that Lore Cha was petrified at the thought of being alone. And she had no one to go to.

Elise took her hand.

"Come on," she said. "Come with me."

3 6

Kroll undressed in the garage and threw everything, including his shoes, into the trash. Wearing only the flash drive hanging from the lanyard around his neck, he went up the stairs to his bedroom, threw the flash drive on the bed, and stepped into the shower.

Half an hour later, he walked up another flight of stairs in his bathrobe to the main floor of the house and went into the study that overlooked China Beach. The room was bare except for a chrome and glass table and an Aeron chair. There were three laptops on the table. He sat down at one of them, plugged in the flash drive, and opened the latest document.

#248/Jane8

Today's session with Jane8 left me deeply distressed. Her deteriorating relationship with RK continues, and seems to be undergoing a radical evolution. (She still refuses to tell me anything about him that would help me understand—or even imagine—what might be behind these dramatic changes.)

But regardless, his uncanny ability to drill down to the softest core of her pain is undergoing some kind of change, taking on a distinctly darker hue. Unfortunately, I failed to recognize these new developments for what they were, failed to see quickly enough what they foreshadowed. As a result, this precipitously cruel turn has taken me by surprise. I'm frightened, though I didn't admit this to Jane8.

I've been questioning her closely the last few sessions about what I see happening. She hasn't denied that something is going on, but she wouldn't go into it. Now something terrible has happened.

Today Jane8 told me about RK and the glass bird. [See session notes.] She is absolutely traumatized. It was an unimaginably vicious thing for him to do, but even more than that, *how* he might have known the significance of this symbol to her is unnerving in the extreme. I said she surely must have alluded to the incident in her childhood, must have made some reference to it that enabled him to infer the significance of that symbol. She swears that she didn't, but I could see in her eyes that she had begun to doubt herself: had she done this and forgotten? *How* could she have forgotten such a thing?

Today she even alluded to RK's "special powers"—the first time she has ever used those words—a phrase that tells me she's beginning to look beyond reasonable explanations for an answer to his abilities. This is a dangerous turn for her, heading toward a disconnect from reality.

Her accelerating emotional instability has been nothing

less than an implosion . . . sudden and deep. For the first time since she's been seeing me, I'm afraid that she's approaching the same suicidal state of mind that preceded her attempt to kill herself nearly two and a half years ago.

I'm shocked by this dramatic reversal. I've never seen anything like this. I've consulted with Dr. S.J. several times on these developments, and we are in agreement that I should tell Jane8 that her relationship with RK is becoming alarmingly destructive, and that she should stop seeing him.

One final point: Today Jane8 related this dream she had last night, the night after the incident with RK and the glass bird. (The dream is so startlingly blatant, it hardly requires comment.)

Jane8 and RK are driving along a country lane at night. The lane is narrow with sweeping turns, woods crowding in close on all sides. As they come around a long curve something appears in the middle of the road at the farthest reach of their headlights. RK slows, and as he drives closer they realize the object is a black, high-backed wooden chair. They pull up close, the chair square in the headlights.

For some reason the chair terrifies Jane8. RK seems perfectly calm, as though he understands everything. Jane8 has no idea of the significance of the chair, except that it's threatening to her. He tells her to stay in the car, and he gets out and goes to the chair in the glare of the headlights. He turns to her and gestures to her to pay attention to what he is about to show her.

He sits in the black chair, facing her, knees together, posture straight, square in the headlights' glare. He takes something out of his suit pocket and puts it into his mouth. He takes something out of his other pocket, a pistol. Looking squarely at her, he bends his arm and puts the gun to his head . . . and shoots himself—the pink mist lingering in the beams of the headlights, before drifting gracefully away into the darkness.

Jane8 is not horrified by this, or by the fact that RK stands up in the road, his head blown out on one side, a flap of skull dangling behind one ear. He approaches the car, opens her door, and she steps out into the chill night air. Holding RK's hand, she walks to the chair and sits down, knees together, posture straight, blinded by the headlights. RK gives her what he had in his mouth, something smooth with a cold, familiar shape. She puts it into her mouth. He hands her the pistol and steps out of the light.

Suddenly she realizes the object in her mouth is the green glass bird. She begins crying hysterically, raises the gun to her head, and pulls the trigger.

She startles awake, sobbing.

When I asked Jane8 what her thoughts were as she sat in bed, afterward, remembering the dream, she said, "I felt relief. Finally, there was an end to it."

Kroll stared at Vera's entry on the computer screen. It was even more than he had hoped for. Elise's frame of mind was primed for the last act. She had approached the darkness of the idea and, in the end, she had embraced it. And with Kroll himself playing the role of a mentor. Damn, she couldn't have gotten the message any clearer if he had written it down for her. Elise was within his reach.

As for Vera List deciding to warn Elise not to meet with him again, he was in luck. List's calendar showed that she had canceled all of her appointments for the next day, when she would normally have sessions with Lore in the morning and Elise in the afternoon. But now she wouldn't see them again until Monday. By then, it wouldn't matter.

He clicked through to the latest entry for Lore Cha.

#62/Jane12

Jane12 came to today's session absolutely petrified after an episode of fantasy role-playing with "Robert" took a menacing turn. [See session notes.]

Jane12 has discovered that "Robert's" driver's license is counterfeit: she doesn't know who she's been having an affair with these last four months, and that discovery is driving her to distraction. Not only that, "Robert" informed his last interpretation of her fantasy with bits of information that she claims only I know about her, secret fantasies that she's revealed in analysis.

While I find this concerning, I'm not totally convinced that she remembers precisely who she may have shared some of these fantasies with. I know that she has, incredibly, forgotten some of the fantasies she's shared with me. I was incredulous the first time this happened, but it has happened a couple of times now, so I can't be too shocked when she tells me that "Robert" has miraculously crawled into her mind and knows even the fantasies she hasn't told him.

But there's no mistaking her fear. She hasn't slept well since this happened five days ago. She's agitated, has no appetite, and cries easily. And most disturbing, she's having

fantasies of suicide in which Robert plays various and inte-
gral roles. [See session notes.] With her history of depression
and attempted suicide, I'm worried that this instability could
accelerate quickly, even too quickly to address.

Remarkably, after going into weeping jags while telling
me about "Robert's" betrayals and abuses, she neverthe-
less feels irresistibly drawn to him. She insists that the next
time he calls and wants to meet, she will do it, even if it
means more disturbing revelations. This is a willful embrace
of self-destructive behavior that she admits is obvious
even to her.

I know this is her history, and that she's fighting an uphill
battle, but I thought we had been making good progress.
These latest developments, however, appear to be turning
all of that progress upside down.

I have an appointment with Dr. S.J. to discuss the sudden deteriorating condition of both Jane12 and Jane8.

Kroll was relieved. He had been concerned that his last
sessions with Elise and Lore had pushed both women too
far, too fast. He was afraid they might even suspect that he
was reading their files, and confront List. But apparently he
had been wrong about that. In fact, it seemed he had judged
both women correctly. He had ratcheted up the pressures on
them to precisely the right degree, pushing them closer to
the breaking point.

Vera List, however, was no fool, and it was with her that
Kroll may have made his mistake. Another session or two,
and she was going to connect the dots. She was already just
about there. He was going to have to work fast.

. . .

Fane's BlackBerry woke him. He had been asleep on the sofa in his office, still in his clothes. It was 2:15 a.m.

"Here's something interesting," Roma said, sounding sleepy. "Bücher just called. Around one o'clock Elise and Lore left their homes and met at Blaine's Grill near Larkin and Sutton. They left Blaine's just a few minutes ago and ended up at Elise's place."

"Damn it, if Kroll's watching either of them, this can't be good."

"He'd have to be live on them," Roma said, "because Libby drove by Elise's house and neither car is visible. I guess Elise had the presence of mind to put them inside. So, do you still think these two didn't know each other before all this started?"

"Yeah, I'm still okay with that. My guess would be that our session in Vera's office this afternoon raised a ton of questions. Finally they couldn't stand it anymore, had to talk, compare notes."

"And who do you think initiated this?"

"Lore, I imagine."

"And why did they end up at Elise's?"

"You've got me there."

"Well, the longer they're together, the greater the risk," Roma said. "It's bad timing."

Fane agreed.

She paused. "I can't stop thinking about the suicide thing. It's wild, Marten, but I think you may be right about it. And if it's going bad for him, who knows what he'll do."

Fane agreed with that, too, but before he could respond Roma was off the phone. Actually, he wanted to listen a few more minutes to her voice, listen closely, to get a feel for how she was handling Celia Negri's disappearance. He was worried that she was more affected by it than she wanted him to know.

He sat on the edge of the sofa and ran a hand through his hair. He thought about calling her back on some pretext, and then rejected the idea. She could smell a pretext a mile away. But then, maybe that would have been okay.

But he didn't do it. Instead he stared through the darkness and the fog at the scattered lights along the bay, and let the emptiness of the house gather around him.

Fane was still sitting on the sofa, the BlackBerry in his hand as he stared at the floor, when it rang again.

"This is Shen. I just got a call from Parker, and I've got a message for you."

FRIDAY

37

At dawn the city was in the grip of a full-blown Pacific front that had been threatening to move ashore for days. Thick, lowering clouds and intermittent rain colored the morning in a deep, gray mood as Fane drove down Steiner Street to Rose's.

Again, there was a sparse crowd in the café. Fane called Roma while he waited for his breakfast. She had already checked with her people, and they were taking turns sleeping, pacing themselves for the long haul.

Then he called Vera and told her about Elise and Lore.

"That had to happen," she said. "I completely understand it. But, to get together last night . . . ?" Suddenly she said, "Is this a problem?"

"I thought you might have a thought about that."

"No, not . . . not from my perspective. Is it for you?"

"I don't really know," he said. "I'll call both of them in a little while and check in, but I don't want them to know that we know that we've got people watching them. But I'll be curious to see if they tell me."

"And if they don't?"

"I'll be a little worried about that."

"Why?"

"There's room for only one plan here," Fane said.

"Oh, Christ," she was shocked. "You can't believe . . . should I call them?"

"No, I'll do it. I'll keep you up to date."

He waited until he got back to his study to call Elise. He told her that Kroll had picked up the files last night as anticipated, and reminded her of how they were planning to handle the process whenever Kroll called. She was calm enough, though her voice was edged with concern. She didn't mention that Lore was with her.

He called Lore. Same routine, but she was uncharacteristically subdued. She didn't mention where she was, either, and Fane let it go at that.

He ate lunch in the kitchen, a glass of Mourvèdre, some Spanish cheese, ciabatta, olives. The fact that neither Elise nor Lore mentioned they were together bothered him. Was he missing something here?

He sat in the gray light washing into his study and listened to Erik Satie's *Trois Gnossiennes* while he pored over his photography books. The dreamy piano music drifted through the hours of the long afternoon punctuated only by intermittent rainstorms and occasional phone calls as he monitored all the players. From time to time he glanced across the room at the colored dots on one of his computer screens. There was very little movement.

Late in the day he put on Tom Waits's *Alice* album and pulled another photography book off the stack of them on the ottoman. Despite the music and the books, his mind kept wandering. Like Vera, he couldn't leave the possibilities alone. They were as intellectually seductive as dreams begging to be untangled.

"This is Ray."

Elise flashed a look at Lore. "Ray?"

Lore froze in the middle of the room like a cat startled in midstep. They were in the sitting room/study just outside Elise's bedroom and had just poured their first drinks of the evening.

"How are you?" Kroll asked.

She didn't expect that. It wasn't a Ray kind of question.

"You've got to be kidding." She was surprised at the acid in her voice. Lore signaled her frantically to put the speaker on. She did.

"What?" Kroll asked, surprised.

"How *am* I?"

There was a pause, as if he had been caught off guard, too. She imagined him correcting his thinking, resetting his instruments.

"Am I on speakerphone?" he asked, suspicion in his voice.

"Yes, you are," Elise said, and somehow she thought of it: "I'm wiping my nose. I've been . . . I've . . . I'm upset," she finally said.

"Have you been crying?" He didn't sound concerned, just curious.

She didn't answer.

"What's wrong?" he asked.

"Oh, Christ!" she snapped, couldn't help herself.

"Look," he said, "if you're still upset about—"

"Still? God, Ray, what do you mean 'still'? I should be 'over it by now'? Is that what you mean?"

A few beats. "Look," he said again, "what . . . what was going on there? You, you just . . . what happened? What am I supposed to think about that?"

Elise paused. What the hell was she doing? She couldn't say what she was feeling. She had to stay with the script they had established at Vera's office the day before. She had to remember the context of the scenario they had laid out in the bogus notes from the bogus session and stay with the tone required by that script. She was depressed, suicidal. Not angry, not belligerent.

She thought back to the meeting in Vera's office: Townsend's words, his instructions. Just get him to meet somewhere, give Townsend's people a chance to lock onto him.

But, suddenly, hearing his voice, knowing how intimately this man knew the way she thought . . . and felt, the way he had manipulated her, and how she had fallen for it, she was livid—and petrified. He would see through this, no matter what she did.

"Ray . . . I'm . . . I can't talk about it. It's . . . just . . ." She stopped, surprised, confused, and surprised to be confused. The role-playing was just too involved, calling him Ray when she knew he was Ryan, thinking inside the bogus context when she knew the reality was otherwise; pretending to be in despair when she was actually furious, hurt, bewildered, afraid. Damn him, why hadn't he called Lore? *She* could role-play; *she* could suck him into a meeting. Why hadn't he?

She gave a desperate glance at Lore, who was gaping at Elise's silence with baffled anticipation. What? What?

"I can't do this," Elise said, speaking to Lore as well as to Kroll.

Lore's eyes opened in wide desperation, and she cocked her head with a get-a-grip expression: You've got to! she was saying.

"Okay, fine," Kroll said, calming her, backing off. "Fine, but still, we should talk. I need to understand what happened. . . . You owe me that, don't you? To help me understand this."

Elise froze. His tone was as sincere as she had ever heard him, the inflection in his voice was heartfelt, deeply caring and genuine . . . and it sent a chill through her. This was the kind of emotional fraudulence that he had manipulated her with from the very beginning of their relationship, and she was mortified by the naked cruelty of it. It was shocking.

"Elise?" Kroll's voice reflected a concern at her silence, a fear that he might be losing her. "We can't . . ."

Lore hurried to Elise's writing desk and found a pen . . . a piece of paper . . . began scribbling.

"—leave it like this," Kroll was saying. "We have to talk about it . . . resolve whatever . . . whatever's upset you so much."

Lore whirled around to Elise and held up the piece of paper for her to see the huge words in a hasty scrawl:

MEET HIM IN <u>PUBLIC</u> . . . HOTEL LOBBY??!!!

"Elise?"

"I'm here," she said.

"Let's get together and talk."

Long pause. "Where?"

"There's this house . . . it's quiet, out of the way—"

"No!"

Pause. "Okay." His voice was cautious. "How do you—?"

"In public," she said.

"Public? Well, okay, how about—?"

"The Fairmont," she said. "In the lobby. There are private corners there where we can talk . . . in the lobby."

Kroll didn't answer immediately. "I don't understand. Why in public? We've never done this."

"I don't trust . . . myself . . . with you"

Was that the wrong thing to say! She threw another desperate glance at Lore, who gave her a reassuring look.

Kroll was silent.

"Okay," he said finally. "I'll be there. Nine o'clock."

3 8

There was a flurry of phone calls. First Fane told Elise to just sit where she was, and he would call her right back. Then he called Roma, then Vera. Then Elise again. They would meet at Vera's office.

Within half an hour everyone was either there or on the way to other points for the surveillance setup.

Elise and Lore arrived together and explained at the outset that they had met and talked the night before, and that Lore had spent the night at Elise's and would stay there tonight as well. The whole thing was awkward and raised a host of questions, but there was no time to go into it.

Kroll had set the time to meet at the Fairmont at 9:00 p.m., a curious three-hour delay from their phone call. Curious to Fane. No one else seemed to note it. Still, it gave them time to get ready.

Bücher and Roma arrived together. Fane provided cursory introductions, then Bücher explained that he was there to install a sensitive wire mic into Elise's bra, if she would please go to the bathroom and remove it and let him have it for a few minutes.

"Can you do it while I'm wearing it?"

"It goes next to the inside curve of the left cup wire," Bücher said stiffly.

"Then this is easier," she said, standing and unbuttoning her blouse and opening it.

Not looking at anyone, Bücher opened his little bag and produced the wire, which resembled a flexible hat pin with a small pearly bead on one end. With a trembling hand and Elise's assistance, he had the wire installed in a couple of minutes.

After explaining to her the things to avoid that could interfere with transmission, and answering a few questions, he put on headphones and tested the wire. Satisfied, he gathered up his bag and left.

Fane explained the surveillance setup and how it would work.

"Jon will be in the control van, and the rest of us will be in cars, six vehicles in all."

"Who will be able to hear what's being said?" Elise asked.

"Everyone," Fane said. "We all have to be on the same page at all times. That way when a decision is made to do something, everyone knows why; tactics don't have to be explained. These people have worked together a long time, so a few words go a long way."

Elise glanced at Vera.

"I understand your concern," Fane said to both of them.

"It could get awkward for you. But just remember: your exposure to these few people is nothing compared to what could happen if we don't stop this guy. It's not much of a trade-off when you think about it."

Elise nodded. "I understand that."

"Also," Fane added, "if Kroll happens to call you on your phone, put it on speaker. That way we can hear his side of the conversation, too."

"He'll be able to tell. It's going to make him suspicious."

"If he says anything about it, make an excuse. It's essential that we hear both sides of the conversation. Make it work. We need you to do it."

Roma asked, "Have you decided what you're going to say to him, how you're going to approach the conversation?"

Elise shook her head. "I'm not sure. . . ."

"Just keep this in the back of your mind," Roma said, moving over in front of Elise, who was sitting on the sofa next to Lore. "We need to follow Kroll to find out where he lives. But if we don't find the files there, then we have more work to do. So keep him interested; don't burn your bridges with him just yet."

"I understand," Elise said.

He was slumped on the sofa watching the rain pelt the glass wall overlooking China Beach. He felt strangely euphoric with undercurrents of anxiety. It was weirdly exhilarating.

The conversation with Elise wasn't at all what he had expected. Vera's notes had led him to believe that she would be unstable, vulnerable. That was, essentially, the bottom line of Vera's assessment. But the woman he had just talked to didn't seem susceptible to self-destruction; she wasn't despondent. Rattled, yes, but she wasn't the emotional shambles that he had hoped for.

Did she seem disturbed? Yes, but at the beginning of their conversation she had also been belligerent, challenging. Then that gave way to confusion. What was going on with her? Not wanting to be alone with him—that was fear. She might have been alienated by what had happened at their last meeting, by the gift, but he hadn't expected fear to be part of the mix. What he heard tonight was fear.

So, where did that come from? He had to admit that this development hadn't shown up even on the remote edges of his radar screen of possibilities. It blindsided him as if he were a rank amateur, as if he hadn't planned the damn thing at all. Why didn't he see this coming?

Suddenly Kroll was stunned to see the rain on the glass wall stop. It didn't trail down the glass. It splashed and stuck and began piling up rapidly in a translucent coagulation. He could no longer see out; not even the far-off, rain-drenched lights in the bay penetrated the gelled rain that was accumulating on the glass like a slather of petroleum jelly.

Robotically, he punched the voice recorder and played back pieces of his conversation with Elise.

> . . . private corners . . . where we can talk . . .
> . . . public . . . I don't trust . . . myself . . . with you.
> . . . I don't trust . . . myself . . . with you.
> . . . I don't trust . . . with you.
> . . . I don't trust . . . you.

He was hot. He was oily. Every pore seeped. He punched the replay again, and this time Elise's voice had slowed to a rate that allowed syllabic distinction. Suddenly he was *inside* her words, phrases, sentences . . . ellipses, viewing, touching, tasting them, walking through their smells and sounds as he examined the near molecular structure of their meanings.

When he was aware of himself again, he couldn't move, and he had to wait for his heart rate to regulate so he could breathe.

He forced himself to look at his watch. Only a moment had passed. All of that in a moment.

The sweat was real, though, and the gelled rain had liquefied again and once more drizzled down the glass wall.

He quickly stood, fighting claustrophobia, unable to suck enough oxygen from the air.

Inexplicably, and entirely against his will, Kroll felt himself slowly being sucked into the maw of uncertainty, that gloamy sanctum of his worst enemy: self-doubt.

39

The past two and a half hours had been like mainlining adrenaline. By the time Kroll found himself walking up the steep slope of Sacramento Street in the chilly rain to the Fairmont Hotel, his legs were wobbly. He had worked through his bout of excessive suspicion, calmed himself enough, come down enough, for his training to reengage.

Not showing up at the Fairmont Hotel was impossible to imagine, even though something didn't ring true, and all of his training told him to cut and run—right now. But somehow his carefully laid plans had gone awry, and he needed to know why and how. The phone conversation he had had with Elise a couple of hours earlier just didn't add up to what he had read in Vera's process notes. He wanted to see for himself what lay in the distance between the two impressions. Curiosity was trumping discipline . . . and common sense.

• • •

Fane told Elise that a woman named Libby would be in the hotel to monitor her conversation with Kroll, and the rest of the surveillance crew would be on the streets around the hotel.

When she turned off California onto Mason and drove her Mercedes under the hotel's porte cochere, Elise was scarily close to hyperventilating. The thought of coming face-to-face with Kroll again was unnerving. It seemed an eternity since he gave her the gift three nights ago, and she had no idea how she was going to behave.

It was a busy time of the evening for the valets, with people leaving in groups for dinner, others arriving to have cocktails with friends, the end of a work day, and the beginning of the night's social events.

Elise tipped the valet and asked him to keep the Mercedes available in front. Then she entered the grandiloquent old lobby, resisting the temptation to look twice at every woman she saw in the hope that Libby would reveal herself with a reassuring nod. She scanned the cavernous space for an isolated sitting area that wasn't occupied, and spotted one near the grand staircase.

She headed toward it across the busy lobby. Halfway there she caught another figure in the corner of her eye angling through the scattered crowd in the same direction. Kroll was looking at her, anticipating where she was going.

They arrived at the same time. He reached out to greet her with a polite kiss, but she shrugged away.

She sat in the middle of a settee, leaving no room for him. He took an armchair next to her.

"What do you want?" she asked immediately.

He gave her a puzzled look. "What's going on, Elise?"

She studied him in silence. Her chest was so tight with conflicting emotions, their alternating ebb and flow coursing so quickly through her, that she hardly recognized or understood anything she was feeling.

"After we finish this conversation," she said, "We're through. I never want to see you again. Ever." She was astonished by her own words. Christ! But she literally couldn't help it.

Kroll froze, his face a mask.

"What's happened?" he asked, his tone and expression were stoic.

"You weren't smart enough," Elise said.

"What?"

"You overreached . . . you failed, and you'll never know why." She regarded his bewildered expression. "That's pitiful . . . isn't it? Being lost inside your own scheme."

"Scheme?" he lunged at the word. "Failed at what? What in the hell do you think you know?"

"You're confused?"

"You're not making sense."

"Oh, but I am," she said. "You're just not understanding it."

She had awakened a withering anger that she didn't know she was capable of. Kroll's flummoxed expression was beyond his control. He was trying to figure out what he had missed and how he could react to it. Pretending not to understand only made him look stupid, something intolerable to him.

Whatever was happening, Kroll was frantically trying to figure out a way to get beyond it. Suddenly he didn't control the situation, and for a man who had been presenting himself to Elise and Lore as all knowing, to be suddenly, helplessly confused, was galling.

"That fucking glass bird," he said, staring at her.

She hated him for saying it, for bringing it out in the open again.

"You're a failure, Ray," she said, goading him. It was something new to her, this desire to cause anguish in someone else. She had absorbed so much of it over the years, from so many people, for so many reasons, that being on the other side of the pain was shamefully exhilarating.

"That one thing," he said, "whatever 'that' was, whatever it meant to you, just that one thing and it's over?" Then, almost under his breath, "It must've been a hell of a stunner."

She wanted to scream what she knew. Her stomach ached to do it, to see the shock on his face, to see him unhinged. But there was too much at stake to risk derailing Fane's plan . . . if, God help her, she hadn't already done it.

"As long as I've known you, Ray," she said, keeping her voice even, emotionless, "you've always been able to anticipate me, to 'see' what I was thinking, to know *why* I was thinking it. Your amazing insight was . . . unassailable."

She stopped and raised her eyebrows at him as if to say, Right? Isn't that right? He knew what she meant.

"Why don't you rely on that amazing insight to figure this out, to understand what you seem not to understand right now?"

She could see in his face that he knew she was taunting him, and she understood him well enough to know that it was ripping him apart. She imagined that it took all of his willpower to maintain his rigid demeanor.

They looked at each other in silence, oblivious of the teeming lobby. It was as if the sound had been turned off and everything around them blurred. The only thing they knew was all that had passed between them, all that had brought them together, and, now, all that was pulling them apart.

"You've made a mistake," he said.

He stood, looked at her with empty eyes, and walked away.

Libby followed Kroll out the front door of the hotel, where, luckily, a group of friends was getting into a Range Rover that was the first in line under the portico. Kroll spoke to the valet, who hailed a cab.

The cab pulled up under the portico behind the Range Rover, where the guests were talking over one another as they tried to agree on where to go for a late dinner, taking forever to get into the vehicle. Kroll went for his cab, followed closely by two businessmen heading for a second cab pulling up behind Kroll's. Libby was close behind the businessmen, and cut between the two taxis.

As Kroll bent to crawl into the backseat, Libby dropped her car keys. As she stooped to pick them up, she wedged a GPS transmitter under the bumper and continued away from the hotel toward California Street.

"He's in the cab, and it's tagged," Libby said into her mic.

Roma and Lore were just around the back side of the hotel, and as soon as the cab's icon popped up on Roma's screen and moved away from the Fairmont down California Street, Roma pulled around the corner. She let Lore out and went on to join the others following Kroll.

"Jesus Christ!" Roma wasn't on the group communication, but on the phone to Fane. "What the hell happened there? That was totally unexpected. I didn't expect it anyway. She's been the level-headed one."

"I don't think Elise expected it, either," Fane said. "She just couldn't handle confronting him, knowing what she knows now—it changes everything. We can't fault her for that."

"No, God, you're right. I just . . . don't want to lose this guy."

Fane was watching the colored icons on his screen. "We're okay. He's covered. Everybody's in place."

The surveillance team kept to the parallel streets, strung out a block apart so that when the cab turned they could roll around it a block away and never be observed by the surveillance-obsessed Kroll.

They had no idea where the cab was taking him, maybe into the peninsula and Silicon Valley, maybe out to Marin County, or maybe just a few streets away. But at last, they hoped, they were heading toward Vera List's files.

4 0

Kroll gave the taxi driver his address, sat back in the corner against the door, and immediately started questioning what had just happened.

This wasn't good. The second he had turned and walked out of the Fairmont lobby, he lost control of the events. That was no good. What the hell was going on with her, anyway?

Damn! She had actually taunted him! Did she really know something? How could she? It wasn't possible. Only two days earlier she had been falling apart in Vera List's office—what could have possibly happened between then and now that would have wiped out six months of his careful work?

The fact of the matter was, this sudden change was wildly suspicious. This was some kind of a setup. Elise was already upset by what he had done the last few times they were together. Damn, he should've realized it while he was standing right there in front of her: she had hired a PI, just like she did to check up on her husband. That was it. But why? What had caused her suddenly to do that?

Shit.

He swung around and looked out the back window of the cab. Several cars strung out along the long slope of California Street, a trolley rattling up the hill in the opposite direction. He studied each of the cars, the nearest first: the make, the model, the color. He turned around and sat forward in the seat and spoke to the driver.

"Here," he said, handing a hundred-dollar bill over the seat. "In about ten blocks you'll be coming to Temple Sherith Israel. Make a left onto Webster, speed up, take the first right onto Pine, and let me jump out in the middle of the block. You just go on like normal, all the way out to Sunset. At Thirty-second and Ortega there's a little mom-and-pop grocery. Tell the fat guy behind the till that Wes sent you. Wes, okay? You'll get another hundred."

"Got it," the driver said, as if it was the most normal thing in the world.

Ten minutes later Kroll was standing in the dark entrance to Orben Place, a short alley-like lane between Pine and California, watching the cab's taillights brighten as it turned onto Fillmore. He didn't know what the hell was at Thirty-second and Ortega, but if the cabby was gullible enough to go there, he would lead the PI a long way from Kroll.

He waited a while without seeing anything that made him suspicious. Then he walked the half block to Fillmore, where he caught another cab back to Nob Hill.

. . .

Elise sat where she was and waited for Lore Cha, her heart still hammering. That's what he did to her, but she no longer knew if it was anger or hatred or fear that caused her to hyperventilate when she talked to him. And it was even worse when she met him face-to-face. She hadn't anticipated the intensity of emotion that rushed through her when she saw him walking toward her across the lobby.

"Elise."

She flinched, and Lore sat down beside her.

"That was a hell of a conversation," Lore said.

"I didn't know what I was doing. I think I blew it."

"You sounded cool to me. But I was riding with Roma, and she was a little freaked out. I was proud of you."

Elise looked at Lore, surprised by the remark.

Lore motioned to Elise's chest and put a forefinger up to her lips. Then she made a motion for Elise to slip the mic out of her bra.

Surprised again, Elise glanced around the lobby and reached between the buttons of her blouse, found the nub end of the wire, and carefully pulled it out of the piping around the bra cup. Lore motioned for Elise to give it to her, then Lore stepped around to the stairway and inconspicuously laid the wire next to the carpet on the tread.

"What's happening out there?" Elise asked.

"As far as I know they're following Kroll."

"And Vera, where is she?"

"I don't know if she's still at the office, or if she's gone home."

Elise was suddenly drained. The confrontation with Kroll had sucked everything out of her.

"Let's get out of here," she said.

Fane sat in his car watching the colored dots on his monitor and listening to Libby's team follow Kroll's taxi down from Nob Hill, through Fillmore, the Western Addition and Haight Ashbury, and then into the foggy flats of Sunset. Finally, suspicious at the taxi's meandering course, one of the team pulled up beside him and saw he had no passenger. A quick interrogation of the driver got the story and the address Kroll was going to before he changed his mind: Sea Cliff Avenue.

The minute Fane heard the address, he called Elise.

"Where are you?" he asked.

"We're at home. Lore's with me."

"That's good. Listen, we located Kroll's address, and we're headed there right now."

He told her where it was and asked her if either she or Lore had ever been there. If they had, their knowledge of the layout could help Bücher's people find their way around when they got there.

But neither of them knew the address.

"Well, there's something else," Fane said. "We lost Kroll. Something made him suspicious enough to dump our surveillance. I'm guessing he's spooked and he's running. My hunch is he'll go home first."

"Oh, God," Elise said. "I'm sorry, I'm so sorry. I . . . I just lost my temper. It's my fault—"

"Forget it," Fane said. "It doesn't matter, but since we

don't know where he is, make sure your security system is set."

"You don't think—"

"No, there's no reason to believe he's going there. Is the security system on?"

"Yes it is, but should we leave, go somewhere else?"

"Has he ever been there?"

"No, never."

"Okay, but that doesn't mean anything. I still think he's running, but as soon as I can I'll pull someone off surveillance and have them go over there just to be safe, and until we know what's happening."

Fane stayed well away from the migration of dots as they turned toward Sunset Boulevard and headed to Sea Cliff. He needed to stay out of the way and let Roma's people do their jobs, but he wanted to be close enough to get to them quickly in case of an emergency.

He tried to imagine the mind-set behind Kroll's disappearance, and he kept coming up with the probability that he was running. Most likely as Kroll gave more thought to his meeting with Elise, and realized that her behavior just didn't match up with what he had read in Vera's files, he had decided to pull the plug on the whole thing. He was probably headed home to collect his cache of forged documents, passports, and cash, and to clean out Vera's files.

At least, that's what Kroll would be doing if he was thinking straight. Fane only hoped that they could get there before he did.

He thought, too, about the unlikely relationship developing between Elise and Lore. Their differences were melting

away in the fierce heat of their common experience with
Kroll. They both had to be more than a little curious about
the patterns that Vera had observed in Kroll's interactions
with them that led her to her discovery.

As they drew closer to Sea Cliff, Roma parked her car and
joined Bücher and Kao in Bücher's van.

What would Kroll do when he came home and found his
computers missing? Fane had already made a decision about
what to do about Kroll, but until Roma's people were safely
out of the picture, he didn't dare make that phone call.

If they beat Kroll to the files, then Fane's phone call could
end it all. If it was the other way around, all bets were off.
There were still too many possibilities, and too little information.

It was going to be a while. Fane stopped at a coffee shop,
bought a cup, then headed back to Sea Cliff. He found a
parking place on Lake Street and settled in to wait.

41

As the taxi cruised by the front of the Fairmont, Kroll wasn't surprised to see Elise's Mercedes was no longer parked in the valet section in the front of the hotel.

He gave the driver an address in Pacific Heights and sat back to review the logistics ahead of him.

Kroll knew that Elise's relationship with Currin had deteriorated to the point that their routine communication consisted of only brief conversations once or twice a week. Often a week or two would go by without either of them speaking to the other.

As her alienation from Currin continued, Elise grew increasingly reclusive. By the time Kroll began seeing her, she had given the cook, housekeeper, and gardener three-day weekends. That meant she was entirely alone in the old mansion Friday through Sunday.

In short, no one in particular kept tabs on her very much. That was why she depended so much on her sessions with

Vera. And it contributed to the ease with which Kroll was able to insert himself into her life. For the past four months, apart from Vera, Kroll had been the person she saw more than anyone else.

On Fillmore he asked the driver to pull over at a corner store, and he ran in and got an umbrella. Twenty minutes later the driver dropped him off two blocks from Elise's home.

After the cab disappeared around the corner, he crossed the street and headed up the hill. A light rain dribbled off his new umbrella. The trees dripped softly all around him as he passed pristine Victorian Queen Annes to the top of the hill.

At Broadway he stopped and looked at the old three-story neoclassical house on the corner. It was dark except for the lights in the third-floor corner windows angled toward the bay. Elise was there.

He crossed the street to the Broadway side of the house and approached a wooden door in the vine-covered garden wall. Crouching at the base of the wall, he fished in the wet ivy and found a small plastic packet. He took a key out of the packet and unlocked the garden door.

At the same time that Kroll began breaking into Vera's office on a regular basis, before he started using cutouts, he also began breaking into Elise's house. Patiently doing his groundwork, he studied her routines, learned when the staff was there and not there, and ascertained the details of her security system so that he could come and go with ease. Often he was there while Elise was asleep.

He stood in the tree-covered garden, listening to the light

rain, and gave careful, last-minute thought to what he was about to do.

He didn't know what had happened to Elise between the time Vera recorded her thoughts about their session and Kroll's meeting with her just hours earlier. But something had jolted her, interrupting months of careful planning during which he had cultivated a mind-set in her that had primed her for a moment of exceptional despair.

He didn't know what had happened, but he believed that he could reverse it. He had all night, and he knew the inside of her head better than she thought he did. If he could catch her completely by surprise, shock her, and shatter the confidence she had displayed at the hotel, he could take her thinking back to where it had been when Vera made the notes describing her despondency. A shock would do that.

And if it didn't, then he would handle her the way he had handled Britta Weston—just get rid of her to eliminate the distraction of an unraveling plan and move on to Lore Cha. That one he could deal with.

Thirty-two minutes had passed when Fane's BlackBerry came alive again.

Roma said, "Okay, we're past the security system and we're going inside on the lower level . . . practically empty, garage, empty rooms. Second level, more empty rooms, his bedroom. Bücher and Kao going on upstairs."

The heavy mist was turning to drizzle now, and Fane had started the Mercedes for a little warmth.

Libby's voice came over the headset and computer.

"I've been checking the address," she said. "The house is owned by Morgan Searcy, Nassau, Bahamas."

Fane shook his head. When they got into Kroll's computers they were going to find that he had layers of fake names attached to real estate, offshore accounts, cell phones, passports, Web sites, e-mail accounts, credit cards. That was his life, living in multiples of himself.

Roma came on the BlackBerry.

"This guy lives like a monk," she said. "There's hardly any furniture in the place, and what's here is only in a couple of rooms. Closet full of expensive clothes and shoes, but no junk laying around, no iPod or DVDs for his flat-screen television. From what I'm seeing here, I couldn't tell you anything about the guy who lives here except that he's super low maintenance.

"Going into the bathroom. Nothing—okay, here's Jon. . . . They've got three laptops—nothing anywhere else in the house. We could do a search for possible concealments—"

"No," Fane said. "I think you've found what we're looking for."

"Okay, then," Roma said, "I'm going to send Kao to the van to get started on the laptops, and I'll have Jon get started on the cameras. I think three should cover it."

Fane waited while Roma put Bücher to work.

"What about Libby's team?" she asked.

"Have them stay in the vicinity and report on anybody going into the area. We can't miss him if he comes back. And keep Bücher's van nearby, too. Kao's got everything he needs in there. Stick with him and get a look at the contents of those computers as soon as you can. Maybe something in there will give us some idea about what Kroll will do next."

Fane stayed in the Mercedes until he saw Bücher's van pass through the intersection in front of him on the way out of Sea Cliff. Then he started the car and turned back toward Elise Currin's house in Pacific Heights.

42

There was a small trellis shelter in the garden, and Kroll went to the third beam nearest the gate and retrieved a key wedged between the beam and the runner. He went to the servants' entrance door and unlocked it with the key and entered the house.

Putting the key in his pocket, he went straight to a security panel and entered the key code to turn off the alarm system. He was standing in a small wet room, dripping where the dripping was supposed to be done. Methodically, he hung his umbrella on the stand, removed his raincoat, and hung it on the stand as well.

He reached into his pocket and took out a pair of powder-free latex surgical gloves. Small. Tight. He pulled them on and walked through the pantry and large commercial kitchen into the dining room. He paused and listened as he absently snugged the gloves around his fingers.

He went into the living room, an old museum of a place

in which the only thing that ever happened was that the maid cleaned its surfaces once a week. The wan light from the tall rain-streaked windows provided him with enough illumination to move easily through the room.

A seven-foot grandfather clock stood near the entrance of the room, its pendulum motionless. The crown of the clock was surmounted by a cornice, and in that recess lay a black CZ-75 automatic with a full clip. It had been there nearly two months.

Kroll took down the CZ and walked out of the living room and across the broad entrance hall to the grand flight of stairs that swept upward to a second-floor mezzanine. His wet shoes were soundless on the carpet runner as he ascended. His latex-covered fingers gripped the CZ as if it were glued to his hand. He crossed the mezzanine to a second flight of stairs that took him to the third floor.

Elise spent most of her time in a suite of rooms on the northeast corner of the old house overlooking the bay.

He paused in the small foyer outside her suite and listened at the door. Nothing. The door opened into the sitting room, so he had to be prepared that he might surprise her there.

He turned the doorknob, felt the free movement of the door in the frame, and shoved it open quickly.

Elise flinched, her arms raised behind her head as he caught her in the process of tying her hair at the back of her neck. She froze, shocked. She wore an emerald nightgown; a fresh drink sat on the coffee table in front of her. He saw her eyes register the latex gloves, the gun.

· · ·

"Ray!"

Elise's shout stopped Lore in midmotion, her hand on the handle of the toilet where she sat naked, except for her panties pulled to her knees. Elise's borrowed chemise lay within arm's reach on a small table.

She heard a man's voice. Deep, modulated. Unhurried.

A clammy warmth enveloped her.

Elise's voice, raised, but Lore couldn't understand anything. The bathroom door was closed, and there was the distance of the dressing room beyond that.

Trembling, she carefully lifted her hand off the brass handle and stood. She forgot the panties around her knees and nearly tripped but caught herself on the back of a chair that almost tipped over. Shit! She pulled up the underwear, reached for the chemise on the small table, and slipped it over her head.

Creeping to the bathroom door, she carefully put her ear against it.

"A gun, Ray?" Elise's voice was unnaturally loud.

Lore's mind lurched . . . Kroll!

If she opened the bathroom door, the wide passage through the dressing room would expose her to some parts of the study, and Kroll could see her from any number of angles.

Her cell phone was in the bedroom.

There was a window, but three floors to the ground.

"What's going on, Elise?" Kroll asked. "What was all that about back at the Fairmont?"

She sat straight-backed on the sofa, legs together, hands

clasped and resting on her knees. She was aware of looking at him blankly. He was going to kill her.

"I've had enough," she said. "I can't do this with you anymore. It's sick, and I'm sick of it."

"Can't do this? What's this?"

She looked at him. "I'm not really sure, Ray. What is this that you've been doing?"

Kroll was still standing just inside the door, which he had closed behind him. Now he moved into the room and approached her. He still had his gun in his right hand, hanging straight down at his side. He picked up her drink with his left hand and sipped it.

Elise found the surgical gloves more horrifying than the gun itself. They were ghoulish. She could see the hair on the back of his hand as if shrink-wrapped in the latex.

He stood over her, looking down at her as he drank.

"You haven't figured it out, have you?" Kroll said. "Back at the hotel I wasn't sure. You don't know what the hell's going on, do you?"

"What do you want from me?"

"Everything."

"I don't understand."

They stared at each other, and she saw his eyes trying to glimpse her breasts through the gown.

"Slowly . . . eventually, you will."

Elise felt naked. She didn't want him to touch her. If he was going to kill her . . . then not that, too.

"It . . . it's not going to happen," she said. "I do know more than you think, Ray."

He looked at her and sipped from her glass. It was vodka. And lime. Ice.

She watched him looking at her, repulsively relaxed. Enjoying the drink and the view . . . relishing the anticipation of something more. She knew that before he did whatever it was he was going to do, he would try to get between her legs.

"I've got to go to the bathroom," she said.

"Forget it."

"I've got to go, Ray."

"Piss on the sofa," he said.

She dared him with a look. She stood slowly, without fear, without defiance. "Shoot me if you have to."

She stepped around the end of the sofa and turned toward the bathroom. She heard him behind her. This was insane.

The lights were out in the dressing room, but they were on in the bedroom. She went through the dim dressing room passage to the bathroom door. It was closed. She opened it and saw a petrified Lore standing to the side and behind the door, out of Kroll's sight. Elise didn't look at her. She turned to close the door.

"Leave it open," Kroll said, just outside the door now. "I'll watch." He was still holding the glass of vodka.

Elise walked to the toilet, turned around and lifted her emerald nightgown, and slipped her fingers into the sides of her panties. Kroll came closer into the doorway to watch and raised his glass to drink.

At that instant Lore lunged against the door with all her

might, smashing him in the face—shattering glass, a pained howl, his body hitting the floor.

"Lock it! Lock it! Lock it!" Elise screamed, dropping her gown as Lore scrambled and fumbled at the door.

The door exploded open, slamming Lore back against the vanity as Kroll hurtled into the room, fighting for his balance, bleeding profusely from the gashes on his face from the shivered glass.

He stood dazed, gaping at the woman on the floor, blind in one eye, his legs spread as he tried to remain standing and conscious. He aimed the gun on Elise to keep her back but turned his bloody face to the woman on the floor. He gaped at her, recognizing Lore, his confusion apparent on his face even through the bloody mess of lacerations.

"Fucking hell!" he slobbered through the blood. The glass had ripped a gash from the corner of his mouth upward into his cheek, and shards of glass were splintered all over his face.

Lore was petrified and didn't move or answer.

"Get up," Kroll croaked.

She pulled herself off the floor, leaning against the vanity.

Kroll moved the gun from Elise to Lore. He lowered it to her crotch and mashed it hard into her while he looked at Elise.

"You stay there," he blubbered to Elise, spitting blood, "or I'll blow her all over the damned room."

43

While he drove, Fane unlocked a side pocket in the car door and took out his old Walther, checking the load and the action. Roma would have exploded. This was not, by mutual agreement from the beginning of their partnership, the way they did things. But then, Fane never imagined they would be dealing with someone like Ryan Kroll, either.

He needed a description of the layout of Elise's house. He called Vera.

When he arrived, he drove past the intersection several times. The only lights on in the dark old house were in the upper corner windows, where Vera said Elise's suite was located.

He parked downhill. Deciding against an umbrella, he grabbed an overcoat and an old fedora out of the backseat and got out. There was only a light drizzle now as he started uphill.

He went straight to the door in the garden wall that he had observed two days earlier when he checked out the property before picking up Elise for their first meeting. Aside from the public front entry and the garage, this was the only street access to the property.

The door would surely be locked. If it wasn't, that was a bad sign. He put his hand on the iron lever, pressed down, and felt the latch snap open.

Carefully he pushed open the door and went inside. A path to his left led through another garden wall gate around to a front-side entrance. A path to his right, under a trellised pergola, led to the garage. He went to the servants' entrance door and tried the knob. It was unlocked, too. Christ.

He reached under his suit coat and pulled the Walther from the waistband of his trousers in the small of his back. He slowly pushed open the door and entered the wet room. A man's raincoat hung beside an umbrella on the rack against the wall. He touched them. Both were still wet.

Quickly moving through the pantry and the kitchen, he avoided the dining room and walked through the broad hallway to the front entry foyer. Without pausing, he hurried up the turning stairs to the second floor, then past the mezzanine and up the second flight.

It wasn't hard to find his way to the door of Elise's suite. Now he stopped and pulled off his overcoat and fedora and dropped them quietly on the floor in the corner of the small foyer. He approached the door and put his ear carefully to the surface. Nothing.

This was the truly stupid moment. If he was lucky, and

the study was empty, his odds of hearing them in one of the other rooms without them knowing he was there were much better. But this moment was entirely dependent on dumb luck.

Kroll sat on a bench next to the vanity sink glaring at the two women who sat on the floor against the glass wall of the shower. He was still bleeding from the wound where pieces of glass had been driven into his cheekbone just below his left eye. His mouth was swollen on the same side, but the bleeding there had stopped.

Lore had removed the biggest pieces, having done the best she could with the barrel of the CZ jammed into her crotch. No one talked. Kroll nearly had been knocked out by the door, but his head was clearing with every minute that passed. The excruciating pain of Lore pulling glass out of his face had helped.

Now he was just staring at them, the CZ pointed their direction.

"What's going on?" he said.

They looked at him, petrified.

"Elise, how the hell do you two know each other?"

Her face was blank.

"Damn it!"

"Look . . . look," Elise said, "the truth . . . the truth is we're having an affair."

"What?" How the hell could he have missed something like that? "Shit." He didn't believe it.

"It's . . . it's been going on for a while," Elise continued. "Nobody knows, and—"

He slowly moved the CZ over to Lore, again pointed between her legs. They were both sitting with their knees drawn up in front of them, their panties showing underneath their short nightgowns.

He spoke to Elise.

"I'm in no mood to fuck around. Tell me what's going on here. Don't lie to me."

Fane slowly turned the knob and opened the door.

No one there.

He quickly took in the lay of the rooms, comparing them to what Vera had described: a passage to the bedroom through a huge closet/dressing room, straight through to a door to the bath on the left, the bedroom on the right. The lights were out in the dressing room but on beyond that.

He heard Elise's voice, but it was low and he couldn't distinguish her words. Then a man's voice. Conversational tones, not argumentative or threatening. But why in the bathroom? And where was Lore?

The path to the bathroom door led through a wide passage in the dressing room. There was a Persian rug runner the whole length, quiet. His eye caught something near the bathroom door. Glittering. Broken glass.

Fane eased into the darkened dressing room and stopped only steps from the bathroom door.

Lore's voice. Somebody was moving around. This was as

close as Fane could get, and he still couldn't understand what they were saying.

He had to assume Kroll was armed, so Fane had to confront him suddenly. Unfortunately he would be surprising all of them at the same instant, and that could be a problem. Regardless, he needed to get them out of the bathroom, and he needed a tactical advantage.

He took out his BlackBerry and dialed Elise's number. It rang in the study.

Elise froze, her eyes locked on Kroll's as the phone rang again and again.

"You expecting that?"

Elise shook her head. "No."

"Who knows you're here?"

"Nobody . . . I mean, I'm always here. . . ."

Kroll's face was continuing to swell in a lopsided way, his left eye sealed shut, the left side of his mouth bloating out of shape. Still she could tell that he was agitated by her answers to his questions. He must know in his gut that she was lying.

Right now he seemed to think the ringing phone was a deliberate effort on her part to confound him. He sat in silence, his one good eye boring into her. She felt as if each ring was goading him closer to an explosion.

The ringing quit.

Incredibly, another phone rang. This time in the bedroom.

Lore looked shocked. "My phone," she said.
"What's going on here?"

Kroll listened to it ring . . . five times, then silence. This was
no coincidence. This was seriously coming apart. Suddenly
he was disoriented; then his mind caught traction.

"Who the hell knows you two are together tonight?"

"Nobody," Lore said. Too quickly.

"I want to know who the hell that is," Kroll said to Elise.
He stood and waved the gun toward the door. "Get up."

He backed out of the bathroom and stopped, standing
on the pieces of broken glass. The ringing quit.

"I'll stand right here," he said to her, pointing the gun at
Lore and nodding toward the study. "Get it."

The phone was on the coffee table in front of the sofa
where Elise had been sitting when Kroll arrived. She
stepped past him and walked through the dressing room to
the study. She picked up the phone and looked at the caller
ID. "Townsend." God, now she would have to explain it to
Kroll.

She started back to the bedroom through the dressing
room. The second she hit the shadows she saw Fane's gloomy
form standing to the left of the door. Her reaction was
obscured from Kroll by the relative darkness of the dressing
room and by Kroll's poor, one-eyed vision. Fane held up a gun
for her to see beside his face and a vertical forefinger over his
lips.

She didn't even break stride, but her heart lurched and went crazy.

Kroll took the phone from Elise and held it in front of his good right eye. Looked at her.

"Who's this?"

Suddenly Lore's phone rang again.

"Get that damned thing," Kroll snapped to Elise, and she turned into the bedroom, went to her bed where Lore's clothes lay, and picked up the phone.

She took it to Kroll. He looked at the screen and turned it to her. It said "Townsend."

"Who the hell is this?"

"Townsend," Elise explained to Lore.

"She's going to keep calling," Lore said without missing a beat. "We were going to have a threesome."

Elise was surprised by Lore's quick thinking. Her heart was slamming. Kroll was facing the dressing room shadows. It was up to her to give Fane a chance. Kroll had to be turned away. Fane needed a blind side.

Fane could tell if Elise was giving him what he needed only by listening. Kroll was just a couple of steps away now, lingering at the bathroom door.

"Okay," Elise said suddenly. "I've had it. Either shoot us or let us get something on. Look at her," she gestured to Lore, who was still sitting on the cold marble floor hugging herself. "She's freezing. Come on, Lore."

"Stay right there," Kroll said to Lore. Then to Elise, "You go get two robes."

She turned and stepped into the dressing room, glancing at Fane as she got the robes off the hangers. He raised both hands as if holding up clothes. She nodded.

She walked out of the dressing room holding up the two robes in front of her.

"I've got two—"

Fane threw Elise out of the way into the bathroom doorway and slammed the Walther down on Kroll's surprised face. Kroll staggered and stumbled backward, screaming in pain and anger, firing a wild shot into the bathroom wall as Fane drove him back, pounding his face with the Walther a second time, trying to stun him. Kroll fired wildly again, and Fane hammered at his gun hand, smashing Kroll's wrist and fingers and knocking the CZ across the floor. Instinctively Kroll's free hand grabbed at Fane's clothes, latching onto his lapels as he buried his bloody face in Fane's shirtfront in a desperate effort to protect himself from Fane's punishing blows. With incredible endurance, Kroll tried to fight back using his crippled hand to flail at Fane's head as he continued to hold fast with his good hand.

Suddenly Fane grabbed Kroll's hair, jerked his head back, thrust the Walther up between them, and jammed the barrel into Kroll's throat.

Kroll stopped, slobbering blood, fighting for breath. They stood locked together, face to mangled face, the Walther wedged between them, its barrel stabbing hard into Kroll's throat. Kroll was calculating his odds.

Fane felt him slowly loosen his grip on his clothes, heaving loudly for air, spluttering, trying hard not to drown in his own blood. He began to sink, gagging, his head still wrenched back by Fane's grip. His knees hit the floor.

Fane jerked the Walther from between them and slammed it down hard on Kroll's uplifted face again . . . and again . . . and again, pounding him senseless.

Roma answered her phone immediately.

"Marten. Hey, you're not going to believe what we're coming up with here—"

"Tell me later. I need some help."

There was a pause of a couple of beats and she said, "Okay."

In an instant they were on the same page.

"I'm at Elise's. There's a garden wall door on the Broadway side of the house. Come in there; call me."

"What's happening?"

"I've got Kroll here."

He disconnected. Twenty minutes, at least.

Kroll was still unconscious on the floor and bleeding like crazy. The barrel of Fane's Walther had laid open Kroll's existing wounds in a nasty way and had cut new gashes on his head and above his good eye, which was now also swelling.

When he came around he was going to feel like one of those prisoners he had interrogated at his black sites.

Fane was pressing a damp washcloth against the most serious wounds, and Lore was standing in the middle of the bathroom gaping at Fane and Kroll, still shaken by Fane's sudden assault.

"This . . . is . . . crazy . . . shit," she was saying. "I don't believe this."

"You have Valium, anything like that?" Fane asked Elise, who was standing near the door.

She went to her medicine cabinet and got the prescription bottle and gave it to him.

Fane said, "Lore, get me a glass." To Elise, "Do you know if there's anything like duct tape anywhere, maybe in the garage, a work room?"

"I think so," she said, and left.

"Lore, get me the strongest robe sash you can find. Or a belt, something."

"Yeah, yeah," she said, beginning to think now, getting her head back into the moment.

The twenty minutes went fast, and by the time Roma called from the wet room downstairs and ran up the two flights of stairs, Kroll was sitting in a chair in the bedroom with his wrists duct-taped together and his feet tied in a way that would allow him to shuffle along when the time came. Fane had given him only one of the low-dose, five-milligram tabs, and it had already kicked in. He sat in numb silence, his horribly swollen face held together with a patchwork of bandages.

Roma looked aghast at Fane's bloody, disheveled clothes, and then at Kroll, and Fane could tell that she was livid.

"Jesus Christ, Marten."

"We need to go in here and talk," he said, motioning to the study. "Elise, watch him, stay away from him."

She shook her head, averting her eyes from Kroll.

"I can't be in here with him," she said, retreating to the bathroom. "I'll be in here."

"I'll watch him," Lore said quickly.

"Stay where I can see you," Fane said to her, and he and Roma went into the study. Lore stayed away from Kroll but stood in the dressing room door where she could see both him and Elise, as well as Fane.

"What are you finding in the files?" he asked Roma, lowering his voice as they entered the study. His mind was whirring. He knew what he was going to do with Kroll, but he hoped that Roma might have found something in Kroll's files that would give him an alternative course of action.

"Are you okay?" Roma asked, looking again at his clothes. But she wasn't asking about the clothes, and he knew it.

"Yeah, I'm okay."

She nodded; they had to keep moving.

"Well, there's a lot in the files that's hard to believe," she said. "First of all, he kept a log in an encrypted file on one of his laptops," she began, speaking quietly and quickly. "Not a diary exactly, but a log, like he was just trying to keep things straight. I went back almost a year. Your speculation was right on target. While he had access to Currin's files at Vector, Kroll discovered that Currin's wife was in psychoanalysis. That was nearly a year ago.

"Within a few weeks of his first break-in at Vera's office he started compiling names of targets from her files. It's about this time that Stephen List is murdered—though Kroll never mentions this in his logs."

"Stephen and Vera used to share a suite of offices," Fane said. "Stephen must've discovered something that threatened Kroll's scheme in some way. We've got to—"

"Wait," Roma stopped him. "There's a lot more. Kao found something on another computer that answers a lot of questions. Kroll's 'experiments' while he was with the interrogation programs was to see if he could create a more subtle form of prisoner manipulation. He had access to the psychological files of several of these prisoners. . . ."

Roma shook her head as if she couldn't believe what she was about to say.

"It seems that they 'gave' these prisoners to him after they thought they had gotten everything they could get from them. Kroll would use the information in their files to . . . sort of drive them to despair. He designed a program of his own that manipulated these poor men until they killed themselves."

Fane was pulling every word from her.

"Incredibly, he was successful in doing this in eight cases before he was brought back to the States. Then he and the CIA parted ways. The creepy thing is, Vector knew all this before they hired him. No wonder his 'official file' has been reduced to one page."

Fane was incredulous.

"So," Roma continued, "after he disappeared from Vector, his log shows that he started compiling an odd file, recording all these bullet points about 'BW,' kind of a psychological profile. Vulnerabilities. Insecurities. Obsessions. One was a list of 'exploitables.' I can tell from the context of his notes he's talking about a woman, one of Vera's clients."

Fane knew. "Britta Weston."

"It's got to be. Finally he talks about 'pushing her too fast,' about the complexities of adjusting his system for the psychological differences between conflict-hardened subjects and civilian women—it's just insane. Then he says BW was freaking out, can't be salvaged, and he'd have to start over. He drops her."

"He killed her. . . . It wasn't suicide."

"And then his logs show that he immediately starts compiling profiles on Elise. A couple of weeks later, Lore enters the picture."

Fane was stunned by the efficiency with which Kroll had plundered Vera's clients. They were pitifully easy targets for him.

"What else?" he asked. Under the circumstances, it was a grim question.

"That's where I was when you called. Who knows what kind of insanity Bücher and Kao have uncovered on those computers by now."

Fane shook his head again. This was too much.

"This guy was close," he said. "Who knows how much longer . . . they could've handled what he was dishing out."

He looked through the dressing room at Lore standing in the light of the bathroom door in her robe. She was talking in a low voice to Elise, who was around the corner out of sight in the bathroom.

Roma followed his eyes, then looked at him.

"What are we going to do?"

"We're going to get him out of here," Fane said. "Right now."

"Taking care of him . . . how, exactly?" Lore's voice rose anxiously. She had planted herself near the door leading out of Elise's study. Kroll sat in a woozy haze on a straight-backed chair nearby. Lore had stopped their departure, demanding to know more.

"Lore," Fane said, "you don't have to worry about it. That's my job."

Lore went ballistic. "Hey, 'Townsend,'" she snapped, and the "Townsend" had a mocking tone to it to let him know she wasn't impressed with his damned alias, "this is my *life* here! And my *life* trumps your *job*. I want to know what you're going to do with him. I don't ever want to see this insane piece of shit in front of me again—ever! After all the . . . *hell* I—we"—she nodded at Elise, who was standing in the dressing room door—"have been through with this animal, I don't think you have any right *not* to tell me what you're going to do with him, 'Townsend'!"

Fane looked at Roma, who arched an eyebrow at him that said, Hey, the woman's got a point. And Fane knew she did, too. But it was a bad idea to tell her as much as she wanted to know, and he wasn't going to do it.

"You already know why we can't turn him over to the police," Fane said. "So it's got to be something else."

Lore frowned.

Fane said evenly, "I'll take care of it."

"That's it?" Lore was insulted.

"Read between the lines," Fane said evenly. He didn't have time for this.

"But how the hell will we *know*—?"

"Lore!" Elise had come across the room. She put her arm around Lore and pulled her away, "Come on. Let them get on with it. They'll make sure—"

"But—"

"They *can't* tell us, Lore!" Elise snapped.

Lore's eyes flashed at Elise, and for a few seconds they stared at each other; then Lore jerked away and stormed out of the room.

"Thanks," Roma said to Elise. Fane already had the door open and was getting Kroll out of his chair.

45

At half past ten o'clock Fane placed a brief, hurried call to Moretti: a question, a run-by, then precise instructions.

He called Bücher and told him to meet him and Roma at a parking lot near California and Twenty-seventh Avenue. Fane needed to pick up a bug from Bücher.

At the same time, Roma called Libby to let her know that she and Fane were coming back into the surveillance area. She told Libby to pull her crew completely out of the neighborhood and wait for further instructions.

When Fane and Roma pulled up behind Bücher's van in the parking lot of a coffee shop on California Street it was shortly after eleven o'clock. He got the bug from Bücher and told him to turn off all the camera and audio feeds except to the one in Fane's Mercedes. Bücher was used to this drill. What he and the others didn't see and hear, they didn't know . . . and shouldn't know.

With Bücher and Libby's surveillance team completely

out of the Sea Cliff neighborhood, Fane and Roma entered the drive of Kroll's home on Sea Cliff Avenue and parked at the lower-level entrance. They wrestled the woozy Kroll out of the Mercedes and began the laborious task of getting him into the elevator and upstairs to his bedroom.

At eleven-thirty Fane and Roma dragged Kroll onto his bed, his feet and hands still bound, and then Fane installed the bug in a corner of the headboard.

Fane and Roma sat in Fane's Mercedes on Sacramento Street across from the Pacific Medical Center, where a parked car with two people in it attracted no attention. They were drinking coffee and watching the inert Kroll on the portable monitor, which was divided into quadrants, three of which were carrying live feeds from the cameras Bücher had installed a few hours earlier.

"How long do you think it'll take them?" Roma asked.

"I don't have any idea. After Parker told Shen that Vector wanted him, and I agreed to it, I assumed that at that point they put a team on standby. It shouldn't take them very long. If I were in their shoes I'd already be there. As far as they're concerned Kroll's a ticking bomb. And we don't even know the half of it."

"They know his condition?"

"I told Shen. I even told him the time frame on the Valium. If they want to get to him before he becomes a flight risk, they've only got a couple of hours."

"But you didn't tell him about the camera or the bug."

"No. I didn't have to. They'll know that whoever's giving

this guy to them will want to know he's been picked up, that he's not going to get away."

They sipped their coffee. The drizzle was now mixed with fog. It had been a hell of a night, and Fane was beginning to feel the weariness that drifts into the wake of an adrenaline purge. Roma was admirably withholding her scolding. She would blister him for what he had done, but not until the timing was right. Her sense of him in that regard was impeccable.

The woman floated into the frame of the picture like a wraith. Fane and Roma both saw her several seconds before they believed their eyes, before they could react.

"Oh . . . oh . . ." Roma sat up in her seat, rigid.

Fane tensed.

She was only a moment in the first quadrant, the downstairs entry then she was gone. They leaned in closer to the screen.

The woman entered the second quadrant, the central corridor on the second floor. She was wearing a raincoat and a shoulder-length blonde wig—it had to be a wig—that fell close to her face on both sides, hiding her features. She checked the empty rooms and turned a corner out of sight.

A minute later the bedroom camera picked up her smeared silhouette standing in the doorway of Kroll's bedroom. Then she moved into the uneven light.

"Oh, my God," Roma gasped.

She stopped midway across the room, her hands in the pockets of her coat. After that brief hesitation, she approached the bed and stood there looking down at Kroll. If she was surprised by the condition of his face, they couldn't tell.

"Ryan," she whispered.

No reaction.

"Look," Fane said, pointing to the first quadrant again. A figure in a hooded jogging suit was partially visible at the edge of frame, waiting near the outside door.

In Kroll's bedroom, the woman in the blonde wig took a hand out of her pocket and touched him on the chest.

"Ryan," she said. Enough time had passed now that Kroll was coming out of his Valium haze, and he turned his head toward the woman.

"Can you hear me?" she asked. Kroll nodded, grunted.

The woman bent down and carefully leaned in so close to Kroll that her lips must have brushed his ear. His chin lifted slightly as he listened. The mic in the headboard picked up nothing but whispered sibilants, fricatives, plosives, breathy vowelish sounds.

As Fane watched and strained to hear what the woman was saying, every unintelligible syllable she uttered was torture for him. But it didn't last long.

The woman straightened up, pulled a gun from her raincoat, put the barrel between Kroll's eyes, and shot him twice.

She turned and walked out of the room.

The hooded jogger downstairs jerked around toward the stairway at the sound of the two shots.

Fane and Roma were riveted to the monitor as Kroll's life spilled onto the bed, turning the covers black around him.

"What just happened?" Roma was appalled.

"Wait," Fane watched as the woman flashed through the

second quadrant of the monitor, then a minute later into the first quadrant, where the jogger was already holding open the door.

Then they were gone.

Roma said, "You don't think—?" She started dialing.

Fane put his hand on hers and stopped her. He knew she was dialing Elise. They looked at each other.

"It could've been Vector's people," he said. "We don't know. We don't want to know."

He reached out and disconnected the feed to the cameras. It was over.

46

They sat for a while without saying a word. The rain began again and pummeled the roof of the Mercedes with a dull rumble. It fell hard in the streets, creating a foot-deep layer of roiling splash.

Absurdly, Fane was thinking that he didn't know what Kroll looked like. His face was already misshapen when Fane got his first glimpse of him in that millisecond before he slammed down the barrel of his Walther. After Fane was finished with him, he was unrecognizable. No photograph of him had ever surfaced, and probably never would. Kroll's autobiography, his face, was his last secret.

"My God," Roma said again.

Fane would have preferred to continue in silence, but Roma's mind was churning.

"What bothers me is that this business with Kroll, this was just a glimpse behind the curtain. What else . . . what would we have seen if we'd been able to hold the curtain back for a longer look?"

Fane shared her frustration. He couldn't shake the feeling that they had gotten damned close to something terrible but missed it just before they understood what they were seeing.

"Let's start with our anonymity," she said, staring straight out the windshield into the rain. "We're not vulnerable through Elise and Lore. You always used 'Townsend,' right?"

"Yeah."

"We are vulnerable through Vera."

"As we always are with our clients."

"But this time there's Vector."

"They don't know about Vera. They only know that someone was looking for Kroll. They don't know why. This someone had found him and wanted to give him up to them. That's all they know. They still don't know who we are."

"But Kroll's death isn't going to stop them from continuing to try to find out who was offering Kroll to them. They've got to assume that Kroll had computers that contained information damaging to them and that whoever gave them Kroll now has those computers."

"Yeah."

"So it's not over."

The rain drummed a little harder for a moment, then resumed its steady rhythm.

Roma was quiet. Despite the shambling way the case had ended, the identities of Fane and his team remained unknown.

The only exception was Vera List, who wanted to keep it secret even more than they did.

But Vector, the behemoth of black work, was still out there, the stain of its dark concerns having seeped into Fane's orbit through Kroll's delusions. Fane knew he would not find it easy to remove its taint from his affairs.

He looked at Roma's profile against the shattered light on the rainy window. She tried to be stoic about this business of secrets, but it had left her bereft of family, a high price to pay for living in its uncertain margins. He knew she must be considering the somber possibilities they had created by awakening Vector—and how close they had come to revealing themselves.

But for Fane there was nothing alien about secrecy. He didn't fear it or hate it. He accepted it for what it was: another moral quandary that defined what it meant to be human. Man was inseparable from the ethical dilemmas of his secrets, from what they were, of who kept them, who didn't . . . and why.

He no longer remembered when he had stopped wishing that life was different than it was. But he did remember how much it hurt to wish it. As he looked at Roma now, he realized that maybe he was still even a little nostalgic for the pain.

Roma turned her face away to the rain, and Fane started the car.

It was just after midnight when Fane pulled the Mercedes to the curb behind Roma's SUV in Pacific Heights. The rain had stopped for the moment. Tired of sitting in the car, they got out and stood on the sidewalk under the dripping ficus trees.

They were both exhausted, and whatever the hectic events of the past five days would eventually mean for them would have to wait for later conversations.

"Are you going to see Vera now?" Roma asked, pulling her keys out of her shoulder bag.

"It's no good putting it off," he said. "She needs to know that Kroll's dead, that it's over."

He couldn't see Roma's face clearly in the street's rainy light, just a pale highlight on the bridge of her nose, a sallow wedge of a high cheekbone. Neither of them was able to read the vocabulary of the other's face. But Fane could feel her gaze from the dark cradles of her eyes. It was a mixed communication at best, open to interpretation, like so much else that had happened in the past few days.

She stepped closer and put her arms around him. Surprised, he embraced her.

If, in looking back, it seemed that they held each other a little too long, if he remembered too well the warmth of her face against his neck, and the smell of her, then it might have been a mistake of remembrance, a feint of memory.

Without a word, Roma turned from him, unlocked her SUV, got in, and drove away. Fane watched until she was out of sight. In a minute he would go see Vera List. It didn't matter what hour it was. He knew she would be waiting to hear from him. But he didn't move. He took a slow deep breath and tried not to think at all, his attention drawn to the fog-orbed lights along the falling street.

And then it began to rain again.

He got into the Mercedes and started the motor. He made a U-turn and headed toward Vera's place on Russian Hill.

EPILOGUE

(THREE MONTHS LATER)

47

It was late at night, and I was in the study ending a long conversation with Roma, who was in New York following a line of research that we hoped would add more pieces to a puzzle we had inherited. After we disconnected, I sat back on the sofa and returned to my dog-eared copy of e. e. cummings. Then the phone rang again.

"Marten, are we secure here?" It was Shen Moretti. He knew the line was okay, but it was a heads-up that this was going to be serious, if for any reason we shouldn't be talking right now. I told him to go ahead.

"I just got a call from Parker," he said. "Someone at VS wants to talk with you."

Vector Strategies hadn't been at the forefront of my thoughts in a good while, and I didn't want it to be. After Ryan Kroll's death, it took me a month or so to get the whole Vera List operation out of my head. There's always a period of readjustment after a job ends. It's your whole life for a while, and then suddenly it isn't. But Vera's ordeal had lasted only a week, a short, endless, intense week, and the way the thing stayed with me afterward was disproportionate to the time I had spent on it. It had been unsettling.

In the meantime, Roma and I had been making plans to move on to other projects, though we stepped a little more carefully now and read more closely the nuances that waited silently between the lines. Shen's call was an unwelcome whiplash back to three months before.

"Someone?"

"He says it's a person of significance. A major player. He wants to arrange a meeting."

"Why should I do that?" I asked.

The prospect of a meeting with a Vector player, even one that I had reason to believe was well-placed in the corporation, gave me pause. I already felt that my anonymity with these people was tenuous.

"Answers, he says."

"And why would he want to give me answers?"

"I don't know, Marten. You don't want them?"

That hardly deserved a response, and I didn't give any. But Shen waited. He was in a delicate position. He knew both sides of this awkward arrangement and was keeping each of our identities secret from the other. By letting him be our intermediary we were demonstrating to each other that we trusted him. Shen wouldn't be bringing this to me if he didn't think there were legitimate reasons behind it.

I knew what Shen was doing, waiting quietly as if there were any real question about what I would do. He knew me too well, knew what was coming next.

"I decide on the security," I said.

"No problem."

The meeting happened two nights later on Powell, at a place where the street fell sharply toward Market. Shen and I had used the spot before for similar situations, and he was familiar with the routine. I was already in my parking place uphill when Shen's SUV turned onto Powell from a cross street below me and pulled to the curb beyond a row of ficus trees.

The person I was meeting had no idea where I was, though he surely must've assumed I was close by. My BlackBerry hummed. Shen told me he was handing the encrypted phone to the man in the passenger seat. There was silence, and I watched Shen get out of his Land Rover and walk diagonally across the street to Roxanne Café on the corner, where he would wait out our conversation.

"You okay with this?" the man said. His voice was a mellow baritone, without tension.

"Go ahead."

"The mutual anonymity works for me," he said. "It'll be easier to maintain if we both want the same thing."

I didn't quite grasp the remark, and he didn't give me time to respond.

"My people are assuming that the deceased had computers and that they contained a lot of information about our shop. Information that compromises us."

He paused just in case I wanted to confirm anything. I didn't.

"When this guy came to us he was offering a pretty . . .

peculiar skill set," the man said. "You know what I'm talking about? I mean, not just his background, his training. We have lots of those guys. But he was offering something specific."

He paused. "I don't know what you know . . . what you got from his computers. Do you understand me?"

"About his 'peculiar skill set'?"

"Uh-huh."

"You talking about his experiments?"

"In another country, yeah."

"Yes." The veiled language was threatening to get cloudy, but neither one of us was willing to clear it up. Paranoia, like a low-grade fever, always lingers just below the surface in this business.

"Okay, well, he was offering that to us. It wasn't for every situation, of course. It was esoteric. Complicated. Dependent upon his insight, on how he played it. But it was artful, ingenious. And in those circumstances where it could play, it was brilliant; it was perfect.

"But the proposal was heatedly controversial inside our shop. So, in the short term, we hired him as we do scores of others with his background, and put him to work on high-value accounts while we argued over his offer."

This was a revelation. Vector was entertaining hiring an assassin? And the "we" was telling, too. If this man was in a position inside Vector that required him to be part of an internal debate about whether or not to hire an assassin, then I was impressed. He was definitely in the upper echelon of this global corporation, maybe one of only half a dozen people, if that many.

"Eventually we split over taking him up on his offer. I was

on the 'we don't do it' side. We lost. But the people who pre-
vailed wanted assurances from this guy. Since he had only done
this in those special places in other countries, they wanted him
to prove he could do it under 'normal' circumstances. He
agreed to show them.

"He'd been working on this one account and knew that
the subject's wife was seeing a certain kind of doctor. He
put his finger on the wife and on another woman. He could
use them, he said. Incredibly, our people gave him a green
light."

The man paused. When he spoke again, I could hear in
his voice that he had taken a long, deep drag on a cigarette.
I saw a waft of smoke lift out of the passenger-side window
of Shen's Rover.

"Let me get this straight," I said. "Are you telling me you
were opposed to taking on this guy's line of work, or were
you just opposed to his peculiar technique?"

This was a huge question. Was he objecting to Vector
establishing an assassination department, or did they already
have one, and he was just disapproving of the way Kroll was
proposing to do it?

But the question was too direct, and he ignored it.

"So it started," he continued. "We wanted distance from
this guy. If the wheels came off this thing, we didn't want the
blowback. So we came to an agreement with him, and one
day he just disappeared. We pretend to be shocked. Dis-
mayed. Our CEO met with her liaison on the executive committee of the board and gave him the bad news. We created a
bogus manhunt, which we played out for several months
before letting it gradually slide into the background."

"Then your board didn't know the real story here?" I asked.

He paused again, and this time I gathered that he was double-checking himself, making sure he wasn't saying too much or too little. He was checking his balance. By choosing to have this conversation, he was stepping out on a tightrope. A fall would be fatal.

"We had no contact with him for six months," he went on, again ignoring my question. "He had fingered the women, and we were waiting to see if it happened the way he said it would."

I couldn't believe what he was saying, and I couldn't believe he was telling me. There was a pause and another puff from the Rover's window.

"Then Moretti contacted his friend with us, and we learned that somebody—you—were onto this guy and knew about his ties to us. I didn't, and don't, know who you are. I didn't, and don't, know why you were after him, but it didn't matter. He was now radioactive to us, a disaster waiting to happen. I got my people to pull the plug on him."

Another ambiguity. What had I seen at Ryan Kroll's house the night he was killed?

While I was gathering my thoughts, trying to discover a way to get a more direct answer out of him, the bright arc of a cigarette shot out the Rover's window onto the wet sidewalk.

"That's it," he said.

"Wait a second. I think you'd better explain to me why you wanted to have this conversation."

Another hesitation.

"Let's just continue the mutually anonymous arrangement. I think we'll find it'll work very well for both of us."

Then the phone went dead.

I sat there a moment trying to get a grip on what this man had just told me. It was shocking.

He must have signaled Moretti, because at that moment Shen stepped out of Roxanne Café and crossed the sloping street to the Rover and got in. Its brake lights popped on, and it pulled away from the curb and disappeared down the hill into the wet lights of the night.

I thought of the cryptic observation by Diane Arbus about the nature of a photograph. It was "a secret about a secret. The more it tells you, the less you know."

In the end, there was more shadow than light in what had been said, all of it suggesting uneasy associations that I couldn't quite discern or understand. I had been in this line of work too long to expect that I could always coax clarity from shadows. I knew that I'd gotten involved in something much larger than anything that had surfaced so far, and I knew that I probably never would understand everything that had happened during those five days of the Vera List affair.

But I also knew that time was the crafty guardian of revelation. Sometimes answers came when they were least expected, and sometimes the best way to dispel the darkness was simply by being patient and waiting for the light.

ACKNOWLEDGMENTS

A book is conceived in solitude, but its birth is in the hands of talented midwives without whom it could never survive. I am especially indebted to three people who were committed to nurturing these pages to life.

David Gernert, my agent, whose alchemy and imagination have worked magic for me, from distant beginnings to now.

Steve Rubin, my publisher and the president of Henry Holt and Company, a visionary of possibilities, from distant beginnings to now.

It is my good fortune to have come full circle with these two men.

And finally I am indebted to Lauren Culley, my editor, whose guidance, persistence, and insightful understanding of my pages were, simply, invaluable.

ABOUT THE AUTHOR

PAUL HARPER is the pen name for *New York Times* best-selling novelist David Lindsey. The author of thirteen critically acclaimed thrillers—including *Heat from Another Sun* and *The Absence of Light*—and a nominee for the Edgar Awards Best Novel, he lives with his wife in Austin, Texas.